LOTTY
ENTERS THE
BUILDING

LOUISE EMBLING

author**HOUSE**®

AuthorHouse™ UK
1663 Liberty Drive
Bloomington, IN 47403 USA
www.authorhouse.co.uk
Phone: UK TFN: 0800 0148641 (Toll Free inside the UK)
*   UK Local: 02036 956322 (+44 20 3695 6322 from outside the UK)*

Published by AuthorHouse 05/11/2021

ISBN: 978-1-6655-8931-4 (sc)
ISBN: 978-1-6655-8932-1 (hc)
ISBN: 978-1-6655-8930-7 (e)

Print information available on the last page.

This book is printed on acid-free paper.

DEDICATION

This book is dedicated to my beloved mother, Glynne, who was my support bubble throughout the 2020–21 global pandemic, during which I finally found enough time to finish writing *Lotty Enters the Building*, which I started fifteen years ago. Glynne couldn't have done more to make me laugh and feel loved.

It is also dedicated to all my friends and family members. I was humbled by your kindness during the pandemic.

Throughout this book, the reader will come across certain people who exhibit characteristics that are not meant to be derogatory; the aim of these characters is to celebrate the fact that everyone is unique, is special, and should be loved. Nobody is "different"; it is just that we are all equally not the same.

CHAPTER 1

Lotty looked up at the clear sky thoughtfully as, unsubtly, she pulled her tight black lace thong down from where it had ridden quite far up her arse crack. Thankfully it wasn't a front wedgie; she found those considerably more painful, and they were much less socially acceptable to remedy in public. She let her mind wander, musing on the exciting world of fashion, the endless parties, the champagne on tap, and the abundance of pointlessly small morsels of food on shiny trays …

Lotty pondered, therefore, how *her* choice to enter the field of forensic science instead of fashion had been a good one, as she stood knee-deep in smelly pig excrement. Having coughed so hard on the stench at one point that she had very slightly wet her pants, she strongly questioned if she had indeed entered the right vocation. *Then again,* thought Lotty, *those fashion folks must surely suffer a lot with gout and bad cholesterol.* Furthermore, Lotty's fashion faux pas were legendary, including the time she had pulled down her strapless dress that was too short when attending an upper-class horse racing event, which had resulted in her flashing an ancient floral-print bra at the very surprised steward. Then there was the time she had worn a pair of new knickers, taken straight out of the delivery parcel that morning, to visit her hip surgeon, unaware that they were decorated at the back, in glitter, with three-inch-high letters that spelled out the word *spank.*

A couple of decades ago, Lotty's school career counsellor had sat her down to discuss her "wildest dreams", which had led to an awkward discussion on what were appropriate thoughts for a young teenager to be having about David Hasselhoff.

Having desperately wanted from such an early age to follow in her aunt and father's footsteps in the field of criminal justice, Lotty knew deep down in her heart that she had, in all honesty, found her true calling. She did often feel, however, that the closest she currently came to be being anywhere near to Magnum PI was her need to get back to the beautician for another lip wax. She absent-mindedly stood midthought with a few fingers of her hand on her upper lip. She was attempting to prove her hypothesis that she could now plait her lip hair.

She raised her arms above her head and stretched them fully upward, feeling rather too old to be spending hours bending over and searching through the wet soil that served as her work environment for the day. Needing to get back to her chiropractor, she had even tried sleeping on her bedroom floor recently because someone had told her that's how you fix a bad back. Lotty felt sure that anyone who advised you to sleep on the carpet like that didn't own a cat and had no idea what it was like to have such a creature rub its arse across your eyelids at two o'clock in the morning.

She waded deeper into the thick, pungent dark animal waste around her feet and settled into a new area of the field that she had recently marked out in a square using white tape and small wooden poles set into the ground. As she bent down and started to sift through the disgusting waste, carefully cataloguing any larger debris, something caught her eye. In her latex-gloved hand, she held what she was confident was part of a human bone.

"Sir, it looks like we have something here. I'll bag it and carry on," she called over to her superior, Arthur Ray. Arthur hated to be called "sir", but she refused to break the habit. Neither Arthur nor Lotty was a law enforcement officer, with many countries, including the USA and Great Britain, now conducting crime scene investigation using civilian officers. Long gone were the days of scene-of-crime, or SOCO, officers. "It looks like this part of bone escaped being digested, it looks like part of a tibia."

"OK, Lotty, good work. Bacon sandwiches all around, eh?" he joked with her, winking as he did so.

He was fun to work for, but she sometimes did wonder if he ever took his job seriously.

Arthur Ray was a very good boss. He was never firm, was always fair, and had a very bad cabaret-style sense of humour. He did his best and was very supportive of his subordinates and their decisions. He had known

Lotty's father, Gordon. Lotty loved to hear the many anecdotes about him that Arthur offered. Arthur had once tried to pursue a career in the mainstream police force himself, but he did have to finally concede that it wasn't for him after an embarrassing incident on an assault course where he'd slipped while traversing a rope-walk and had fallen directly onto his groin and suffered a dramatic testicle-related injury. He would never forget the emotions he'd felt that day because of having to endure a nurse pressing an ice pack against his engorged testicles for several hours.

"Lotty, why don't you go home now? It's past ten by my watch, and you look hungry and tired, love."

"OK. I am actually finished with my section, so if you don't mind, I think I will make a move. I've set the cat feeder, but no doubt Arabella is waiting for more, and I don't fancy another mutilated bird incident."

Arabella was Lotty's faithful cat; she was a beautiful Russian Blue who didn't care for anyone or anything other than Lotty. Arabella had once made a vet cry, not through fear but because she was adept at struggling, and it had taken this vet over an hour to remove her from the cat carrier that she'd been taken to the clinic in. Arabella had also made Lotty cry once when the cat launched herself from the top of a wardrobe onto Lotty's face at two in the morning.

Lotty took her leave, grabbed her field kit, and started towards her car, carefully packing her kit into the boot neatly and removing her muddied green wellington boots. She carefully cleaned the boots off with a stick she had found nearby, wiped them with a cloth from her field kit, and placed them also in her boot. A close-up smell of the stick told her that she may have trudged through a cowpat on the way to the car, so she left the stick in the field. There was a time and a place to be tidy, and it wasn't as if the stick weren't biodegradable. Lotty got into her car, unaware of the large smudge of cowpat that now resided on her face.

CHAPTER 2

Lotty drove her bright red Nissan GTR home, the car itself having only made a partial dent in her recent inheritances. While Lotty was not prone to frivolous wastes of money, she had believed the purchase of her favourite vehicle would help to cheer her up slightly. And it had. There was nothing Lotty liked more than to take the Beast out for a drive through the picturesque Thames Valley countryside, with ABBA blaring out from the stereo when she was sure no one else would hear her terrible singing. As the car's mighty turbocharged engine roared down the countryside towards Lotty's house, sticking like glue to the forever winding road, Lotty wondered when she would ever enter the realms of being a glamorous sleuth like Aunt Molly. She wondered if Aunt Molly and Daddy were watching down or her right now and feeling proud. She also wondered whether the tuna steak she had purchased at the weekend had been in the fridge too long or if it would be OK to eat when she got home.

A short stop-off at the petrol station allowed Lotty to grab some white chocolate to eat later as a treat. It was here that she suffered the embarrassment of the very attractive cashier pointing out that she had cow manure on her face.

Finally reaching home, and with her body now full of fatigue from hunger and cold and suffering slightly from dehydration, she dragged herself out of the car and packed her field kit away carefully in her spotlessly clean and well-organised garage cupboard, then quickly hosed down her boots outside. She took a long sniff, fought the need to wretch, walked back into the garage, grabbed her car air freshener, sprayed her boots with it, and then went inside the house to a very hungry cat. As Lotty walked towards the also spotlessly clean kitchen, she navigated carefully around the grey furry obstacle weaving adeptly through her legs as she took each step. Arabella was making funny little growling noises, which meant she was annoyed, presumably because she felt Lotty was late home and tonight was cat-brushing night. The fact that this was actually in Lotty's calendar as a monthly recurring appointment served to highlight the state of her social life. Lotty had been right about Arabella being hungry again, so she grabbed a can of luxury cat food and served it to the very fussy Arabella, before starting on her own supper of grilled tuna steak with coriander and a dressed green salad. Lotty's hunger overcame her like a wave of nausea as she finally sat down to eat at her dining counter while watching the enormous plasma-screen television she'd had installed in her kitchen last year. The fact that the meal hardly even touched the sides of her empty stomach as she wolfed it down, coupled with the accompanying coriander and with a faint waft from the cow manure still on her face, ensured that she was not quite able to detect the odd taste to the tuna.

CHAPTER 3

The next morning, Lotty's house was overcome with an air of tiredness. Lotty had given up with her incessant running to and from the toilet and had taken permanent residency in the bathroom at about four in the morning. Lotty's hypothesis of the tuna steak having been in the fridge too long had been more than proved by the subsequent urgent expulsion of said tuna steak, erratically and violently, throughout the night. As a result, the house was also filled with an air of pooh and vomit, the lavender air freshener having run out by about seven in the morning.

By nine in the morning, Lotty had already placed a call to Arthur and explained her predicament.

"Lotty, don't worry. We can cover for you while you're sick. Stay in bed and eat mashed apples and eggs. That will bind you up nicely. You know there is pectinase in apple skins. It's the same enzyme that's used to bind jam."

"Arthur, that's very kind of you, but I am actually coming in today. I am just going to be a little late as I will be swinging by the chemists on the way to work to pick up something to help settle my stomach and replace my lost salts. I feel pretty dehydrated."

"If you say so, love. The option is yours. You've already worked a lot of long days this month as it is. Perhaps you need a rest, eh?" Arthur debated.

"It's OK. You know I hate taking time off for sickness. I'll be fine. I'll see you soon."

As Lotty walked out of the parade of shops later, having stopped on her way into the office, her mobile phone rang. Before hitting the answer key, Lotty checked out the caller ID. It was Bruce, a very dear family friend whom Lotty treated as an uncle and, now, as a replacement father figure.

6

Bruce was quite happy to oblige with such responsibilities given that he had never fathered children of his own. In Bruce's world, children were something that happened to people other than him. He adored them, and he would happily take the progeny of his various friends out for day trips, but he felt that it was his role to hand them back when the effects of the sugar that he often treated them to had set in. If your children got back from such a trip screaming, jumping onto a mattress, and rebounding off it into a shelf so hard that it knocked your expensive ornaments onto the floor, it was referred to by his circle of friends as "having been Bruced". Many of Bruce's friends had been the victim of receiving their child back from him in a heightened state of exuberance, and one of them had been forced to point out to Bruce that Ferrero Rocher wasn't considered a food group.

"Lotty darling, I need you to come to a party I'm hosting this weekend," Bruce explained, without even saying hello or asking how Lotty was. "I need to talk to you about your father and Aunt Molly's estate. And the dress code is black tie," he continued. "I want to complete my executor task so I can put it all to bed and move on. I feel the administration of it all is making me feel so sad still." Bruce had been as devastated as Lotty at the loss of Bruce and Aunt Molly so close together.

"OK," replied Lotty. Before she could ask anything further, Bruce had disconnected the call, clearly in his normal rush.

Lotty, quickly checking her reflection out in the shop mirror, cringed. She headed back into the chemist to buy some facial hair remover as she wondered what it was *specifically* that Bruce wanted to discuss about the estate.

CHAPTER 4

Lotty's main interest lay in forensic anthropology, despite it not being her job. She concentrated on fingerprint analysis when in the laboratory. Outside the lab, she assisted in evidence collection along with many of her peers. Her hunch was that the bone she had discovered last night was from the missing wife of a farmer named Bill Gardener, who owned the farm that she had been called out to yesterday. Further investigation by the coroner, as well as her esteemed colleagues in the laboratory, would validate her assumption. Furthermore, Lotty hoped that the various specialists, many of whom she referred to as dear friends after working with them for so long, within the network of laboratories across the UK who supported the police would be able to prove later under a specialist microscope that the minute cuts that she had discovered during her initial on-scene visual inspection were marks from a saw. This would allow the police officers assigned to the case to demonstrate to a judge that the body was cut up prior to it being fed to the farm pigs. Lotty wasn't a huge fan of pigs since visiting a petting zoo last year with her friend and their children. Her friend had been forced to explain the birds and the bees quicker than they would have liked because Lotty had been mounted by one of the larger hogs in the pen. One of the staff had tried to placate her as she helped remove the hay from her hair, but Lotty would never forget the squealing noises and could never entertain the notion of eating a sausage ever again.

As she took a long swig of chalky-flavoured antacid to settle her distressed stomach, Lotty drove into the vast expanse of concrete that was the parking area of the Oxfordshire-based laboratory where she worked. She got out of her car and touched her upper lip gingerly as she checked herself out in the rear-view mirror. Waxing her lip earlier in the shopping centre car park had seemed a perfectly good idea at the time, but she was worried it was quite noticeable now what she had done. There was a fierce line of red adorning the area between her lips and her nose.

The police had first been alerted to potential foul play on the farm that Lotty had visited the day before, when Farmer Gardener, known for his violent manner, excessive drinking, and gambling, had made the mistake of disposing of a bag of bloodstained clothes. The vigilant dustbin men spotted the blood on the clothes when one of the waste bags had split. Having seen Farmer Gardener just the week before having a blazing row with his wife in the supermarket, the dustbin men had connected the dots and alerted the local police station.

The local police, having wasted no time, approached a judge to obtain a search warrant for the farm after further investigation, having spoken to several locals who knew the Gardeners and having demonstrated that Farmer Gardener had been seen buying new meat cleavers in the local hardware shop.

"Violent and stupid," muttered Lotty to herself as she walked to the laboratory from her car, still touching her upper lip gently in an effort to soothe as well as cover.

Cally, a black and fluffy miniature dachshund and working cadaver dog, had been taken to the sprawling expanse of farmland yesterday afternoon but had proved unsuccessful in locating a body, while Hercules, a highly experienced giant German shepherd search dog, had led his handling officers to a new, bloodstained knife buried at the back of the farm. While the farmer's scheme seemed categorically premeditated, he did not seem highly organised, having left the offending murder weapon on the farm. Lotty had struck gold. Early last night, under the bright beam of her trusty head-mounted light, she could clearly see latent prints on the knife. The knife wouldn't even require further augmentation using chemical treatment to show the prints.

A paper receipt had also been discovered by Lotty's esteemed colleagues, still in the farmer's wastepaper basket, documenting how, just a day before, the farmer had purchased that very knife from the same hardware store in which he had been seen by a witness purchasing the meat cleavers. He hadn't even shopped around in other shops in the area to allay suspicion, apparently.

Lotty stopped her mind from wandering, mentally chastising herself, and placed her field kit on her clean work desk. She walked over to the newly collected farm evidence, took out the knife, and walked back to sit down. Having misjudged the location of her ergonomic office chair, she only just managed not to fall completely onto the floor and stab herself in the process, as the chair had shot back when she tried to sit down.

Latent prints are generally far from visible to the naked human eye and are left as traces from the transfer of the skin's oils and salts. Lotty was hoping to prove that the prints on the bloodstained knife were from Farmer Gardener and that later on, laboratory analysis would match the blood on the knife to that of his wife, Grace. The excitement for Lotty was in watching all the evidence gather momentum, weaving a conclusive story for the police to tell a set of jurors in court. She was proud of every one of her well-trained colleagues, especially those who could actually work a chair properly.

Touching her lip once more, Lotty then gently fluffed her faithful fingerprint brush, shaking it adeptly between her two palms. She gently and meticulously laid her first brushstroke across the latent print on the knife. Halting her work, she held her breath while keenly observing in which direction the print was running. She carefully blew away any of the excess print powder and photographed the revealing print. Then she reached down into her forensic kit, lightly farting as she did so, and drew out her professional lifting tape, which she placed evenly over the entire print, starting at the top then working her way down. She executed this technique swiftly yet carefully to avoid any wrinkles; she had done this thousands of times and could perform the entire process with her eyes closed.

Lotty pressed down hard on the knife's cold, hard surface. Again to avoid any wrinkles, she swiftly removed the lifting tape from the knife and carefully placed the tape on a piece of white card. To avoid the current aroma of rancid second-hand tuna that was inflicting itself upon her, she attempted to take slightly shallower breaths through just her mouth. While still nursing her injured lip, unaware of the transfer of the fingerprint powder to the sticky remnants of hair-removal wax that still resided there, she documented on the evidence card certain data points, including the object that the latent print was lifted from, the date, and the case the evidence related to.

Next, Lotty bagged the knife, placing it in an evidence bag on which she wrote her name and the case number, before sealing it and signing that neat seal with her initials. She walked down the long, well-lit corridor to deliver the knife to the desk of one of her absent colleagues. Hoping that her colleague was just out to lunch, she became increasingly concerned that people in the office were avoiding her as they'd heard about her stale tuna breath. She quickly scribbled some notes onto a notepad, asking her colleagues in the laboratory to analyse the blood type on the knife, which she could then hopefully match to that of Grace Gardener. Her co-workers would then be able to pass on the knife for further testing.

While Lotty's UK-based colleagues were a far cry from the extremely coiffured, St Tropez–tanned actors found on the popular American crime investigation television shows, they were a great bunch of people to work with. Teresa Riley was the most outgoing member of the team and was Lotty's best friend. While extremely skilled in her field of forensic computer science, Teresa was also the queen of the double entendre and had a laugh like a castrated hyena. When Teresa was not in the office, the air became slightly less blue and incredibly boring. Teresa was currently taking her lunch break and was unintentionally making the act of eating a banana totally and utterly obscene. Lotty walked up to Teresa to discuss the Farmer Gardener case.

"Hey, sweets," Lotty said to the masticating Teresa. That verb alone was worthy of one of Teresa's famous "comedy honks".

Teresa finished her mouthful and swallowed.

Don't even go there, thought Lotty.

"Hi, Lotty. You are going to be pleased with my work on the farmer's desktop computer," enthused Teresa.

"Already? You are good!" complimented Lotty to her friend. She put her arms around Teresa's shoulders and hugged her.

Teresa hugged her back and smiled, beaming with pride. "Well, I have spent all morning working on the hard drive, and I have found a spreadsheet which basically documents Farmer Gardener's finances. It seems he was pretty short of cash. He'd been running at a loss for a while due to some issues around losing customers. Judging from what I heard about him, his violent reputation was seen as cause for putting more senior detectives on the case. They have already discovered a life insurance policy that the farmer took out on his wife just last year. I guess he was going to bide his time and scrimp and save until he could eventually cash in on the policy under the missing persons clause. Apparently, there's going to be a new investigator being brought onto the case. The person I spoke to is struggling with bandwidth. They've got someone new joining their team who has just moved into the area."

"Jackpot," complimented Lotty. "This case has become so airtight that the only thing that could make it any worse for the guy would be if he had inadvertently videoed himself chopping up his wife's lifeless corpse and then uploading the video to social media."

"Well, I'm still scanning his media files," replied Teresa.

"I'm joking. I really do *not* think he would have done that, babes. But these days, nothing surprises me. I've just lifted some prints to compare to the farmer's when I have his sent over from the police station. It was a clear set actually."

"Great. Are we still on for tonight?" Teresa winked.

"Oh, do we have to?" whined Lotty, displeased at the prospect of another dreadful evening of the worst pastime known on Planet Earth: speed dating. Lotty inwardly and outwardly groaned.

"It will be excellent fun," urged Teresa reassuringly. "You'll enjoy it. And I am not taking no for an answer. The taxi is picking me up at seven-thirty, so be ready for your pickup at about a quarter to eight, please."

The last session of speed dating clearly hadn't put Teresa off. Lotty had, in the space of less than two very painful hours, been exposed to such a gaggle of bizarre individuals that she'd very nearly had nightmares afterwards. One particularly lewd man had directed his entire conversation at her breasts; another man had initiated their encounter by asking if she fancied some this evening; and another had simply spent their entire discussion explaining his fetish for hairy women. The third man had requested a callback from Lotty upon returning his forms to the organiser, thus reinforcing her need for the long-overdue lip wax. Lotty, considering whether it would be within the bounds of speed dating etiquette if she were to take along her personal alarm this time, wondered how many other speed daters had ever used pepper spray during their encounters. This evening did not bode to be a good one. At least she might get a mojito at the bar, though.

In true Teresa fashion, her friend had noted Lotty daydreaming and had simply walked off midsentence to finish having sex with her lunch and worry about why it looked like Lotty had been snorting cocaine.

CHAPTER 5

Much later that evening, at the trendy and subtly lit bar, Lotty was not a happy camper. She had already spent one mini date being so repulsed that she was struggling not to vomit on one individual. Another of her mini dates had left her wondering how many more times she should let this man touch her arm before she inserted her drink into him rectally. She had, however, finally started a very interesting conversation with a man named Jim, who was a client relations manager in a bank. The two of them appeared to have a lot in common and were both at ease conversing with each other. He was intelligent and articulate and appeared to have all his own teeth, so Lotty had agreed to let him buy her a mojito in the bar where the speed dating had taken place. Teresa was seated at the same bar table, wobbling unsafely on the bar stool because she had consumed an excessive amount of alcohol, and trying to seduce Jim's friend Tom. She was currently sucking on a plastic cocktail stirrer so hard that she had very nearly swallowed it. Teresa's seduction technique did not seem to be working solely on Tom. Several other hapless men in the bar now seemed to be rather taken with Teresa's actions, with one man having to place his cold pint in his crotch area to abate any embarrassing activity, as well as serving to hide it should such activity occur.

Cupid's beautiful bow was hurtling towards Lotty at quite a speed as she gazed into Jim's sexy brown eyes while he gently stroked her hand and asked her to dance.

As Jim took Lotty's hand and confidently started to lead her to the dance floor in the corner of the bar, the music blared. Lotty was rather excited, despite having worn extremely uncomfortable shoes, and was really starting to feel that her love life was taking a turn for the better. Jim, now hideously drunk, leaned in rather unsteadily, yet still suggestively, towards Lotty, grabbing hold of her small waist and shouting loudly in her ear.

"God, you're so hot. I really want to kick your back door in. How about it?"

In Lotty's head, the angels stopped singing, the harps stopped playing, the clouds darkened, and it started to rain. She was already dialling the number of the local taxi firm on her mobile phone as she walked towards the nearest exit, with Teresa walking unsteadily in tow and with the tune "Sisters Are Doing It for Themselves" playing in her head.

CHAPTER 6

It was the day of Bruce's party and the morning after the speed dating debacle. Lotty had awakened on this fine Saturday morning feeling slightly broken from last night's experience and with the need to scrub herself violently in the shower. Her upper lip had thankfully calmed down to its normal pale tone.

After feeding Arabella and making herself a hazelnut-infused coffee, Lotty drove slowly yet purposefully to the gym of which she was a long-standing member and partook in an energetic martial arts–inspired aerobics class. Imagining that the air she was punching was Jim's face made the class go very quickly indeed. After a swim, a sauna, and a steam, Lotty showered once more and went home to finish her housework and personal correspondence. It was a glorious day of pottering about her neat, moderately sized house, one of her favourite type of days—a day when she didn't have too much to do, so anything achieved was indeed a bonus. As she ironed the clothes that she'd let pile up in her airing cupboard, she watched television, then treated herself to a short power nap. Her constant need to exercise and burn off calories left her constantly dehydrated and in need of both sustenance and naps wherever possible.

At about five in the evening, she set about the task of preening herself in case of any potential "man candy" who may also be attending the party tonight. She was forty-three years old and *very* single. Her list of men who hadn't quite made the cut was possibly greater in length than a Premiership football coach's, but that didn't deter her in the slightest. Lotty was always waiting for Mr Right. The attributes that she sought in a man had now been narrowed down at this stage of her failed love life to

(1) likes cats, (2) must be toilet-trained, (3) doesn't mind helping put the bins out occasionally, and (4) has a pulse.

Lotty's mind wandered to Arabella, her beloved feline friend, as she finished putting on her rather fabulous glittery blue eye make-up, accompanied by a deep black flick of eyeliner. Arabella, despite being a typically independent and arrogant creature, fickle towards the person currently feeding her, was still Lotty's most faithful friend. The cat sensed when Lotty was feeling down and in need of a bit of tender loving care and was always happy to supply it. Lotty wondered what adventure Arabella was having right now. O to be a cat with the ability to roam all over the expansive local countryside and almost invisibly enter any situation and observe unnoticed. Arabella could be out there right now watching the early evening sunset as its warm hues gently transformed into the pitch-black of night, or perhaps watching an al fresco dinner where two separate lonely souls were merging into one as love unfolded. Lotty grabbed her keys and purse and then performed her post-make-up stray nasal hair inspection. She spotted, on the edge of her peripheral vision, Arabella investigating a puddle of her own sick. Doubling back into the kitchen, Lotty got some disinfectant from the cupboards, took out a cloth and some kitchen paper from the sideboard, and set about an emergency removal of the offending cat vomit, while trying not to add to the puddle herself. She desperately held her breath.

CHAPTER 7

The drive to Bruce's had been fairly noneventful, apart from a brief to-do with her in-car satellite navigation system. Bruce had recently moved and had texted his new postcode to Lotty earlier that afternoon. The annoying little gadget had at one point been uncomfortably close to being launched by Lotty out of her window and thrown violently into the river that ran parallel to the road at several points of the journey.

"For the millionth time," Lotty screamed at the piece of hardware, "I will not be able to drive through cement bollards. Pick a different buggering route!" As she cruised into South Stoke and towards the large country seat occupied by Bruce, Lotty's mind raced as she wondered out loud to herself, "What if I do fit Daddy and Aunt Molly's shoes but have a lot of foot room to spare?"

Lotty certainly had a lot to live up to because, while her beloved father had forged a fruitful career in the police (including when he had once appeared on crime watch picking his nose), cut short during his path to retirement by sudden death from complications associated with a brain tumour, her aunt Molly had been a highly acclaimed private detective. *Acclaimed* was not used at all lightly when referring to Aunt Molly in this manner; the detective agency that she had solely set up and run until her recent demise had been successful in bringing to justice a myriad of bad eggs. Molly had, by the end, been employed by many high-profile departments of law enforcement to advise when it was deemed fit. Molly was also the go-to person for any celebrity who was subject to burglary, Molly herself having been elevated over the years to hold her own celebrity status. In fairness, Aunt Molly's mind had begun to wander quite badly during her twilight years. She had died doing what she loved and did best. Aunt Molly's final thoughts, as her trap had lured, as expected, her prime suspect into entering her house to silence her, had entailed the niggling worry of whether she had advised her enforcement colleagues to turn up at eight or nine in the evening. The officers, having actually been advised nine at night by Molly, had actually belatedly caught the suspect red-handed, clearing up the mess—the red on their hands having been supplied by poor Aunt Molly.

As Lotty pulled into Bruce's long drive then parked her car, she performed a final cleavage manipulation to make it so that her evening dress sat right. She smoothed her blonde hair into place and rang Bruce's doorbell. The party was already in full swing. Lotty was happy, but not surprised, when her darling Bruce answered the door already holding Lotty's favourite cocktail. While she keenly took the perfectly mixed mojito into her hand and lovingly smelled the fresh mint in it, Bruce walked her through to meet the various other guests at the party.

"Lotty darling," Bruce gushed, "there is the most gorgeous gentleman I want to introduce you to. He's your age, single, and a very successful lawyer. His name is Mark."

Bruce was already waving the handsome, well-dressed Mark over in their direction. Lotty quickly set her cocktail down on the table nearest to her and reached into her clutch bag. She still had time for applying emergency lip gloss, she thought, reaching deep into the mess that constituted the contents of her handbag. Her lip gloss was hiding rather far down at the bottom of the bag, and everything between the gloss and her hand seemed to be catching, rather annoyingly, onto her Tiffany's charm bracelet, this evening's jewellery of choice. As the stunning Mark came and stood next to Lotty, his short brunette hair shimmering under the lights and accentuating his stunning brown eyes, he smiled sexily at Lotty and held out his hand to introduce himself.

"I'm Mark Lynam," he said, flashing his perfectly straight pearly white teeth.

It was as if time had stopped and her actions were made in slow motion as Lotty, all too late, noticed that her now outthrust hand, finally free from the mess of the clutch bag, ready to receive Mark's, had dangling from her bracelet a stray tampon that had managed to escape not only her purse but also its wrapper.

"Er, I'm Lil-Let … er, I mean Lotty."

Lotty's face flushed red. *Oh God, kill me now,* she thought.

CHAPTER 8

Later on at the party, the decadent buffet was set out in the large temporary dining room created in an area of the main marquee for guests to help themselves to such luxuries as lobster tails, caviar blinis, and scallops wrapped in prosciutto ham. Mark Lynam was now chatting to a rather stupid yet stunningly beautiful woman as far away from Lotty as possible. Lotty couldn't blame him; he was probably in fear of having a sanitary towel thrown at his head. In any case, Lotty was very doubtful whether the stuffy Mr Lynam would appreciate her outrageous humour, especially her popular flaming Sambuca party trick. While it was impressive to watch, Lotty had been known to remove the odd eyebrow or two of any spectators who may have wandered too close for a better view. Lotty was busy catching up with Bruce and, hence, was happily preoccupied.

"Lotty, I need an answer regarding Molly's estate. As executor, I need to know what you want done with the detective agency. Are you going to run it, sell it as a going concern, or asset-strip it? We need to bottom this out." She was waiting for Bruce to bulldoze rapidly towards making a joke about bottoms, but he managed to maintain the appropriate level of seriousness that the discussion required.

"Well, I have given it a lot of thought and was hoping that I could employ someone to manage the detective agency and all of their cases. Perhaps one of Daddy's retired colleagues? Many of them were also great friends of Auntie Molly and would want to do her proud. I would, of course, be on hand to advise with any forensic matters or provide management direction when required. What do you think?"

"I think that's an excellent idea, darling." He pecked her on the nose lovingly. "It would be nice for Molly's business to be kept on. And if you ever choose to wander full-time down the path of private sleuthing, there will always be room for you at the agency as lead investigator. Having been hoping this would be your final decision, I have already taken the liberty of approaching Calum Summers, one of your father's old colleagues, on your behalf. He seems quite keen to take on the role of general manager as he is already rather bored of endless rounds of golf since he retired more than five years ago. I'll set up a meeting with us all next week, my dear."

Lotty settled back comfortably in her chair with Bruce alongside her. They reached a comfortable silence and started people watching, one of their favourite party pastimes.

"This marquee is really warm, considering how windy it is outside," commented Lotty.

"Yes, darling, it's the heaters I have had delivered. They are fab, but if you stray too far from one, then you can feel the chill. Consequently, I have stacked a lot of heaters out here," replied Bruce.

"Who is the woman positively dripping in designer clothes?" asked Lotty, who had spied a very well-dressed middle-aged woman who was also people watching.

"Oh, that's Evangeline DuVoir. She is a gossip columnist and socialite. She tends to write inordinately catty columns for the broadsheets."

"You're kidding me. That cannot possibly be her real name?" asked Lotty, laughing hilariously.

"Well, she is actually from a very good background, Lotty—very old money. It wouldn't surprise me in the slightest if that *were* actually her real name. You know how eccentric wealthy people can be. Anyway, we mustn't be unkind. Evangeline is just recovering from surgery due to recent kidney failure. We must be nice, darling, and not mock her name or her dreadful taste in shoes."

Lotty's eyes dropped in a catlike manner to the offending shoes. She screwed her nose up in disgust. Her eyes then met Bruce's, and the two of them exchanged mocking and conspiratorial glances.

Evangeline's own piercing eyes were scanning the marquee like a hawk's. She was dictating into a small voice recording app on her mobile phone, clearly making notes for future columns. Lotty could hear Evangeline's voice but could not quite detect the words being said.

As a huge wind struck the garden and ripped into the marquee, tables, drinks, and chairs were flung haphazardly across the dance floor and dining area. Hairpieces, scarves, and various other items of clothing and accessories were blown around the marquee. Lotty noticed that something immediately caught Evangeline's attention with the speed with which a shark senses blood in the water.

More than fifteen minutes later, as the party guests were still recovering their various items that had been misplaced by the wind, Evangeline was still talking frantically into her mobile phone. Then the power suddenly went out in the main marquee.

"Don't panic," shouted one of the catering staff. "We have called the maintenance team down to the marquee. The lights should be back on very shortly. In the meantime, we are going to relight all the candles that were previously blown out by the strong wind, as well as bring down more candles to illuminate the room."

Lotty, having annoyingly lost sight of the shark-like Evangeline, wondered what exciting gossip point could have caught Evangeline's sharp eye. Lotty noticed that people had started forming small intimate crowds in the romantic candlelight being created by the candles. Mark Lynam was now subtly fondling the buttocks of the woman he was speaking to. The subtle light in the marquee was still not quite strong enough to display all the faces deep in the various conversations going on around the room, but from somewhere in the marquee, Lotty was sure she heard a whispered argument between two individuals, and the louder of the voices involved in the conversation, she was sure, was Evangeline's. She recognised her voice given how she had been dictating earlier so loudly it was audible over the band. The band struck up again just as Lotty heard Evangeline ranting something about mail. She thought nothing more of the argument as she headed back over to the buffet area to shove profiteroles into her mouth as quickly as humanly possible to satisfy the hormones raging inside her. Lotty didn't worry too much that her menstrual issues might cause a dampener to any later part of the evening, based on her sanitary success with Mark. Lotty sucked on the dregs of the nonalcoholic cocktail that she had now been ordering because of her decision to drive home, not embarrass herself too much more, and avoid Mark, who would be staying in one of Bruce's many beautiful rooms at the manor house.

Lotty was introduced in the delicate semidarkness at about eight in the evening to Greg Alberny, an aging ex-playboy who, it was explained by Bruce, owned the *UK Chronicle*, one of Great Britain's leading daily tabloids.

"Actually, Greg is Evangeline's boss," Bruce went on, waving his hands and spilling some of his drink that he was holding in one of them. As Lotty smiled politely at Greg and extended her hand for the exchange of an unnecessarily firm handshake, she noticed the tall, long-legged, muscular blonde woman attached to Greg's arm like an insecure limpet. Lotty recognised her as the woman who had nearly knocked some drinks over, the one she had been sitting next to at the bar when she was hit in the face by someone's scarf earlier that evening when the wind had caused havoc.

"This is Melissa Bantley, my wonderful fiancée," gloated Greg, stroking Melissa's hair. (*Extensions,* postulated Lotty in her normal catty manner.) Greg crooned at Melissa with his eyes displaying the characteristics of a mix between a randy-dog and a lovesick kitten. Lotty inwardly threw up.

Melissa nodded demurely as she held out her hand to Lotty in what also turned out to be a surprisingly firm handshake.

"I'm also an assistant to the photographers on the paper, and general all-round intern," boasted Melissa with pride.

"Nice to meet you both," gushed Lotty falsely as she contemplated if they had any more than a bushel of brain cells between them both. It sounded to Lotty that Melissa was a general dogsbody at the *UK Chronicle*.

"So, what do you do, Lotty?" questioned the clearly disinterested Melissa as she picked at her bright red nail polish with her teeth. Lotty, germophobe that she was, struggled not to recoil in horror.

"I'm a crime scene investigator actually," replied Lotty, in the vain hope that she could drag the limp conversation into her personal field of interest.

"Wow, excitement." Melissa coughed up her mai tai with what seemed to be genuine sincerity.

"A gavver, eh?" Greg said, laughing. "I thought I could smell bacon."

Not over your aftershave, which, I'm pretty sure, contains rat's piss, thought Lotty.

Melissa seemed embarrassed at her crass significant other.

"Actually, Greg, I think you'll find Lotty is not a police officer but a civilian. Am I right, Lotty?"

"Yes, you are, Melissa." Lotty smiled, immediately promoting Melissa from "complete dumbass" to "slight dumbass" status.

"Greg, maybe we could do a piece on Lotty as part of our series highlighting government spend?"

"Great idea, gorgeous."

"Maybe," offered Lotty politely as she considered that they would have more of a chance shoving a woolly mammoth up their arses than getting her to spend any amount of time with a tabloid journalist. Lotty, having had significant experience with having her words twisted by journalists in the past, avoided engaging with them at all costs these days.

"We should do lunch." Greg shoved his business card at Lotty. It was a very expensive one, so Lotty chose to take it and planned to keep it in her purse, in order to make her look important in case anyone ever saw it.

Lotty took her leave from the group. *Do lunch?* she thought. *Do lunch?* Yuck; she wasn't a fan of buzzwords. Lotty couldn't help but pretend to shove her fingers down her throat as she turned to laugh with Bruce, who was at her side and had also escaped from Greg and Melissa. His tanned face staring back at her showed his disappointment at her behaviour.

"Lotty," he reprimanded, "this is why you are single. You are far too judgemental and fussy, darling."

Lotty couldn't help but think that surely she was single because most of the men she had dated had fewer cultural or social graces than a pubic louse, but she bit her tongue, knowing when not to annoy Bruce any more than actually necessary. She also felt he was being rather hypocritical, considering he was one of the most judgemental people she had ever met.

Bruce's voice hushed down to a faint conspiratorial whisper, which generally signalled the extraction of gossip from Bruce's loose lips. Having noted that this evening Bruce's lips were also glossy, Lotty wondered if he had been rummaging around in her make-up bag again. She stifled a giggle with her hand and let Bruce continue. He had accidentally used the gloss that contained a glittery shimmer.

"I've heard that Evangeline has been causing waves at the *UK Chronicle* while negotiating her latest exorbitant salary. She is grossly overpaid to be a gossip." He spat the last word.

Lotty chuckled at the irony.

"Bruce, people like reading that kind of stuff, me included, if I'm honest." Lotty felt ashamed at her confession, but she was actually interested in who was wearing what and who was doing whom. She felt an element of distraction from work when she succumbed to her occasional craving for a gossip magazine. When Lotty was at the hairdresser, she always flipped straight to the more gossip-related articles in the magazines.

"Well, anyway, I hear Greg had to fork out an absolute fortune to retain Evangeline, on the back of a previous airtight contract that she had made him agree to quite a while back when a rival tabloid was aggressively trying to poach her."

"So, are you going to introduce me to any more potential suitors?" asked Lotty optimistically. Bruce sat on a nearby chair and mentally scanned his list of guests. He suddenly sat bolt upright, looking very pleased with himself.

"OK." He counted on his hands as he spoke: "I can do a mobile phone mogul, an accomplished investigative reporter, and an IT wizard."

Greedy bastard, nosy bugger, and geek, translated Lotty. "Can we not bother with the reporter though? Thank you.

"OK, start with the most eligible suitor, please." She plumped her small yet pert breasts and checked her hair in a nearby mirror, then let Bruce lead her over to another clique of men and women standing by the buffet. Lotty was distracted and wondered if she had time to grab a few of the miniature burgers that had just been brought out to the buffet table.

"Sir Ralph!" called Bruce to a very tall and peppery-grey-haired man who, Lotty disappointingly calculated, was old enough to be her father— and that was being kind. She smiled politely and fought to hide her sadness.

"This is my darling Lotty, about whom I have told you so much." Bruce's chest expanded like a proud cockerel who was trying to impress a hen, which made Lotty smile. In reality, Bruce would be far more interested in another cockerel.

"Lotty, what an absolute pleasure." One could literally see the plums falling out of Sir Ralph's slightly wrinkled mouth. "I'm sorry to hear of your family bereavements. I do hope you are coping?"

"As well as can be expected, thank you. It's certainly been a tough year." The reminder of losing her father and Aunt Molly, and in such a short space of time, once again hit her as hard as if she had actually been punched in her stomach. Lotty felt winded by the sadness. A sudden feeling of nausea swept over her as a violent tidal wave of emotion. She held back her tears and continued. "Bruce and Mummy have been absolute rocks."

"Yes, I hear your mother is taking an extended trip to recharge her spent batteries."

"Mummy is currently staying with some dear friends in South Africa. She is utterly devastated, just like me."

"I hear you're quite the accomplished woman at work." Sir Ralph chuckled, trying to steer the conversation with a far more cheerful yet extremely patronising tone.

Lotty wondered just how far she could shove the condescending Sir Ralph's vol-au-vent down his throat without causing too much of a scene at the party.

Bruce attempted to cut through the cloud of awkward conversation that was building up in front of him. "Sir Ralph owns a chain of mobile phone outlets, Lotty."

"Oh, a shopkeeper? How interesting," she spat through her firmly gritted teeth.

Bruce recognised the fire burning in Lotty's eyes and laid his hand on her arm gently enough to calm her, yet with enough pressure for her to know that she was being kept in check.

"My lovely Lotty is rather excelling in her field of forensic work, and she has just taken over her Molly's detective agency. She's quite the sleuth to be reckoned with." Bruce's volume had increased and had started to attract attention from a wider audience, causing Lotty to blush.

"Well, I would be interested in contracting out my employee background checks, if that's something that your agency could become involved with?" offered Sir Ralph in a blatant attempt to ingratiate himself back into Lotty's favour. He felt an urgent need to prevent her nostrils from widening any further and was becoming increasingly more uncomfortable with Lotty's unblinking eyes, which were now staring daggers at him.

"Yes, that's fine. I will get Bruce to pass on my telephone number."

Sir Ralph breathed a long sigh of relief. The atmospheric tension reduced instantaneously. Lotty was appeased.

Bruce recognised this as an appropriate time to get Lotty as far away as possible from Sir Ralph before she kicked off again. Also making a note to encourage her to join him at one of his relaxing tai chi classes that he had been enjoying recently, he took her gently by the arm.

Lotty's approach to making conversation never ceased to amaze Bruce, and not in a good way. She didn't work a crowd but preferred to hit it like a social tornado. She could decide in a matter of seconds if she disliked someone, often before the individual had even said anything to her.

"Right, I'll introduce you to Alexander Rowley, the IT consultant I told you about."

Bruce led her to the end of the marquee and towards a group of people doing tequila slammers. A very drunk man about Lotty's age was attempting to lick some salt off another partygoer. Lotty cringed as Bruce tapped him on the shoulder. "Alexander, can I introduce you to Lotty? She's the forensic scientist I told you about the other week."

"Lotty, hi. Nice to meet you." It looked as if Alexander were attempting to be debonair and charming. He was being very successful, but he was so inebriated that his eyes were half closed.

"Likewise," replied Lotty, feigning interest.

"You'll have to forgive me, I'm a little drunk. Let's say we bring on the Sambuca?" shouted Alexander to the crowd gathered around him. He was quite the opposite of the geek that Lotty was excitedly expecting. Despite her lack of sexual attraction towards him, she decided she liked him as he seemed fun at least.

"Bruce, I think I'm going to stay and chat to these guys, if that's OK?"

"Of course, darling. But promise me that you will go over and talk to your accountant at some point this evening. He has some matters to discuss with you. And he is here somewhere."

"I promise."

CHAPTER 9

The power to the lights of the marquee had been restored much later on that evening, but the revellers were enjoying the candlelight and the ambience that it was creating, so Bruce had instructed the staff to keep the lights very dim in the marquee to maintain the intimate party atmosphere that had been accidentally created. Alexander had finally passed out about an hour ago in a temporary coat cupboard that had been installed in a spot at the back of the party room, and Lotty's attempt to walk the room after her fun with Alexander's crowd had proved fruitless. The conversations she had joined at different points during the party had been dull to say the least. Lotty knew it was probably time for Alexander to call it a night after he had accidentally burnt his mouth when he forgot to blow the flame out on his flaming Sambuca. Lotty, feeling that she would rather lick her own anus than discuss interest rates any further, had therefore just left a crowd of very boring financial types, including her own accountant, in the search for more enjoyable conversation. As she neared the back of the party, manoeuvring a conga line full of drunken revellers, her attention was drawn to what appeared to be a beautiful coat that had been left carelessly, and rather haphazardly, on the floor of the giant tent. As Lotty progressed closer towards the abandoned apparel to rescue it to Alexander's temporary bed, a member of staff had also spotted it and was attempting to pick it up. The young waitress dropped to her knees on the floor and let out a blood-curdling shriek that caused the band to stop playing and all heads at the party to turn. As a rather embarrassed conga line steadily halted behind Lotty, she could see that under the discarded jacket was the limp body of Evangeline DuVoir, deceased. In the depths of Lotty's mind, she heard the immortal tune "Another One Bites the Dust".

In an attempt to secure the crime scene and preserve any of the physical evidence, Lotty called for quiet and started ordering the staff members to stop any catering activity. She called over a rather spotty greasy youth who had been deeply engrossed in excavating his nasal passage. Lotty made a mental note not to shake his hand.

"What's your name, young man?" asked Lotty.

"James, Miss." She could just about cope with younger people calling her Miss. If he had called her "ma'am", she may well have punched him in the face.

"James, please run up to the main house as quickly as you possibly can and call the police and an ambulance. Please inform them that a sudden death has occurred at the party. Add that a civilian employee of the Thames Valley Police Force is at the party and is currently working to preserve the scene."

"Yes, Miss," answered the already scared and retreating James, still picking his nose, but now more furiously, in a state of either shock at the death or euphoria at having now unearthed some hidden treasure from up there.

As first responder to the crime scene, Lotty's first thoughts were to remember that the crime may be ongoing. She therefore ordered the lights to be turned up to full and for all the attendees of the party to remain seated and still. She compromised that the now nauseous-looking Alexander should just remain still, as he was clearly having a problem with the *seated* part of her request, having fallen off the chair several times before his crowd of friends conceded to leaving him on the floor in a heap. Lotty felt slightly despondent in the knowledge that many people had already left the party or left for their rooms in the manor house. Having secured a notepad from a staff member, she observed the immediate scene and documented the persons within the perimeter of the marquee, using Bruce as her oracle of names. She completed the next task of noting all paths into and away from the area. She finally wrote down her sensory observations, stating the lack of any overpowering smells of gunpowder or chemical compounds and noting the very poor version of "Disco Inferno" that the band had been playing at the time of discovery of the body. This served mainly to highlight the band's awful taste in music and not to contribute anything of investigatory worth.

As Lotty's tiredness began to overcome her, she heard the sounds of sirens coming up the huge expanse of shrubbery and rocks that Bruce called a drive.

CHAPTER 10

Much later on that fateful evening, Lotty was making a statement to several uniformed police officers in the presence of her superior, Arthur.

"Oh, don't be such a bore, Lotty. The Trammps were a band well ahead of their time. I'm sorry, but that song's a classic," argued Arthur, unaware of his constant disturbances to the statement being finished.

"If you have finished with Lotty, I would like her to be allowed to drive home now. She has been suffering with the most chronic runny tummy recently and needs her rest."

Lotty flushed redder than red in the presence of the more attractive police sergeants in the group whom she had been attempting to flirt with.

"Yes, Arthur, we're done," replied the officer, unable to hide his distaste very well at the mention of Lotty's recent bowel issues. Men did not like to think that women carried out any form of rectal activity. Well, nearly none.

"Lotty, I would like you to watch your back for the time being, please. Evangeline had several enemies, and we are yet to determine a cause of death. Bruce has been boasting at the party that not only did you and the waitress discover the body of Evangeline together, but also that you will not take long to unearth the guilty party if it's foul play, seeing as you are God's gift to investigations and were in attendance."

"Well, I will be careful, but I'm sure that it was Evangeline's kidneys that failed her. Bruce told me she had just had rather serious surgery."

"Well, you are probably right, but I will have a uniformed officer follow your car home and see you into your house just to be sure." Arthur leaned in close enough for Lotty to smell the heady mixture of curry and stale beer that wafted from his mouth. He attempted to whisper. "Which one do you want me to ask to 'accompany you home'?" asked Arthur, winking at her about as subtly as an erection in a convent. Lotty groaned and turned ever redder.

CHAPTER 11

Having waved off the strapping blond police officer whom Arthur had asked to accompany her home, while nudging said embarrassed officer in the ribs, Lotty was now tucked up in her cosy and warm double bed. Thick sheets of rain crashed relentlessly against Lotty's upstairs windows near where she lay, and the black of night stripped away any cracks of light from her bedroom. Above the eerie and menacing wind enveloping the house, Lotty could just make out the incontinent scrabbling of Arabella in her litter tray, which was located in the kitchen. *What had Arthur meant?* she thought. Lotty surely was not in any real danger, she reassured herself.

Just as her thoughts drifted to soft presleep fuzzy ones, Lotty heard a noise downstairs. She had distinctly heard glass break in the back door. Someone was in her house. She held her breath and gently untucked herself from beneath the warm covers. Lotty started to panic as her mind went into overdrive. *Who is in the house?* she thought. *Did someone at the party hear Bruce mention my address to the accountant when he joined them to discuss the detective agency's finances? Will I die tonight? Did I leave the iron on?* She quickly grabbed her work mobile, dialled 999, and made a mental note to check the plug next to her ironing board later. Lotty, hearing "The Final Countdown" being played in her head, felt her sphincter loosen somewhat.

As she heard the intruder navigate somewhat gracefully through the house, Lotty's distress call was dispatched by the police control room to the nearest squad car in the area where Lotty's house was located. Meanwhile, DS Mason Andrews, assigned earlier that very evening to the murder of Evangeline DuVoir and already on his way to Lotty's house to take a statement, heard the alert over the dispatch radio and accelerated a great deal faster into Lotty's neighbourhood. His right foot pushed down firmly on the pedal as the car lurched forward and the speedometer raced rapidly around its dial.

"Thit," he muttered under his breath.

Swearing with his speech impediment tended to detract from DS Andrews' profanities somewhat and caused much merriment with some of his more childish colleagues. Those fellow officers tended to use the phrase *suspicious circumstances* more often that DS Andrews felt was wholly necessary in the statements that he often had to read out in a courtroom setting. DS Andrews was new to the Berkshire area; he had recently relocated from Bath, seeking a fresh start. He'd spent so long progressing his police career that he was yet to find true love. He had been on dates and had had several short-term relationships, but unfortunately, he had spent more time studying for his police exams or on tactical operations than on meeting women. As a result, love had simply passed him by. His head and his heart were both ready to meet someone special. He was unaware that fate had just directed him right into the path of a very suitable candidate. Lotty was about to cartwheel into his life at great speed and change his life forever.

Back in the house, a very worried Lotty was breathing in harsh, deep breaths and attempting to minimise the noise she was making. She was trying to delay being found by whoever was in her house until the police arrived. She heard the quiet yet urgent padding of footsteps through the carpeted hallway, pausing to trip over Arabella's pile of toys and moving up the staircase. As the anonymous assailant finally stepped into her room and loomed over her bed with gloved hands moving slowly yet forcefully to grab at her neck, Lotty struck. The only implement Lotty had near her bed was already primed in her clamped, sweaty hand. She violently pounced up from the bed like a startled tiger and struck out, screaming repeatedly and maniacally at the intruder as she did so. While Lotty couldn't help respect the use of strangulation over stabbing, demonstrating a distinct mark of respect for her prized soft furnishings, thoughts of the smarmy traffic warden who had written her a ticket earlier that week as she ran back to her car from the gym overcame her and enabled an extra hint of viciousness in her defensive attack. The intruder's hands limply released her throat.

"I was only two minutes later than my ticket's expiry time!" she continued to scream at the bewildered attacker. The intruder stumbled, having been caught off guard by such a frenzied set of strikes by Lotty, and fled from the bedroom, running down the stairs and out the back door, only faltering briefly to step over Arabella as the cat was cleaning any remaining faeces from her anal area. Arabella hissed at the retreating attacker to display her distaste at being disturbed during such an important and complex task.

DS Andrews ran up the drive to Lotty's house and banged loudly on her front door with his fist.

"Open up. Thisth isth the polith."

Crying, very scared, and already entering a state of shock, Lotty tore down the staircase and unlocked her front door. She opened the door to allow entry to what was possibly the most beautiful man she had ever seen in her life. As she stood in front of the detective sergeant open-mouthed and tearful, she wondered whether she should be more embarrassed about being in her Scooby-Doo pyjamas, complete with a hole in the crotch, or of the fact that she had to now explain to the officer that she had just scared off her intruder by defending herself with a vibrator.

CHAPTER 12

Lotty, now having changed into a high-end blue leisure suit and leopard print trainers to impress DS Andrews, sat bolt upright in her kitchen and cradled the hot toddy that one of the attending officers had been ordered to make her.

"Thee'th bound to be in thock," DS Andrews had explained after making his request for the drink. DS Andrews had waited for his fellow officers to laugh at him or mutter "Sylvester the Cat" under their breaths. Nobody had made a joke; they'd just followed his instructions and nodded respectfully. It was now very clear to him that the bullying he used to be subjected to at his old place of work was a reflection on *those* people and that there was nothing wrong with him. He felt inwardly content, which reinforced that his relocation was indeed a change for the better. His mother had played an active part in alleviating the ferocity of some of the bullying that he used to be subjected to when he was much younger and at school. His peers knew that if they weren't nice to him, then they'd be the victim of a sharp clip to the ear from the boy's mother at the school gates. One of them had gone home utterly terrified after being chased there by the fearsome Mrs Andrews holding a mop. They had later used this as the reason that they broke into a sweat when performing any of their housework later in life.

Lotty chose to not take DS Andrews' speech problem into consideration. She had her own problems anyway. She suffered from chronic irritable bowel syndrome and would never forget her release of a rather loud fart that she had been struggling to keep in throughout her entire meal at a very posh restaurant on a recent date. She had, in fact, never seen anyone eat as fast as her dining partner had done after the incident occurred. She had watched him finish his meal, refuse dessert or coffee, and request the bill to be delivered very quickly, all while he attempted not to breathe too deeply. Lotty was somewhat unsurprised when he never called her again. Lotty's view of life was that everyone had their thing and that these individual things should be celebrated as uniqueness. She believed that no one should ever feel embarrassed by their personal issues. In her mind, everyone should be kinder to each other, as life often is hard enough.

Between sips of the strong beverage she was currently demolishing, Lotty recalled the events of the party, again, to DS Andrews and then the events that had occurred after she had taken herself to bed.

"Well, we don't yet have any potht-mortem rethults, but my gut insthtinct isth that thesth eventsth are connected, I'm afraid. For the time being, I will requestht regular drive-bysth and check-insth with the local officersth."

Lotty squirmed at the mention of guts. The whisky in the hot toddy was already churning her bowels and creating rather too much gas in her stomach. Having become quite adept at handling her flatulence issues, Lotty shuffled her chair nonchalantly and coughed to hide the noisy escape of a pocket of gas from within her leisure suit bottoms.

"I'm really annoyed about Bruce's big mouth at that party," ranted Lotty, shuffling her chair and coughing again. "I should make him pay for a security guard in the short term."

"It won't be necessthary, I'm thure. Anyway, I am going to leave you to get to bed and enjoy the weekend."

DS Andrews vacated the building and pondered how much more attractive Lotty would be without her nervous tic that caused her to fidget so much. He began wondering how she coped with it when she wasn't seated on a chair.

CHAPTER 13

Lotty slept in late the following morning, which was her usual custom on a Sunday anyway. Her weekend alarm call was generally Arabella's claws being drawn gently, yet still painfully, across her face in a display of hunger. This Sunday's absence of feline activity worried Lotty as she rose from her stupor and put on her pink silk nightgown. Having tied the cord tightly around her waist, she walked downstairs and made a note to wear her slippers in future as she noticed the mouse entrails that she had just trodden on. Lotty grabbed a roll of kitchen paper, a cloth, and a bottle of disinfectant from the kitchen and went back to the stairs to remove what was left of the mouse. The danger of Lotty's sleeping in too long was that Arabella often chose to display initiative and feed herself. "Clever girl," she muttered at her cat sarcastically. Having made herself her own breakfast of toast and jam, accompanied by a very strong cup of coffee, Lotty scanned her telephone messages from the night before.

"Lotty darling, it's Bruce. I just got your text. You must have gone back to bed, my love. I hope you're OK and not too shaken up. Call me if you need anything. Well, call me anyway. I want to make sure you're OK. Much love."

As requested, she dialled Bruce's number. He picked up on the first ring. Clearly, he felt guilty for having missed the text that she had sent to him after DS Andrews' departure. Lotty still blamed Bruce for divulging her personal address because his speech became so much louder the drunker he became. After two bottles of Pinot Grigio, Bruce, she was fairly sure, could be used to guide ships lost at sea.

"Lotty, are you OK?"

"I'm fine, just a bit rattled. It may have been a coincidence, but I really doubt it."

"I want you to call my landline in future instead of texting me. It is always by my bed and a lot louder than my mobile. If you ever need me in future, you must promise to do that. Do you promise?"

"I promise."

"So, what are your plans for today?"

"Well, I have DS Andrews' number, and he asked me to sleep on it then call him back to discuss the events of last night again. I was pretty tired when my statement was being taken."

"Or do you think he fancies you, lovey?"

Ever the optimist, thought Lotty.

"I very much doubt it, but fingers crossed."

"Wow, it's like that, is it?"

"Yes, it's like that, Bruce. He was adorable. He has the cutest eyes, and the loveliest hair, and the most endearing speech impediment."

"Right." Bruce tried to think of something diplomatic and encouraging to say. The prospect of introducing this chap to some of his less politically correct friends wasn't too appealing, but then again, at least she had met someone nice whom she seemed rather keen on. Some of his friends could be arseholes.

"Right, I have to go, my sweet. I have a tennis lesson with that gorgeous Spanish coach."

"Is he hot to trot?" She laughed.

"A complete dish, no less. Love you, darling."

"Love you too."

Lotty replaced the phone's receiver and went back to the sofa to finish her coffee. She was nervous about ringing DS Andrews and was thinking how long she should leave it in order not to look too desperate. She then reminded herself it was actually a criminal investigation and therefore was not bound by the normal rules of social etiquette.

She went up to the shower and set about her routine. She jumped into the shower and applied a mint pore-refining mask, which she left on while she washed and conditioned her hair. While her conditioner was left to work its magic on her unnaturally blonde follicles, she rinsed off her mask and washed her face with cleanser. Next, she shaved her legs using her melon-flavoured shaving foam and then washed her body with shower gel, finally rinsing off her sweet-smelling honey conditioner. She brushed and flossed her teeth and then applied her eye cream. "Goodbye, dark circles." She finished her routine by applying her chocolate body lotion. Lotty felt quite sure that if DS Andrews had a sweet tooth, then she was going to be OK. She also hoped she wouldn't pass a wasp nest at any point today.

CHAPTER 14

After making her bed and tidying away her breakfast dishes, Lotty finally felt ready to call DS Andrews.

She went to her handbag and retrieved his number, then walked back to the telephone and noticed her hands were already covered in a film of nervous sweat. "Perspiration," corrected the often absent lady in Lotty.

She picked up her mobile phone and placed it back down, then picked it up again, dialled the number, and placed the phone back down. She was very nervous indeed. While mentally rehearsing the dialogue in her head, she started to dial the number again.

"Mason thpeaking."

"Hi, DS Andrews. It's Lotty. I was just calling you back to go over the case again."

"Right, thanksth for calling me back. Call me Mathon, pleathe. Hope you're feeling OK today. Do you want to meet thomewhere, perhapth for a coffee?"

"Yes, that would be really lovely." Too keen, she mentally chastised herself and bit her lip. "Do you know the Starbucks in Reading, in the main shopping centre?"

"Near the thinema?"

"That's right."

"OK, leth thay one o'clock?"

"Yes, sure. I'll see you then."

Lotty went upstairs to apply her make-up and blow-dry her hair. Then she put on her shoes and went to grab her car keys. After suddenly remembering, in all her excitement, that she wasn't actually wearing any clothes, she went back to her bedroom and put on a pair of jeans and a jumper. She ran downstairs, grabbed her handbag and coat, and started her journey to Starbucks.

CHAPTER 15

Mason was already waiting for Lotty and nursing a coffee when she arrived, so she ordered an Americano with hazelnut syrup, which he then paid for and collected, before joining her again at the table.

"Tho, how are you holding up after laththt night?"

"I'm apprehensive about going back to bed tonight, that's for sure. I had to take a homeopathic sleeping aid last night after you left." *Stop sounding dysfunctional, Lotty. Damn.*

"Don't worry, if they come back, you can hurl thome love eggth at them." He winked at her and laughed. Lotty felt mortified. If you could die of embarrassment, then she'd be six feet under right now.

"Hey, I'm jutht kidding. It'sth perfectly natural. You're not offended, are you?"

"No, it's fine. I can see the funny side, I guess. The vibrator was luckily next to my bed as I had bought it the day before as a joke gift for one of my friends."

"Luckily, you had managed to unwrap it and put the batterieth in before the intruder arrived then."

Lotty flushed a very deep hue of crimson.

"So, have you had any further news on what happened to Evangeline? My boss texted me this morning to say I was banned from going into work and that I had to rest and recover."

"Isth that Arthur?"

"Yes, Arthur Ray. He's my boss at the laboratory. He's really sweet. He thinks I'm in shock, apparently."

"I agree with him. You need to relaxth a bit afthter what happened. Well, I thpoke to one of your colleagueth earlier on at the laboratory. The

44

initial toxicology thcreening performed overnight at the laboratory thowed extremely high levelsth of proteinth in her wine glath."

"I guess they'll have more of an idea why when they perform a detailed blood panel on Evangeline over the next few days. You are essentially saying it's foul play though, right?"

"Yeth. Which heightenth my conthernth over laththth nighth eventsth."

Lotty felt herself warming further towards Mason, her wide doe eyes hanging on to every word that he said.

"Any initial thoughth? You had never thpoken to Evangeline prior to the party?"

"No. And as I said, I didn't even speak to her *at* the party. I got the impression from others at the party, including the host himself, Bruce, that she was the sort of person who could have made several enemies. The elite can get a bit protective of their dirty laundry being aired in the tabloids."

"I agree. I have a team of uniformed officersth going back through the guethth thtatemenh, looking for any dithcrepenthieth, and another team going back for thtatemenh from thoth who had departed prior to our arrival and the dithcovery of the body."

Lotty tried to wipe the spit off her face without DS Andrews noticing. She found him cute, and he made her feel more at ease about her own long list of bodily issues.

"I have some future dealings lined up with some of the guests anyway, so I might do a bit of checking out of my own, if that's OK?"

"I'm going to tell you no, it'sth not OK. If your agenthy wanth to probe into the cathe, I can't thay anything, I gueth, but I would want you to perthonally exerthithe exthtreme caution becauth you already theem to have pitthed someone off a great deal. I am, however, more than happy for you to thare your findingth with me."

"I will, I promise. I have your number. And here is mine." She handed him her card as nonchalantly as possible. She felt herself blush. Her face suddenly felt very hot.

"I'm going to nip to the hospital and try to make the autopsy. They will only have done the blood work so far at best. The coroner is renowned for turning up in the late afternoon on a Sunday as he likes to have Sunday roast with his family."

"Thath Jonathan all over, a real family man. I know him well from commuting up from Bath on an earlier cathe he helped with due to bandwidth ithues with the Bath coroner. OK, call me tonight. Then I won't have to read the autopthy rethulth in too much detail." His smile could melt butter.

She drained the last of her coffee and got up. "I'll call you later then."

She walked out, humming the theme song to *A Love Story*.

CHAPTER 16

Lotty got back into her car and tried to compose herself. She felt in a complete love-struck dither. She called Jonathan on the way to the Wexham Park hospital to ask for his approval to observe the postmortem. She had placed her rose-gold mobile phone into its cradle once in her car and had activated her in-car audio kit. Lotty's life was run from the little gadget; she was unsure what she would do without her faithful shiny friend. Her mind drifted off on a tenuous connection, and she made a mental note to replace her vibrator after the embarrassment of the police having taken it away as evidence.

She had given up on a wall calendar as well as a paper desk diary many, many years ago and had all her social engagements organised by a piece of electronic equipment that was the size of a small chocolate bar. She had taken to backing up her data recently on her home computer after an incident where she had accidentally dropped her beloved mobile phone under the wheels of a large lorry while waiting to cross a busy road. The ensuing effect on her private life in the following weeks had been catastrophic, with Lotty either turning up to events on the wrong dates or missing them altogether. Bruce, who was irritated by all things technological, had been very smug about the entire affair until Lotty had pointed out that he himself had recently spilled a 2000 Châteauneuf-du-Pape all over his mobile phone and had suffered a similar fate. While having been equally as put out as Lotty as to the effect on his own social life, he still complimented his particular mobile phone on having a creamy blackberry and cinnamon nose. *Apparently*, Bruce still preferred the 2001, however, as he had felt that the tannins were far too restrained in the 2000 vintage.

Lotty dialled the number and put forward her proposal to Jonathan, who was speaking from his own car phone and currently navigating the particularly treacherous roads that carved his path to work from his recently renovated farmhouse.

"Are you doing it to investigate the case, to further your forensic knowledge, or to try to get your end away with DS Andrews?" He laughed through the speakerphone.

"Oh, ha ha. All three, if you must know," admitted Lotty matter-of-factly. "I'll meet you in the morgue."

She pulled over safely into a lay-by and scrolled through the numbers on her mobile phone. Having set up a group entitled "Nerd Network" in her mobile phone's contacts list, she was now dialling the number for Jane Wairing, her childhood friend who now worked at the Institute of Food Research in Berkshire.

"Lotty, how are you?"

Lotty heard Jane's two children in the background singing along to *Chitty Chitty Bang Bang*.

"Hi, Jane. I'm really sorry to disturb you on a Sunday, but I have a really quick question for you."

"Don't worry about it; I could do with a break from Disney. What do you want to know? It's not another question about foods that will combat bad breath, is it? You just need to floss more often. We've already had this discussion several times."

"No, I'm investigating a murder, and the initial toxicology report showed abnormally high levels of protein in the victim's wine glass. Are there normally any proteins present in wine at all?"

"Well, yes, to some degree. Proteins are typically present in a wine in fairly low concentrations, contributing a negligible nutritive value and serving to positively affect the clarity and stability of the wine. They're derived from the grape pulp actually."

"So, it's fair to assume that wherever the extremely high-protein concentration came from, it certainly wasn't from the wine then?"

"Absolutely not," Jane replied confidently, while being hit in the head with a child's shoe. "I also cannot think of anything off the top of my head that one would intentionally add to wine that would exhibit such high levels anyway. It's definitely a road to start looking down. Call me if you find out anything else. I miss work at the moment."

"I thought you were taking advantage of daily naptime to write your PhD?"

"Yes I am. And don't get me wrong, I'm loving my maternity leave, but when I do get out of the house, it's not exactly a laboratory atmosphere, which I'm missing terribly."

"I would relish the time at home if I were you. You know how stressed you're going to be when you go back. Just chill and enjoy the Disney. Don't forget the salsa evening that's coming up next month. Can Richard still make it?"

"Yep, he's booked the whole day off work so we won't be late. Not sure it's his thing, but I'm looking forward to it." Lotty heard a thud, followed by a cacophony of children's screams. "I'd best go. Josh has just fallen over into Penny while trying to dance like Dick Van Dyke."

"Ha. OK, babes, give them a big kiss from me. Love you. See you soon."

Lotty didn't know why she even kept going back to salsa. On two separate occasions, she had to dance with men who were incessantly grinding their erections up against her, and that wasn't aligned to her expectations of what it should be like to attend professional dance classes.

CHAPTER 17

Thirty minutes later, Lotty and Jonathan were standing in the cold morgue together, in front of the body of Evangeline, and wearing their required protective clothing over clean surgical scrubs. Normally, the smell endured by any laboratory professional was something that one simply had to get used to. Any chemicals wiped under, or indeed up, their noses, as per most television crime dramas, would only serve to open the airways and exacerbate any offensive odours. Essentially, one would simply be smelling "minty death". Some of Jonathan's global peers in forensic pathology had started to evangelise the use of chemical neutralisers, which were relatively new to the market. These neutralisers, it was claimed, would completely destroy all organic smells on contact. Jonathan didn't need *any* of that. Lotty was renowned around the various laboratories of the south-east, and perhaps even farther afield if he were being brutally honest, for wearing so much of her chosen perfume that it masked any smells associated with the postmortem process. In fact, if you got too close to her too soon after she had sprayed herself, it would make you feel like your eyeballs were actually bleeding.

Lotty and Jonathan were joined by Laurence Lancer, Jonathan's assistant, also in scrubs. Laurence's job as anatomical pathology technologist—he called himself a lab assistant when drunk at parties—was to aid Jonathan throughout the entire process of the autopsy. Laurence was quietly spoken, fastidious, and organised. The only fault that Jonathan could find in him as an assistant was that he would insist on trying to eat his packed lunch during autopsies; they'd once had to explain why someone's ribcage had a dollop of taramasalata on it. Because of the proactive approach he took to his work, Laurence had already noted, prior to Jonathan and Lotty's arrival, on his official paperwork the type of clothes that Evangeline was wearing and their position on her body. That evening, the well-bred socialite had chosen a fantastic pair of Jimmy Choo empires that were finished in a leopard print pony skin. They were so fabulous that if Evangeline weren't already dead, Lotty may have killed her for them. Evangeline's dress was a work of art. Lotty stared in awe at its full splendour, hardly even noticing the mass of bile stains made by Evangeline's vomiting shortly before drawing her laboured final breath. It was a brightly coloured vintage Vivienne Westwood creation that Evangeline had probably picked up in an expensive London boutique.

Next, Jonathan and Laurence painstakingly checked the body for foreign debris using an ultraviolet light, before taking several samples of Evangeline's hair and nails. The lifeless body was removed from the body bag, undressed, and checked for wounds. Nothing was initially visible apart from three small scars, which Jonathan noted as more than likely being from the deceased's recent kidney surgery.

"Is that what those small incisions are there on the abdomen?" asked Lotty.

"Yes," replied Jonathan wisely. He pointed to a stack of papers. "You will see here from her medical history that Evangeline had several kidney cysts removed using a technique called laparoscopy, as she suffered from adult polycystic kidney disease."

"So her kidneys would have been delicate?"

"Yes, *very* much so. In fact, she wouldn't have had that much wine in any case."

"I guess that everyone who knew her could have known that her kidneys were not fully functioning," postulated Lotty while speed-reading the medical notes on the laboratory counter.

"Yes, that seems a fair hypothesis. Hypostasis all looks as standard, but I would expect this given we know the body was transported here so soon after her death."

While Jonathan made detailed notes on his findings so far, Laurence cleaned and weighed the body and then measured it in preparation for Jonathan's next step: the internal examination. Lotty took a deep breath. This was not her favourite part at all. Although throughout her short career she was yet to throw up or pass out at the sight of a dead body, she always felt it was a good idea not to observe an autopsy on a full stomach and had therefore decided against a drive-through hamburger on the way over from the coffee shop to the hospital.

Now using his handheld voice recorder to document his findings, Jonathan gave a general description of Evangeline's corpse, including ethnicity, age, hair and eye colour, sex, and distinguishing features (or lack thereof, in Evangeline's case). Laurence placed a rubber brick underneath the corpse's upper torso area so that the arms and neck would fall backward while serving to push the chest upward and therefore aiding the initial chest incision. Jonathan favoured the T-shaped incision technique and hence proceeded to make a horizontal cut from the tips of both shoulders down to the breastbone. Laurence then handed Jonathan his shears, which he used to cut open the chest cavity of the body before using a scalpel to remove any soft tissue that was still attached to the chest plate. Lotty could now see Evangeline's heart and lungs. Then she had a really good view of Jonathan's ear as that was where she felt it best to stare for a bit while she took a brief moment to compose herself. Jonathan was then ready to start removing the organs. Lotty's brain whirred into study mode, drawing upon her past training. She recalled to herself that while some pathologists used the en masse technique of removing all the organs at once in a large mass, UK pathologists favoured a modified version of the Ghon technique, whereby the organs are removed in four groupings. Jonathan opened the pericardial sac to view the heart and asked Laurence at this stage to aid him in collecting blood from the pulmonary veins for the analysis that would determine, hopefully, what was present to substantiate the claim of abnormal levels of proteins in the glass that Evangeline had been drinking from. The pulmonary artery was then cut open to demonstrate to Jonathan that no blood clot was present, thereby eliminating this as the cause of death. Jonathan then proceeded to cut out the heart, the left lung, the right lung, and the abdominal organs, in that order. Lotty reluctantly moved in closer as Jonathan and Laurence examined the stomach and the contents of the intestines before weighing them carefully and with hardly making any sound. Lotty felt Jonathan and Laurence exhibited a great deal of respect when handling the body parts of the dead. Laurence had once said that these people are parents, children, or grandparents of loved ones and the least he could do would be to afford them the dignity of not making a plopping sound when working with their organs. All three people present in the room were rewarded with a strong odour of tannin, thus indicating that Evangeline had indeed ingested at least some of the red wine from her glass.

Jonathan pointed purposely. "Right, Lotty, if you see here, you will note the fairly empty stomach. Evangeline certainly hadn't eaten very much that evening, thus increasing the effect of any toxins potentially introduced into her bloodstream."

"Waste of a bloody good buffet really. It was one of Bruce's best parties, in fairness."

"Not for Evangeline," commented Jonathan with his typical dry wit. He winked at Lotty and laughed. She would have found it funnier if he weren't holding the insides of a person at the time.

Laurence, being highly experienced in his field and not requiring to be mentored any longer, moved the rubber brick, or body block, without being asked, placing it under the head. Jonathan himself then moved up to the cranial area and skilfully made a cut from one ear over the head to the other ear, before starting to pull the scalp away from the skull in two parts. There was a tearing noise. Lotty squirmed. Using an electric saw, Jonathan then exposed the brain and examined it before finally severing the cranial nerves and spinal cord. Lotty decided at that point that she wouldn't be ordering fresh lobster for a while. She then watched Laurence weigh the brain before placing it, as had been done with the other organs, in preservative solution. It had been a very long afternoon. While Lotty's stomach was telling her she was hungry, her brain was distinctly telling her otherwise. She could still almost taste the repulsive formaldehyde and hence felt very nauseous. Laurence proceeded to start collecting various samples for onwards toxicology testing. Lotty observed how he almost robotically started to fill tamper-free sample pots with blood, urine, and liver sections before extracting vitreous humour from the eyes. He started to sit and label all of the samples carefully as Lotty and Jonathan thanked him and left the room.

"Any thoughts?" asked Lotty as she washed her hands and chatted to Jonathan, who made notes while Laurence continued his work in the laboratory.

"Well, I have got some more work to do here, of course, and I will need to send your laboratory the blood samples and other samples for toxicology testing, but my initial thoughts are that the kidneys suffered significant chemical trauma, and this subsequently brought about fatal renal failure as a result of the introduction of an unknown substance, more than likely in that wine glass that was full of proteins and discovered by the victim's body."

"Thanks, Jonathan. I think Laurence has dispatched the courier to deliver the various samples already, so I will personally chase that up tomorrow for you."

"Well then, thank you, Lotty. It's always a pleasure to have a keen observer, especially one who doesn't puke everywhere. If the morgue doesn't smell of formalin, it reeks of medical students' vomit. I don't know what's worse really. I'm also fairly sure that one of the gentlemen who observed last week was still drunk from his previous night's debauchery. Needless to say, he decorated the floor with what I think was absinthe. Bloody idiot."

"Ew. OK, I'm off home to feed the cat and to try to get my appetite back. Thanks again. I'll send your love to Mummy when I speak to her next." She blew Jonathan an air kiss and waved.

"Your dad would have been really proud of you today, although knowing him, he would have chastised you for working on a Sunday."

"I know, Jonathan. I'll see myself out. And thanks again."

Lotty always left a postmortem internally singing "Heads, Shoulders, Knees, and Toes".

CHAPTER 18

After arriving home relatively late and finally succumbing to her hunger by ordering Japanese takeaway food, Lotty had slept peacefully that night and had awakened early and full of vigour on this bright Monday morning. She always slept well after a good meal, and Japanese cuisine was one of her great loves in life. She had ordered unagi, or freshwater eel, and had finished this off with a large bowl of rice, along with tofu teriyaki, fried soft-shell crab, and a very large glass of plum wine. She was keen to progress further both the case of Evangeline DuVoir and that of the missing, now presumed dead, Grace Gardener. She had received a work text from Arthur late last night updating her on the Gardener case; he had explained in his lengthy text that the detectives involved in the case, including the gorgeous DS Andrews, were yet to extract any tangible reason from Farmer Gardener as to his wife's disappearance. Lotty practically jumped out of bed and nearly stamped on the waiting Arabella on her way to feeding the whining cat. Lotty had been awakened that morning by Arabella chewing on the hair of her fringe. It was the sound that had awakened her more than the sensation.

After a light breakfast of peppermint tea to combat the symptoms of her IBS and a small plate of scrambled eggs with gluten-free whole-wheat bread, Lotty ascended the staircase to her bedroom and put on her light blue skirt suit and a duck-egg-blue silk blouse. Then she went out to the garage, grabbed her field kit from the cupboard, banging her head on the cupboard door as she did so, and started her relatively short journey to work. As she drove to work in heavy traffic, she briefly wavered back to her smoking days and longed for a cigarette to pass the time. Not even her recent bereavements had caused her to fall off the fumy bandwagon, however. She had now gone more than three years without returning to the dirty habit. She instead turned on the radio and helped herself to a boiled sweet from her stash, before finally pulling into the laboratory's car park just shy of eight-thirty in the morning.

Lotty made her way to the laboratory's communal kitchen, where she could hear much post-weekend chatter from her colleagues. She proceeded to make herself a very strong cup of coffee. As well as having a penchant for Japanese food, Lotty loved a good cup of coffee. To her, drinking the gnat's piss that was dispensed from most office vending machines was a criminal offence. She went to the electric bean grinder that she herself had paid for and installed in the hope that her counterparts would also themselves become caffeine aficionados, and ground for herself some arabica beans, then placed them in her very expensive coffee maker. She flavoured a flat white using soya milk to keep her IBS from flaring up, and finished this with a hint of sugar-free hazelnut syrup, which she poured into the ceramic cup. Lotty was yet to realise that there was a strategically placed message of "I love dick" on the bottom of the cup, that others could read as she sipped from it. Teresa had purchased it for her recently. Teresa didn't see the cup as a practical joke but more as a way of expediting the issue of Lotty's lack of penis action. James Nielsen, one of her workmates, was making himself a cappuccino using her coffee machine, he himself being one of her converts who was now unable to drink said cappuccino without a sprinkling of fresh nutmeg, which he was now grating over his cup. Lotty smiled.

"Good weekend?" she asked him over the noisy chatter in the kitchen.

"Great, thank you for asking. My youngest, Ben, used his bike for the first time without his stabilisers. It was awesome. Aggie and I were really proud," he gushed while slurping his coffee and giving himself a frothy moustache.

"Cute alert. Did you get some pictures?"

"Yep, I've already uploaded them to the online encrypted gallery." (He didn't *do* social media.) "I'll send you the link at lunch, Lotty. Aggie wants everyone to also notice her new haircut, I think, so if you could text her and tell her how fabulous it looks, that would be great." James' beloved wife, Aggie, had recently beaten breast cancer, but her recent chemotherapy treatment had sadly caused her to lose most of her hair, which had now only partially started to grow back.

"She's gone for a pixie sort of short crop, apparently," he continued, laughing at his lack of any fashion or beauty acumen, having his own hair completely shaved off once a month by Aggie so as it would not get in the way when he was using his laboratory equipment. "I really have no idea what she's talking about. But to be honest, I'm just glad she's happy and well."

"I'll text her after lunch then. On a more serious note, have you done any work on the Gardener case?" Lotty felt mean steering the conversation so bluntly back to work matters, but she was up to her eyes in cases and was just starting to experience the initial car-crash phase of her caffeine buzz.

"Yes. Sorry I wasn't in the laboratory when you dropped the knife by the other day. I was in a meeting about another case with my boss, plus I also heard you stank of sick from your food poisoning."

"I knew people were avoiding me! Don't worry about it. Did you get my notes?"

"I sure did, and I've already made good progress." James, a forensic DNA analyst, often joked with Lotty after he found out that she had submitted an entry on deoxyribonucleic acid, or DNA, to the Young Science Writer of the Year Award when she was just thirteen years old. She didn't win. Bastards. There were several reasons why she had been single for much of her younger years, as well as now, and submitting articles like that, as well as being a member of the chess club and debating team, was probably rather valid ones. Nowadays, it was cool to be a nerd. She had just grown up in the wrong era.

"So, what have you discovered so far then?" she asked.

"Do you want to pop up to my laboratory?"

"Yes, OK."

They both grabbed their cups of coffee and walked down the long, spotlessly clean corridor to the area of the laboratory where James worked. As was their company policy, the laboratory was neat and tidy, with not a single workspace having any out-of-place equipment on it and all devices being carefully arranged, almost having been straightened using a ruler.

James sat down on his heavy laboratory chair, motioning for Lotty to sit on the spare chair next to him, and pulled out his notes from a metal drawer under his desk.

"I hear Farmer Gardener's fingerprints are being sent over as we speak," he explained to Lotty, while thumbing through his notes to find the sections he wished to discuss. "The judge issued a court order for him to surrender his prints on account of probable cause. Why *are* we all calling him Farmer Gardener, by the way? Did someone here just start that and we all followed suit?"

"Yep! It does make it sound like we are attempting to charge a cartoon character. Excellent news on the prints too. I expect they're already on my desk by now."

"Probably. Right, down to business. I took the knife that you had supplied me with, along with the bloodstained female clothing that was provided to the police by the dustbin men who discovered them. In addition, I was notified this morning that Hercules came up trumps at the farm again late last night and uncovered a considerable pile of clothing in a section of the farm where Farmer Gardener had clearly tried to burn some clothes of his that appear also to be bloodstained. There should be enough material for me to extract the DNA from his clothes to match it to Grace Gardener's. I have already extracted the DNA present on the knife and women's clothing."

"What are you going to use to benchmark Grace's DNA?"

"Well, I've already done it. The gods were smiling down on us."

"Go on." Lotty smiled, now intrigued and happy that this was turning out to be one of the easiest cases she had ever worked on. Lotty's father had always taken a very hard line in domestic abuse cases, and Lotty felt that poor Grace Gardener needed to be avenged as well as put respectfully to rest.

"Grace had a twin." He dropped his bombshell and let it sink in.

"You are shitting me!"

"I kid you not. Her twin, Sarah, already surrendered her DNA to the laboratory with the usual hair and cheek swabs the moment we discovered she existed, and I have confirmed a positive match. We work fast here in DNA extraction, and I have been here for several hours already. You actually caught me making my fourth coffee of the day—and I have been spacing them out! Sarah just wants to get the case closed and find out what happened to her beloved sister. Obviously, they were very close indeed. As you are well aware, I'm sure, the DNA that we inherit from our parents when a sperm finds an egg is absolutely unique to every individual, yet often it's fairly similar between blood relatives, which is known as a familial match. Identical twins, however, such as Grace and Sarah were formed from one fertilised egg, so their DNA is absolutely identical, providing them with a matching genetic profile. It is only by their fingerprints that scientifically we are able to tell them apart. All of this has been rather fortuitous seeing as the one element of organisation that Farmer Gardener had gotten right was to start throwing away the items that we would normally use to extract our DNA benchmark—hairbrush, toothbrush, et cetera.

"Judging from his shoddy approach to date, I guess he was more purging the house of her for personal reasons. He seems to have been pretty slapdash in this whole affair, which is working greatly to our advantage."

Lotty did in fact feel like doing a cartwheel down the corridor, but not only did she feel that this would detract from the professional reputation that she was trying to forge for herself within the department, but also she was wearing her zebra print pants, which she thought her colleagues could rather do without seeing.

"James, you are a star."

"I do my best. You want to come and collect the latest evidence with me? It should have been delivered already. You can assist with the DNA extraction. I know you love helping out in other areas of the laboratory."

"That would be really helpful actually as Arthur wants me to get some laboratory time under my belt in the other disciplines because I have expressed an interest in moving over to the DNA profiling team."

"That's excellent. You know Amelia is going on maternity leave soon, and between you and me, I don't even think she wants to come back to work afterwards. Let's go and pick up the evidence."

CHAPTER 19

Later on, as James and Lotty were walking over to the section of the building where evidence was stored, processed or unprocessed, they bumped into Arthur.

"Hello, my little scientists. What trouble are you both causing today, I wonder?"

"Actually, I was just about to call you. Is it OK if I assist with a DNA extraction for James?"

"Absolutely, love. How are you feeling? I thought I left you a message to stay home and rest. You've had quite the couple of days, haven't you? How's the diarrhoea?"

"Do you want to just stand on top of the building with a loudspeaker so that *everyone* knows?" she asked sarcastically. Lotty was pretty sure everyone did already know, Arthur wasn't a gossip, he just felt the need to tell everyone everything.

"Sorry, pet. You go assist James. Then do the farmer's fingerprints, which are waiting for you in your laboratory. You can document the comparison for me when you are done."

"Yes, of course. It'll be done by the end of the day."

"Thanks," he called, walking off to the men's toilets. Arthur's bowels were as regular as clockwork. He often joked that if the frequency were to increase, he wouldn't really ever need a watch.

Once they had collected and signed out the evidence, Lotty and James walked back to James' laboratory, where they donned their clinically white lab coats and started to get their equipment ready. As they both proceeded to put white latex gloves on their hands, James turned to Lotty. She saw his face shine brightly with pride. "I had the kids perform their own DNA extraction a couple of weekends ago," James explained as they carefully cut out small samples from several of the bloodstains on the various items of clothes in front of them on the hard, metal surface of the workbench, carefully documenting the area from which each sample was removed.

"Huh? How?" James never failed to amaze Lotty. She wouldn't be surprised if both his young children ended up at either Oxford or Cambridge University well before the standard age of eighteen. She also imagined that with James and Aggie's support behind them, they would be the sort of children who would pass exams without having to study and would be the first picked for all the school sports teams. Lotty thought back to the painful, awkward years of her youth; she was never picked for anything and wasn't part of any of the cool cliques. The nicest the cool people at school had, in fact, been to her was when she had been hit by a car and launched twenty feet up a gravel road. This was an extreme method of temporarily breaching the in-crowd. Lotty wouldn't recommend it to others.

"Aggie and I got the kids some spinach and supervised them as they blended it for a few seconds with some table salt and also some ice-cold water. I think they were just happy to be doing anything that involved not eating the spinach, to be honest. Blending the spinach serves to separate the spinach cells from one another. Then we had them strain the resulting mixture themselves. I then added some liquid washing detergent for them, and we left the green slush that was produced to sit for a few minutes while I explained what we use DNA extraction for. We then poured the mixture into a small Thomas the Tank Engine glass; Andrew and Ben were quite adamant that we use that. Next I asked Aggie to add some enzyme solution. What do you think we used from our household for the enzymes?"

Lotty panicked at the question, which was clearly a subtle and informal test of her own skills and her ability to step into Amelia's shoes.

"Pineapple juice or contact lens solution?"

"Excellent. We also could have used meat tenderiser."

Lotty wasn't sure that she had ever even owned meat tenderiser, but she allowed James to carry on.

"The only item we actually had in the house was my contact lens solution, which Aggie poured in. I then took over and gently tilted the glass while very slowly and carefully pouring in some 90 per cent ethyl alcohol that I had been authorised to take home from work for the purposes of this experiment. As I poured it in, it formed a layer over the top of the spinach puree."

"Ah, and because it's less dense than water, it floated on the top!" Lotty chimed in to demonstrate her knowledge further. She did this mainly because, at this point, she was concerned that James' kids were actually on the way to becoming cleverer than she before they even started puberty.

"That's correct. The kids could then observe a white sticky substance at the top of the mixture which was the spinach's DNA."

"Held together by the salt in the contact lens solution, I guess?"

"Correct again. And when DNA, normally dissolved in liquid, becomes salty, it precipitates out to form a layer on the top, and the salt serves to create a chain of DNA, pulling the rest of the DNA out of the mixture."

"I guess if the spinach's DNA was being tested as a suspect in a murder, the victim would have cried out '*Spin-ouch!*' during the attack."

James stared unblinkingly at Lotty. She practically saw the tumbleweed rolling down the corridor.

While they had been talking, they had both prepared their own samples for testing, which they now placed into well plates that were attached to a piece of machinery that would the isolate the DNA for further analysis. James had nicknamed his machine "the Isolator", always said using his worst Arnold Schwarzenegger impression.

James allowed Lotty to assist him in the act of strategically adding several magnetic beads to the plates, before announcing that their work was done and that they should now wash their hands.

"We've got about one and a half hours to kill. I'm going to work on some other evidence I have in the meantime."

"Ok, I'll go and work on the farmer's fingerprints then."

CHAPTER 20

Lotty strode confidently back down the long corridor to her own area of the building, her blonde hair flowing from side to side now that it had been released from the ponytail that was obligatory for her to wear when working in the laboratory environment. She washed her hands once more and reflected upon the day so far. Feeling that the impromptu DNA laboratory session with James had gone really well, she smiled to herself and gave herself a mental pat on the back. She then walked over to her desk to retrieve the piece of card containing the fingerprint sample that she had previously obtained from the knife, and then sat down at her desk and located the farmer's fingerprints, which Arthur had already placed on her desk. Apparently, he had also left her a chocolate bar and a flyer for a singles pottery class that was being advertised locally. She ate the chocolate bar with gusto and, in protest to his lack of subtlety, screwed up the flyer and violently threw it in the recycling bin, rolling her eyes as she did so. Lotty didn't *do* pottery. She had long accepted that she wasn't good at any arts and crafts, having once sewn a sock she was trying to repair to the trousers that she had been wearing at the time.

Lotty examined the thumbprint of the farmer, removing a large flake of chocolate that had fallen out of her mouth and next to the card, and noted that the print clearly displayed a double-loop whorl, which she made a note of before placing the card on the scanner of her computer. Once the thumbprint was scanned into the machine, she removed the fingerprint card from the scanner and repeated the process with the sample print she had removed from the knife. Judging from the section of the knife on which the print was found and the angle at which she found it, she postulated that the print she had extracted was that of a thumb, hopefully the thumb of the farmer. The computer attached to said scanner started to churn away, processing her results, making noises that were reassuring to the user that it *was* actually doing something. There were no fancy flashing alerts displayed on a giant screen as television crime dramas would have people believe; the computer simply stopped making a noise when it was done—slightly less dramatic, but practical all the same.

The computer's findings documented that there was a 100 per cent match. Lotty smiled, pleased with herself, and noted her findings in an email that she then sent to Arthur, who would be put in charge of distributing the information to the relevant stakeholders. After washing her hands once more, Lotty walked down to the kitchen with a confident swagger, her mood dampening only slightly when she forgot herself and quietly broke wind halfway down the corridor. Lotty, looking around to check if anyone had seen or heard it happen, then walked into the communal kitchen. She opened the giant double fridge that was shared by her various colleagues at the laboratory and pulled out her stash of gluten-free bread, butter, and cheese, proceeding to make herself a modest-sized sandwich (only six slices of cheese and a depth of butter that one could leave a deep fingerprint in), before finally sitting down to eat it while reading today's edition of the *UK Chronicle*, which someone had kindly left for others' enjoyment in the kitchen. She briefly scanned an article on the second page of the paper that outlined the Evangeline DuVoir case in graphic detail and happily noted the absence of any information pertaining to Lotty or the events that had occurred during the party, especially the stray tampon incident. DS Andrews had managed to keep many of the details of the evening under wraps at least, and Lotty felt sure that Bruce was currently revelling in his status as Drama Queen at the fallout of the article. Bruce was one of her favourite people, but she had to admit that he went over the top when anything even vaguely dramatic happened either to or around him.

Lotty got up, checked no one was watching, and shifted the zebra print adorning her firm buttocks in order to remove the wedgie that had been annoying her and chafing her all day.

Having eaten her cheese sandwich and cleaned away her plate, Lotty walked back along the corridor to James' laboratory and entered. "Are you ready?" she asked.

"Yep. Coat up and wash your hands, please, then join me over here at the counter," he answered, stacking away a huge pile of journals that he had been reading. James preferred to read in hard copy as he felt it was better for his eyes.

"You're not going to make any more jokes, are you, Lotty?"

"Tch, no. Talk about a tough crowd."

James gestured for her to follow him over to the plates that had been isolated. Between the two of them, they removed the ten liquid samples they had put into the machine earlier, now placing them in a nearby test tube rack. The air-conditioned office was colder than Lotty's laboratory because of the equipment being used in there. Lotty felt herself shiver.

"Someone dancing on your grave?"

"No, Mr Morbid. It's bloody freezing in here."

"Yes, I can tell from your blouse. It looks like you're smuggling Smarties."

Lotty tutted, pulled the two sides of her laboratory coat together, buttoned it up, and followed James over to another area of the laboratory.

"So, remind me of what we have done so far."

Another test. Lotty felt herself go red in the face as her heart raced. She felt ridiculous getting this nervous, considering James was a friend and not just a work colleague.

"The liquid-handling workstation, lovingly referred to as 'the Isolator', is the machine we used earlier this morning. It lowers the pH of the plates to 6.5, which allows the DNA to bind to the magnetic beads that we added to the plates containing the samples."

"Ten out of ten, Lotty. Well done. There's hope for you yet." He laughed. "Right, now it's time for the gel electrophoresis process. So, would you like to place the extracted DNA substance from the first sample onto the gel, turn on the current to the tray, and talk me through the process?"

Lotty did as she was instructed and then narrated her procedures. "The gel acts as a strainer, if you will, and the switch that I have just activated enables the electrophoresis of the sample. The DNA holds a slight negative charge and thus moves towards the tray's positive end. The smaller the DNA fragment, the faster it moves through the gel."

"Excellent. Now I am placing a nylon membrane over the gel as it's easier to work with henceforth than the gel. You will note that I am adding probes to the membrane …"

"Which themselves then attach to the DNA fragments with a specific code?"

"Correct. These probes are radioactively charged and will therefore be displayed on the X-ray film that we are to now place on top of the membrane. Would you do the honours?"

Lotty placed the X-ray film over the nylon membrane and pressed down gently, before handing the film carefully over to James.

"Great work. You already know what you're doing. I'm going to send Arthur an email recommending you for the team during Amelia's absence. It's not for a while though, mind."

"Oh my goodness, thank you so much, James. That's fabulous. I don't mind waiting at all."

"Right, assuming that you don't mind and are relatively free for the rest of the afternoon, you need to repeat the process on the rest of these samples, please. I'll organise for the film to be developed."

Lotty did as she was told, working according to her normal standard of perfection, while James documented the processes that they had carried out in the case notes. Upon completion of these tasks, they walked the X-ray films, now in separate labelled envelopes, over to be developed.

"Lotty, I can deliver these. Why don't you make a move? In a very rare occurrence, we've finished relatively early. Thank you so much for your help today. I really appreciate it."

Lotty beamed at James. "OK, if you don't mind, I will. I was going to call DS Andrews for an update on the case." She inadvertently blushed a very deep red, almost concealing the fact that she was, in fact, wearing blusher today.

"Oh, it's like that, is it? Isn't he the nice chap who rescued you the other day?"

"Yes, he's gorgeous."

"Well, please let me know if anything happens with him with regard to dates et cetera. I am sure Aggie would be very keen to hear all about it."

Lotty blushed even redder and went off in order to collect her various personal belongings from her laboratory locker. As she walked slowly to her car, the vacancy in her eyes was indicative of the fact the she was daydreaming of DS Andrews' strong shoulders and chiselled chin. She almost skipped as she sashayed along to her internal music, this time the song "Close to You": "Why do birds suddenly appear …" Arthur, observing her strange behaviour from his third-floor office window while sipping a cup of strong sweet tea, made a mental note to diplomatically discuss with Lotty the laboratory's policy on drinking alcohol at lunchtime.

CHAPTER 21

Lotty drove home with her music blaring loudly, the roads being relatively clear of traffic because of the time, her having left the office slightly earlier than normal. As Barry White played through her car's stereo, she sang along to the song's uplifting lyrics, navigating the beautiful country roads before finally pulling into her neighbourhood. She parked outside the local supermarket and went in. She felt the need to overshop as her hunger had once again gotten the better of her and her stomach was growling for sustenance.

As Lotty scanned the meat counter, she suddenly spotted in her peripheral vision a man whom she had gone on a very unsuccessful date with a couple of months ago. The unfortunate chap had been so utterly and mind-numbingly boring that, coupled with her fatigue from a late work night the previous evening, Lotty had fallen asleep in her dinner. It was embarrassing all round. He had only wakened her when she started snoring so loudly that a couple at a nearby table became increasingly more irritated at the terrible wheezing noises her sinuses were creating during her nap. Lotty quickly grabbed some lamb cutlets and placed them in her already brimming shopping basket, then literally ran down the other end of the aisle to avoid "Mr Boring" before he saw her. She had never returned his calls, but she had to congratulate his keenness on calling her back at all after the incident, seeing as she had dozed off into, and ruined, an extremely expensive meal of Aberdeen Angus fillet with truffle fries. She now walked at great speed into the vegetable and fruit section, where she grabbed a bag of salad, a cucumber, and some sweet-smelling vine tomatoes. The smell always reminded Lotty of her father, as she would often spend hours sitting and chatting with him in his greenhouse while he tended to his home-grown vegetables. Lotty's brief foray into home gardening had proved more than unsuccessful thanks to her compassion for all things living and her subsequent inability to use slug pellets.

Lotty grabbed some plump, vibrant green limes and placed them into her basket. She felt pleased at being able to walk past the confectionary section without faltering and filling her basket to the brim with the sweet offerings on display. Lotty had another love in life: all things derived from chocolate and sweets. She walked through the book section towards the checkout. Turning, she immediately walked back to the confectionary section and grabbed a bag of fun-size chocolate bars, then walked back to the checkout.

"Damn." She chastised herself and her lack of willpower.

After paying the cashier, Lotty walked back to her car and loaded the boot with her shopping. She continued her journey home, driving into her garage shortly before five-thirty in the evening.

CHAPTER 22

Lotty looked up at the sky and was concerned by the dark, grey clouds that were oppressively enveloping the sky.

She followed her normal daily routine and placed her old, yet faithful, field kit into a cupboard in the garage, then walked into her house to be greeted by the waiting Arabella. Her fluffy friend had been fast asleep on the sofa and, upon noticing the arrival of Lotty, had jumped down to briefly stretch her sinewy limbs and sharp claws before running to her food bowl, thus demonstrating to Lotty what her first priority should be for the evening. The slight odour of eggy cat biscuits hinted to Lotty that the new dry food she was buying Arabella clearly wasn't agreeing with the feline flatulence that the cat often suffered from.

"Just like her owner," said Lotty out loud. She placed some dry and wet cat food into Arabella's respective dishes and topped up the water bowl with some fresh tap water before jumping into the shower. She wasn't sure why she was bothering sometimes, considering that Arabella clearly favoured drinking water directly out of the toilet bowl. That should really come with danger money considering the state of Lotty's bowels.

Lotty relaxed herself from her long day with a nice apricot facial scrub and a hefty loofah session with body exfoliant before jumping out and towelling herself dry. She covered herself in moisturiser, her method of keeping her skin youthful, before donning her warm, fluffy bright pink dressing gown that had come straight from the tumble dryer in the utility room. After tidying away the remnants of a blackbird that she had discovered in the utility room (thanks again to Arabella), Lotty put her gas oven on to heat up. Taking the lamb cutlets out of her shopping bags, which were still on the counter, she proceeded to cover them in a thick layer of mint sauce that would serve to help the meat crisp up. Then she placed the cutlets in the oven and made herself a dressed salad. While she waited for the oven to cook her dinner, she began to mix herself a mojito, using ice shavings from her new icemaker, an essential for the hardened mojito lover.

She sat down on the sofa with her newly washed hair still in a towel to dry. Sipping her mojito, she grabbed her mobile phone and dialled Bruce's number.

"Bruce speaking."

"Hey, it's me. How was your tennis game the other day?"

"Divine." He laughed mischievously. "I was very sore afterwards."

"OK, I don't need any more details, thank you. Mum emailed today. She sends her love. She's been walking on the beach and reading her romance novels. She really misses me and wants me to join her at some point for a bit of a holiday."

"Great. Are you going to go?"

"I might do, perhaps when work calms down a bit. She said you should come as well."

"Sounds delightful, my darling. Any news on the case?"

"We've made some progress with the postmortem and discovered that something was more than likely placed into Evangeline's drink. There are no other obvious signs of trauma as yet. Have you had a think about why anyone would do this to Evangeline?"

"Well, obviously Evangeline's field of work made her a rather venomous and spiteful character, which made people very wary of getting too close. I expect her son's already totting up his expected inheritance."

"Was she very wealthy then?"

"Yes. As I told you at the party, she received a substantial income from her work at the *UK Chronicle*, and in addition to this, she still had her family money, as well as her divorce settlement."

"Do you know her son whom you mentioned?" she enquired.

"We both do. It's Alexander Rowley. He took his father's name when he was born, yet Evangeline always kept faithful to her maiden name or the name she had made up for herself—I'm not sure which was the case. I guess she thought that she had already started a fruitful career with the name of DuVoir and felt that she shouldn't change it."

"What about her husband?"

"Sir Ralph. You met him as well. There was also a previous husband, Bernard Chilton. Oh, there was *rather* a scandal attached to that. They had become estranged when it transpired that he was knocking off his secretary Susan Gibbons, and he had taken to living on his yacht down in Southampton. One day he took the yacht out and never came back. They found large sections of its structure all broken up several miles out to sea. Susan survived as she hadn't taken to living full-time on the boat yet. This was a long time ago. Evangeline met Sir Ralph and had Alexander very soon after. Anyway, when the legal number of years had passed, Chilton was declared as missing, presumed dead. Evangeline and Sir Ralph then made it all official and got married. I believe the executors had been instructed under the terms of the will to distribute the majority of the assets over to Evangeline and to set up a trust for Alexander at the time."

"If you had to suspect any of the people at the party, who would it be?"

"Lotty, there is always the chance that someone I didn't know who had it in for Evangeline could have entered the party and spiked her drink. You're asking me to finger some of my oldest and dearest friends."

Lotty, choosing to ignore the double entendre that Bruce had left wide open to her, carried on regardless. "Bruce, Agatha Christie herself once said, 'Every murderer is probably someone's oldest friend.'"

"Darling, you really need to get out more. You're so very morbid. Anyway, I guess if I had to pick, I would say Alexander, Greg, or Sir Ralph."

"Alexander being for the money, right?"

"Yes, but he does seem an awfully nice chap to me really, darling, apart from being rather a party animal. Greg, as I told you the other evening, was tied in to a very long and pricey working contract with Evangeline. As for Sir Ralph, he was her latest failed marriage. Again, that was a relatively long time ago, and much water has passed under the bridge since then, but even so, it was a bitter and acrimonious divorce. They both still went out of their way to avoid one another in public."

"What was the reason for that marriage break-up?"

"I am not entirely sure, but I think she felt that Sir Ralph was rather too controlling. I also remember that he has always been quite the ladies' man. He has rather a wandering eye."

"Oh, thanks very much for introducing me to *him* then," Lotty retorted so indignantly that she choked briefly on a piece of mint from her cocktail.

"He's still a very endearing and charming gentleman."

"That may be, but he is old enough to be my father. I am not in the slightest bit interested in that patronising old fart."

"Well, quite, dear."

Lotty was grateful to be on a call and not to be looking directly at Bruce's face, thereby avoiding what she imagined to be the rather stern look of disapproval that he was currently wearing.

"Any other suspects?"

She had a brief pause while Bruce pondered the question.

"I would say her agent Emmanuel, whom you didn't meet. Evangeline recently fired her for no apparent reason, but then again, Evangeline did a lot of things for no good reason. I know she also had upset Lorna Brannigan on several occasions."

"Who's that? Did I meet her at your party?"

"No. Lorna rang me shortly before the party started to let me know that she had come down with a gastric bug and would be unable to make it. She writes for a rival paper. She and Evangeline were constantly at one another's throats."

Lotty heard her oven timer chime, which indicated, along with the hearty juicy aroma emanating from the kitchen, that her lamb cutlets were done. "OK, I have to go. My dinner's ready, and I am absolutely starving, Bruce."

"OK. And remember, if you need anything, I'm just at the other end of the phone. Make sure you pop over soon, sweetheart."

"I will. Take care."

She placed the mobile phone down on her lounge table and went out into the kitchen to find Arabella waiting anxiously and staring intently at the oven. Lotty placed the tender pieces of meat onto her plate with her salad and then cut some small pieces of meat off, which she then blew on gently until she deemed that they were cool enough to place into Arabella's food bowl. Arabella ran over to the bowl and started working her way through the juicy morsels.

Lotty watched her and sang "What's New Pussycat?"

CHAPTER 23

After finishing her dinner and tidying up her kitchen, Lotty dialled DS Andrews' number.

"Hi, Lotty. I wath going to call you. How did Thunday go?"

"Very well. Jonathan has concluded initially that a protein-laden substance caused Evangeline to suffer from acute kidney failure. We will be analysing her blood further at the laboratory to investigate what the substance was."

"How come it killed her? Don't we ingetht proteinth all the time?"

"Essentially, yes. We do ingest proteins in small doses throughout the day from the foods that we eat or drink. Bodybuilders and other sporty folk, for example, take highly concentrated doses of protein to build muscles, often as a liquid supplement. Anyway, something with such high doses that it was well above the normal level one would find in something we naturally ingest found its way into Evangeline's wine glass and overloaded her already weak kidneys. Evidently, she suffered from a disease known as polycystic kidney disease, or PKD, for which she had only recently had an operation. She was probably being very careful indeed as to what she was eating and drinking anyway. Jonathan was rather surprised that she was drinking wine in the first place as alcohol can also put undue strain on the kidneys."

"So, do you know how kidney failure occurth from that?" he asked.

Lotty didn't like to point out that she had a degree in biology and so yes, of course, she bloody knew. "Our kidneys act as our body's filtration system, eliminating excess fluid and waste material from our systems. Acute kidney failure such as that suffered by Evangeline is relatively simple to bring about. In some cases, such as deaths related to binge drinking, a person can overload their system with alcohol by ingesting it at a rate much higher than the kidneys can cope with, causing death in the healthiest of people. Furthermore, chronic kidney failure could occur, but over a much longer period of time. This is often related to habitual drinking."

"But you thaid that Evangeline wouldn't have drunk much due to her weakneth."

"Well, that's right. And in Evangeline's case, her already damaged kidneys were subjected to a massive concentration of proteins, not alcohol. Her weak kidneys were unable to break down this excess protein; they became totally overloaded and failed her. Most people who knew that she had damaged and weak kidneys would also have known that putting a dose of *anything* in her drink would have tipped her over the edge. In addition, Jonathan emailed me this morning to advise me that her body displayed signs of a cold. She probably wouldn't have tasted anything in her wine anyway, so the foreign agent would have easily gone undetected. Jonathan estimated that she had allowed herself approximately two large glasses of red wine, and this, mixed with the as yet unknown substance, would have caused her kidneys to totally give out and fail her."

"OK, I underthtand now. Thanksth for that."

"Do you have any other news on the case?"

"A bit. One of the detectiveth told me that a shattered memory card was found near the body. It was in tiny pietheth, unfortunately."

"A memory card?"

"Yeth. It hasth been sent to your laboratory for protething, but I am not thure what help it will be, to be honetht. It isth unlikely that we can retrieve any data from it, and it'sth in thuch thmall pietheth that partial print analythith won't be an option."

"Even if we assume that it was the murderer's and not Evangeline's own memory card, it can be said that everyone and their dog carries around such cards to use in one device or another. The digital camera in my handbag has one, as does my work mobile and work camera. I also have a digital photo frame at home with one in it."

"I know. And we are yet to find any dithcrepenthieth in anyone'th thtatementh."

"I spoke to Bruce earlier."

"To order your bodyguard?" He laughed cheekily.

"No, I haven't put that one past him yet, but I know that he would say yes. I already feel a lot more secure as the police have stuck to their word and have indeed been passing by at regular intervals."

"Good. We aim to pleathe."

"I went over anyone who was or wasn't in attendance at the party to try to start making a list of suspects."

"OK. Do you want to run them patht me?"

Lotty took another long sip of her mojito, savouring the bittersweet mix of brown sugar and lime as it danced on her tongue. She then spent the next ten minutes recalling to DS Andrews the list that she had compiled over the phone with Bruce before dinner.

"OK, I will dithpatch thome officersth out to obtain a thtatement from Lorna, theeing ath thee could potentially be a thuspect despite her abthenthe from the party. Anyone could have thnuck in undetected, I gueth."

"I'd put money on Sir Ralph, Greg, and Alexander if I had to bet. Well, according to Bruce's odds anyway," she offered. "I might check a few people out myself."

"Hmm, really?" His tone denoted that he was clearly very against the idea of Lotty essentially sticking her nose into the investigation and also putting herself further in danger. "Hathn't your latht run-in put you off?"

"Nope. Remember, I'm from good stock. Daddy and Aunt Molly would have done the same. And it will give me a chance to practise my private detecting. I run a business now, you know."

"Yeth, but my friendth down the sthtation who knew your dad told me that you weren't going to take that much of an active role in the agency."

Lotty smiled, knowing that DS Andrews clearly must have been asking around about her. With no one else to see her, she was happy to blush a bright maroon as well as bat her eyelids. She found herself involuntarily stroking her hair and cocking her head to one side.

"Yes, but you never know what's around the corner. And I need some practical experience anyway if I'm going to run the company well, be it just in the background or not."

"Well, leth keep in touch. And do not do anything on your own. Go with your employeeth."

"I will. Shall we meet up later in the week to discuss the cases?" she offered tentatively, trying not to sound too desperate.

"You're working on more than one?"

"Oh, I forgot to tell you, I'm heavily involved down at the laboratory on the Gardener case. I believe that's also one of yours?"

"Oh right, yeth, thath correct. How isth that one going then? To be honetht, I'm yet to catch up on todayth workload. If you can fill me in, then it will thayve me trawling through the thtack of emailth in my inbox."

"Well, as I'm sure you're aware, we have extracted evidence from Farmer Gardener's hard drive pertaining to his financial difficulties."

"Thath right, and he had taken out a life inthurance policy on his wife ath well."

"Yes, and in the last few days we've matched the DNA on the bloodstained knife and female clothing to Grace's. We used her twin's DNA as a benchmark, as twins have identical DNA. In addition, I helped a colleague today with a DNA extraction on some partially burnt clothes that had been found during evidence collection, which we are waiting to confirm shows Grace's blood on them as well."

"I didn't know that—you know, the twinth thing. I've never come acroth it before."

"It was a massive stroke of luck as apparently Farmer Gardener had already disposed of his wife's belongings, which we would normally seize to perform an extraction on. In addition, Jonathan tells me that he has sent off the bone I discovered to be examined further as we need to compare the cuts I observed on it to see if they are consistent with being cut by a meat cleaver or a saw. Oh, and I believe they have extracted some DNA from the bone, which they are analysing tomorrow. This will confirm if the bone did in fact belong to Grace. There will be some further investigations on the evidence later on this week, so I'll keep you posted."

"Thanksth for that. You've been really helpful. I really apprethiate it. Have a good evening."

"OK, you too," she said before disconnecting the call.

Lotty sat on the sofa wondering if DS Andrews' interest was purely professional or whether he wanted to pound her. "God, he's an absolutely bloody dish," she muttered naughtily to no one in particular.

CHAPTER 24

Lotty noted that it was still early evening. She didn't really feel in the mood to watch mind-numbing television, so she went upstairs and changed into a tight pair of black jogging leggings, some black merino wool socks, a baggy hooded jumper, and her new running shoes. She swept her hair off of her face, tied it up in a ponytail, grabbed her smartphone, strapped it to her arm, and started down the stairs. Arabella, having spied the headphone cable, and concluding it was worth attacking, launched herself at Lotty from her precarious seat on the banisters halfway down the stairs. Lotty ducked, but all too late, and both she and Arabella tumbled down the stairs, landing in a heap next to each other at the bottom. With somewhat delayed yet catlike agility, Arabella pounced back onto her feet and sauntered off towards the lounge, looking decidedly embarrassed by the whole affair.

After washing the scratches on her arm, Lotty opened up her kitchen drawer and checked her medical card to confirm she was up to date with her vaccinations. Bloody cat. She made a mental note to purchase some Bluetooth headphones as she opened the front door. She turned on her music and grabbed her foot while bending it at the knee, until her foot touched her buttocks, in order to stretch her quads. She then leaned herself against the wall, placed her toes against it, and stretched out her calves, breathing deeply as she did so. After jogging on the spot for a few seconds to warm up the rest of her muscles, she set off down the path at a steady and confident pace, wincing as she noticed her nice clean running shoes splashing in the muddy puddles from a recent shower of rain. She picked up her pace and continued down the path, giving a passing wave to a fellow jogger, who smiled and waved back, treating Lotty to his revolting-smelling body odour as he passed. As Lotty jogged even faster to escape the offending smell and to enjoy her own body odour instead, she felt her heart beating heavily in her chest like a caged animal trying to escape. More than an hour later, she jogged back into her drive, having worked up quite a sweat. Her eyes were immediately drawn to a typed note that had been stuck neatly, yet threateningly, to her door.

"Stop sticking your bloody nose in or you'll be sorry," she read to herself out loud. She glanced around to see if the perpetrator was still present, with her heart beating even harder in her chest. She felt nauseous and fought extremely hard not to throw her dinner up into her prized rose bush. She quickly ran inside her house, locked the front door, and leaned against it, breathing in hard, deep breaths. Grabbing her mobile phone, she scaled her stairs two by two and dialled DS Andrews' number.

"Hi again. It's Lotty. I'm really scared!"

"Hello again." He sounded pleasantly surprised, yet concerned at her tone. "I agree, Lotty. I am sthcared too. It isth new to uth both, but leth jutht take thingth thlowly and thee where it all goes, thall we?"

"What on earth are you talking about? I need you to come over. I've just found a threatening note taped to my front door!"

When she had finished, she paused for breath and for DS Andrews' comments.

"I'll get patrol over to you now. I'm coming over too. I'll thee you in a thecond." He rang off, hoping that in her blind panic, she hadn't properly heard what he had said.

CHAPTER 25

Less than five minutes later, Lotty heard a squad car, its sirens blaring loudly, pull up outside her house. She ran down her staircase, scaring Arabella as she did so, causing the cat to meow loudly before bolting at great speed under Lotty's sofa. Lotty opened the front door to the waiting police officers.

"I need you to stay inside with Officer Smith, ma'am. I want to just check the perimeter while Officer Smith checks the inside the house." Lotty's heart leapt into her mouth. She ran to the bathroom and was very sick. Afterwards, she sat by the toilet, clinging hard to the cold white porcelain bowl, as her mind darted back and forth to process what the officer had insinuated. She hadn't once thought that there could have been someone *inside* her house with her. As she washed her face and rinsed her mouth with mouthwash, she heard a gentle tapping at the door.

"Who is it?" she asked, not very bravely.

"Lotty, are you OK? It'sth Mathon."

She opened the door and, before she even thought about what she was doing, ran into his arms. *He can't mind too much,* she thought; his arms had already been open to receive her. DS Andrews felt Lotty, now crying, wipe her nose on his jumper as she maintained their tight hug. He waited for what he thought was an appropriate amount of time before diplomatically offering her his handkerchief. As he watched her blow her nose into it, loudly enough to measure on the Richter scale, he quickly wiped her mucous from his clothes before she noticed.

"The officersth have checked outthide and inthide the houthe, and it'sth all fine. They are going to be sthtationed outthide the houthe for tonight ath well. Doeth that make you feel better?"

"Yes," she whispered quietly into the handkerchief.

DS Andrews patted her gently, yet awkwardly, on her arm and hoped that Lotty wouldn't try to give the handkerchief back to him after what she had done to it. "Now leth get you upthtairth and into bed, thall we?"

Lotty looked up, confused and not unpleasantly surprised.

"Obviouthly, one of the female offither will thtay until you're tucked up in bed, and then they'll let themthelvth out. Are you happy if they jutht pull the door closed on their way out?" he asked.

"Of course, that's fine. Thank you for your help and for getting here so quickly. I'm not going to let whoever is doing this get the better of me."

"Thath the thpirit!" he enthused. "Now go on up to bed and call down for Offither Thmith when you're ready for her to let herthelf out. Take care. And I'll have my phone on. Pleathant dreamth."

He found the desire to peck her on her beautiful rosy cheek, and then he let himself out. She watched him walk down the drive. He looked back and waved. As instructed, she went up to her bedroom, undressed, pulled on her dressing gown, and jumped into bed.

"Hi, I'm going to sleep now," she called out to the officer downstairs.

"OK, I'll let myself out. We'll be outside. If you need anything, then just call out. Or my mobile number is down here, written on your telephone pad. Don't worry about anything."

"Thanks so much. I feel much better knowing that you're out there. If you would like to take the spare key next to the phone, you can come in throughout the night and make drinks or help yourself to a snack. Just leave the key on the table when you're done in the morning. You won't wake me; I'm a fairly heavy sleeper once I'm out for the night."

"Are you sure?"

"Definitely. I really appreciate you being out there."

"OK, thanks. I'll be in the kitchen in about an hour looking for your biscuits then."

"No worries. There's a cookie jar on the dining room table. Good night."

"Good night. Sleep well."

Lotty was so exhausted from the evening's events that she drifted off quickly into a dreamless sleep, unaware of the various trips to her kitchen or bathroom that the two stationed police officers made throughout the night.

CHAPTER 26

The following day at work, Lotty caught up on her paperwork. She was still rather shaken up from the previous evening. At about three in the afternoon, she received a call from Arthur. To keep her hands free, she clasped her mobile phone between her shoulder and her ear.

"I'm out at the farm. I have just spoken to DS Andrews, and he told me about what happened last night. Why didn't you call me? You're not having the *best* time of it lately, are you?"

Lotty heard some ducks in the background. "I'm OK. I'm just a bit put out really. I won't let someone intimidate me, Arthur. I just won't. Are you feeding the ducks again?"

"Yes, I just thought I'd come down and feed them for a quick break— very relaxing. You should come down and join me, love."

"Ha, I would love to, but I'm catching up on my office admin today. Is everything going well out there?" She doodled on her notepad absent-mindedly as she spoke; she was trying to curb that habit after she had once sent an entire legal team a copy of her notes as evidence in a burglary trial and one of the pages contained a crude diagram of a penis.

"Yes. We haven't unearthed anything further of great interest yet, but the investigation is coming along smoothly overall. And the team here have dug up more bone matter in the pigpen. It's putting me right off eating sausages in the future."

"I can imagine. I enjoyed the DNA extraction yesterday." Subtlety was not one of Lotty's strong points.

"Yes, I heard. Well, I think we can safely earmark the next available slot in the team for you. As I'm sure you've heard, there's one coming up in the next few months."

Lotty smiled. Then she heard splashing and several ducks quacking in the background. "Hello? Arthur?"

"Yep. Sorry, I'm still here. Just fell in up to my knees. Bloody mudbanks. I had best go, love. I'm drenched and covered in duck shit. Luckily, I keep a spare pair of work trousers in the car."

With that, Arthur disconnected the call.

Lotty laughed and drifted off into a daydream as she heard the theme tune of *Laurel and Hardy* playing through her head. She had already achieved her goal of impressing Arthur; now all she had to do was to impress DS Andrews. She needed a buddy to go out sleuthing with and had just thought of the ideal candidate to go digging for gossip with.

She grabbed her mobile phone back off her desk, dialled, and heard the other line ring a few times.

"Bruce speaking."

"Hey there, how are you?"

"I'm OK. I've just come from an early lunch actually, darling. How goes it?"

"Well, I kind of had a nasty note pinned to my door yesterday." She deliberately downplayed the previous evening's events. "I'm OK though."

"Lotty, I want you to come and stay with me. It's not like it's going to cramp your sex life; you don't have one." Tactful.

"I can't do that; your house is way too far from the office. What about if I agree to having private security personnel placed outside my front door until we know more about the case and get some positive leads?"

"Deal. I will have one of the security folk from my office stationed outside yours in a car. They will text you their car make, model, and registration so you know who to look out for."

Bruce absolutely loved the perks that came with owning his own IT consulting business, especially the free lunches. His company had consistently generated a multimillion-pound turnover for several years and had exponentially grown in net worth. To be blunt, Bruce had more money than he knew what to do with and nobody to spend it on.

"What are you up to tonight?" Lotty asked coyly.

"Spending it causing mischief with you by the sounds of it. What do you want me for this time? I simply refuse to follow any more of your potential suitors. It was very embarrassing the last time. *Nobody* follows people into a sauna."

"Oh my god, that was your idea to follow that man into there. You said you were checking out his assets. It's not my fault it was a unisex sauna."

"Well, they should really make the sign bigger. That lady was horrified when I accidentally sat on her naked. I could have died."

"Anyway, I promised DS Andrews that, in the interest of personal safety, I wouldn't sleuth on my own, but I really want to impress him and start getting some dirt on the suspects. Do you want to help me? We can start with Greg."

"Oh, how exciting!" he squealed. "I'll pick you up at seven tonight. We can drive out to where he lives first. He is out most nights and is a bit of a stop-out, so if he is going out, we should arrive early enough to follow him. He lives over in Caversham Heights. I've been there for several dinner parties. It's one of those gaudy new-build properties with tacky iron gates that just scream, 'I wasn't born into money.'"

Lotty laughed. Bruce could make being bitchy an Olympic sport.

"OK, I'll see you about seven, but in the meantime, can you please get one of the researchers in your office to gather up some background on Greg from their sources? He is fairly high profile, so they are bound to dig up *some* information on him."

The rest of her workday proved to be rather noneventful, but Lotty did, at least, manage to catch up on all of her paperwork finally; she had spent the afternoon furiously filling in several forms that were late. To her, they were long overdue in being submitted. The forms were, in fact, being submitted a week earlier than was required. Lotty firmly believed in the adage that *early is on time, and on time is late.*

84

CHAPTER 27

Lotty breathed a sigh of relief. She had arrived home with enough time to grab a quick shower. After she'd fed Arabella, and before putting on some dark jeans and a hooded black sweatshirt, at exactly seven in the evening, Bruce was waiting at her front door for her, bedecked in black slacks, a black jumper, and black Paul Smith brogues.

"We're following him, not performing a fashion show for him."

"I'm dressed to blend in." He added indignantly, "Tastefully."

They jumped into Bruce's shiny Jaguar sports car and shared gossip from their days apart as they made their way towards Caversham Heights. Once they had reached Greg's address, Bruce pulled the car up and parked it on the side of the road opposite the house.

"I hope he doesn't recognise your car. Damn, I'm not ready for all this sleuthing just yet. Clearly, that's only just occurred to me now that we are actually here." Lotty felt disappointed that she was about to fall at the first hurdle.

"No, don't worry yourself. I bought this car *since* I last dined at his house, and therefore he hasn't seen it. And he isn't a close enough friend even to know that I own it. As far as Greg is concerned, I'm still driving around in the Aston Martin."

"It's my guess that he is going to eat first then go out on the town. That's his normal routine."

"While we wait, did you get any background information on Greg?"

"I have some information here for you. I must admit that we are fairly superficial in our friendship and I didn't know all that much about him." Bruce leaned over Lotty, opened his glovebox, pulled out a notepad, and started to read.

"Greg started out his journalistic career as an agony aunt for a ... gentleman's magazine. I won't tell you the title; it's incredibly offensive and made even me blush. Working at such a publication, based in the big city, Greg partied incredibly hard for several years and developed a bad alcohol addiction. He maintained his partying lifestyle until he caused a car crash while very drunk in the early 1990s. Although he didn't harm anyone other than himself during that crash, he suffered several broken bones and the loss of his driving licence, and it really shook him up. He immediately admitted himself into a rehabilitation clinic in London, where he finally beat his alcoholism. After leaving the clinic, he joined a leading sports publication in Los Angeles as a sportswriter, where he received several prestigious awards for his journalism. It was here that he was mentored by the owner of the paper, Roy Shaddup, who eventually passed away childless and left all his wealth to Greg. While considering what to do with his newly found wealth, Greg travelled the world while performing various bits of charitable work, including building houses and digging wells in Africa and building orphanages in Russia. After returning from his global travels, he met a woman, Abbey Raleigh, with whom he fell totally and utterly in love. During their lengthy engagement, they resided on a farm in Southern England, where they bred alpacas for their wool, which they sold to high-end clothing companies, back before alpaca wool was even trending. Abbey unfortunately died at a dreadfully early age; she drowned while swimming off the coast of Devon during a holiday that she was spending with Greg to celebrate her having become pregnant. Greg, as you could imagine, was utterly devastated. He sold the farm straightaway and moved back to London, where he was snapped up by the *UK Chronicle*. Unaware of his wealth, the various senior journalists there mentored him, before he subsequently performed a very hostile takeover. He assumed ownership of the *UK Chronicle* about ten years ago. He is still teetotal and attempts to seek pleasure via other avenues these days, mostly sports orientated. In the last five years alone, he has climbed Ben Nevis, partially walked the Great Wall of China, llama-trekked in Tibet, and also abseiled down the British Telecom Tower, all for charitable causes. He comes from a simple working-class background, his father having been a coal miner and his mum a cook at the mine's canteen. He also has a brother and sister. Nowadays, Greg maintains his parents and his siblings in a luxurious lifestyle, which he thinks they deserve now that there is money in the family. He also bestows a lot of his wealth every year to several charitable organisations. His parents currently live in St Tropez, France, while his brother and sister both live in Southern Italy, all in properties that Greg has generously gifted to them over the past few years. He visits all of them regularly and keeps a very close relationship with them as he maintains it was their emotional support that enabled him to overcome his alcoholism. Two years ago, Greg admitted himself once again to a private clinic that specialises in sexual addiction, declaring at the time that he wasn't that bothered about being cured but felt that his locality would mean easy pickings. He did, at any rate, also successfully beat that addiction, and finally found love just this year, when he met Melissa when she started working at the *UK Chronicle*. The word on the street is that she loves his newly teetotal and chaste lifestyle as she doesn't believe in sex before marriage." He paused for breath.

"How on earth did your researchers dig all that up in one afternoon?"

"Oh no, I telephone Greg earlier and asked him." Lotty stared blankly at Bruce. "I said that I wanted to get to know him better."

"Subtle, Bruce. Really subtle."

"No, darling, he seemed to believe me. I did mention that I wanted him to come over to discuss it over a moonlit dinner in my garden, as I said that at this time in our lives, we should start building more special relationships. He spilt the beans big time—anything to avoid a romantic dinner with me. My ploy worked. I don't know what your problem is, darling. Really, you can be awfully ungrateful at times."

As they sat bickering in their normal manner, they both spotted a car exiting through the gates of Greg's house. Greg was at the wheel, and Melissa was in the passenger seat. Lotty and Bruce ducked down low into their seats as Greg's black Bentley Continental glided effortlessly past them and moved down the road towards the town centre. After leaving it a sensible number of seconds, Bruce started his own car engine, and they began their pursuit. Bruce carefully maintained a safe distance between his car and Greg's, managing to consistently always remain roughly two cars back. He was used to following cars; in recent years he had followed Lotty on several of her dinner dates to check that she was safe, without her ever finding out.

"His car is awesome. That must have cost a pretty penny," Lotty said, her eyes turning a jealous green hue.

"It's a normal car for someone in his position, darling. It is very fancy though. I might get one next." Bruce changed cars nearly as often as he changed his affections. Lotty had found out in the car journey to Greg's that Bruce had become tired of his tennis coach and that he was currently swooning over the patisserie chef from his favourite restaurant. Lotty had warned him to avoid any romantic goings-on with someone who could, if spurned, do something nasty to his food. Crème anglaise could hide a variety of sins.

Bruce and Lotty followed Greg through town, over the river bridge, down a dual carriageway, and into a small suburb of Reading that was renowned for prostitution.

"Interesting," muttered Lotty to Bruce. "Do you think they're swingers?"

"Ew, I certainly hope not. What a vile pastime that is. If someone wanted me to sleep with their spouse, my first thoughts would be that there is clearly something wrong with them or else their other half wouldn't be trying to palm them off onto somebody else."

"No, I watched a documentary on it recently. They get a kick out of seeing one another with different people, apparently. Voyeurism, Bruce."

"I don't want to hear any more about the documentaries you have been watching. I'm still having nightmares since you recalled the documentary on dogging to me, and now I can't walk across the golf course's car park at night without thinking that the cars parked there are all having lewd acts performed inside them. As for the list of top 20 lewd acts that you explained, let me tell you that I have been unable to eat off my antique table as it obviously has had previous owners who could have been doing anything on it."

"No, they do that on glass tables, so you can see from the other side."

"Enough. Really, enough."

Bruce pulled over to the side of the road as he saw Greg's car pull into a car park behind a building. Lotty craned her neck to get a look at the building.

"It's one of those places that has floatation tanks that you go into in order to relax."

"Oh, right. He told me about that at his last dinner party actually. He goes twice a week with Melissa. They go into separate tanks for an hour and a half and they just float, relax, and meditate. It's all the rage, I hear. I'm rather thinking of trying it myself. If I were in a tank all by myself, I'd probably …"

"Please don't!"

He laughed. "What are we going to do for ninety minutes while they are in there?"

"What about having dinner? I saw a sports bar back there. It's like a burger place."

"Dear God, darling, why don't you cut out the middleman and just defecate into my mouth? What about the bistro we saw about a mile back?"

Bruce was a massive snob when it came to food.

"OK, we can go there, I guess." Lotty was more interested in quantity rather than quality when it came to eating out.

Bruce turned the car around on a petrol station forecourt and made his way back to the expensive-looking French bistro that his eagle eye had caught. He stopped his car, getting out to open Lotty's car door for her. Bruce was a gentleman—well, a gentleman's gentleman, but a gentleman all the same.

CHAPTER 28

Bruce and Lotty were seated at their table by an elderly concierge who was sporting the most unrealistic toupee that Lotty had ever seen.

"I hope his hair is toilet-trained." She laughed as he walked off after explaining the evening specials to them. Then she felt bad. She had promised herself after her near-death experience with her recent house intruder that she would stop being mean about people. It simply wasn't nice.

After perusing the extensive menu, Lotty called the waiter over and ordered the scallops on a bed of squid ink tagliatelle, the steak Béarnaise, and a house salad, while Bruce opted for Coquille St Jacques followed by steak tartare.

After studying the wine list closely, Bruce ordered a half-bottle of 2016 Merlot for them to share.

Over their starters, they spoke very little, both clearly very hungry. When they had finished, Bruce topped up Lotty's modestly filled glass as well as his own. "How is that farm case going that you're on?"

"Really well, actually. I can't talk too much about it, but we are making significant headway. I do believe the farmer is going to be formally charged very soon. Did I tell you that I found out today that I'm being seconded into the DNA laboratory rather imminently?"

"Oh, well, that is wonderful. I'm so proud of you. I know that your aunt and father would be very proud as well, darling. Have you texted your mother?"

"Yes. You know how she likes being kept abreast of all my news. I texted her this afternoon. She is really pleased as I mentioned quite a while back that I was interested in moving my career in that direction. It's much more interesting than the work I am currently doing. I'm really excited actually." Her bashfulness, coupled with the glass of red wine that she had nearly finished, caused her to blush again.

"What about this DS Andrews fellow? Have you made any more headway on that little romance? Maybe you should bring him around to mine for dinner so I can vet him for you properly?"

"No way. I don't even know if he is interested yet. And I would wait for a few dates, if I were to have any with him, before bringing him around to yours. You always get my baby pictures out. It's tragic."

"Oh, you do fuss. They're only photos. You were a beautiful baby."

"I'm naked in most of them. It's really embarrassing."

"Nonsense."

As they bickered once more, the waiter came back to their table carrying a large foldable wooden table that held their main courses. Lotty fought hard to prevent her mouth from filling with drool as she impatiently watched the waiter flambé her sauce before pouring it over her perfectly cooked steak and placing it in front of her. She waited politely, yet increasingly more impatiently, as she watched the waiter prepare Bruce's steak tartare. The waiter carefully poured the ground raw beef from the table into a glass bowl and proceeded to add a raw egg, which he then mixed in before finally adding the essential seasoning. Before presenting the dish to Bruce, he laid on top of the meat a single quail's egg and some anchovies, and also furnished Bruce with a bottle of Tabasco sauce to add to the dish according to his own personal taste, if he so wished.

As Bruce leaned over the table to grab the Tabasco, he knocked over Lotty's wine glass, the remaining contents of which spilling all over her lap. She jumped backward out of her chair all too late, then attempted to clean the strong-smelling stain with her napkin.

"Don't panic. I think that you're meant to pour white wine on red wine stains," Bruce said apologetically. He called over to the waiter and asked for him to bring Lotty a glass of white wine, which Bruce proceeded to dab gently on her jeans upon its arrival at their dining table.

"I think it's working, but you do unfortunately smell like a wino now. Sorry, darling, I'm just a bit clumsy sometimes."

"Oh, don't worry, it was only an accident. And I'm a lot clumsier than you. It's perfectly fine."

Lotty was, in fact, so used to spilling anything and everything down herself that she really couldn't care less when other people did it as well.

Lotty and Bruce sat back down and finished their delicious supper, again in silence. Then Bruce, after asking for the bill, gallantly helped Lotty out of her chair. "Shall we, my lady? Time is getting on. We should be getting back to check out the floatation centre to see where they go next."

"OK, let's go. And thank you very much for dinner. It was utterly divine. I may need to undo the top button of my trousers when we get into the car."

"Me too, and we didn't even have a dessert!" He laughed.

CHAPTER 29

Bruce and Lotty got back into Bruce's spotlessly clean car, which stood out in the car park like a beacon amidst the other, much dirtier and much more normal-looking cars, and both undid their top buttons to make the short journey back to the floatation centre, arriving just as Greg and Melissa were walking out the door.

To avoid being seen, Bruce swerved the car into the car park of a shopping centre next door and rode straight over the bicycle of an unlucky policeman who had been standing there eating a chocolate bar while on his break. The annoyed police officer walked over to Bruce's window and angrily tapped on it. Bruce wound down the window to speak to the officer, looking very embarrassed.

"I am dreadfully sorry, Officer. I will of course pay for any damage."

"Do you mind telling me what you've both been doing?" the officer asked, after noting that both Bruce and Lotty had their trousers undone.

"We've just had dinner actually," Bruce replied innocently.

"Can you step out of the car, please, sir? I can smell wine on you. The entire car stinks of it actually. I'm going to have to call for a squad car to come and breathalyse you."

"Oh, right, that's the wine that I spilled over my young friend here. I can assure you, Officer, that I am well under the legal limit."

"I'll be the judge of that, sir."

"I don't want to cause any extra work for you. I can see that you were clearly very busy when we interrupted you," Bruce snipped at the policeman, getting rather more annoyed at clearly now having missed their chance to follow Greg and Melissa any further.

"Are you trying to be funny, sir?"

"Why, are you trying to be attractive?"

Lotty held her head in her hands as she watched the blue lights arrive behind Bruce's car.

CHAPTER 30

It was much later when Lotty, at the local police station, dialled DS Andrews' mobile phone number, which she had now learned by heart, a clear sign to her that she was very smitten indeed.

"Mathon thpeaking."

"Mason, it's Lotty."

"Oh right, thorry. I didn't recognithe the number that you're dialling from. Are you OK, Lotty?"

"No, not really. I'm calling you from your police station as my battery has died. I've just been brought in with Bruce. He's being breathalysed. There's been rather a mix-up with me smelling of alcohol and him getting the blame. He had spilled wine on me earlier over supper; we only had one glass each. He has been his normal curt self and has upset the police officers here. Do you think you could call them?" Lotty heard Mason's riotous laughing down the line. "When you've quite finished …"

"I'm upththairth. I'll come down and laugh at you—I mean vouch for you. Hang on, I'll be right down."

As Lotty was walking back from the police station's payphone, she saw DS Andrews walking down the corridor towards her, laughing, with a uniformed officer. An attractive *female* officer. Lotty's eyes burned a jealous green as she fumed on the inside.

"Hi, Lotty. I have thomeone here who can help you and Bruthe."

"Hi. Nice to meet you. My uncle and I are in a spot of bother, and I haven't brought my work pass with me."

"Hello, babes. I think it was my husband whom Bruce was rude to. And he owes Mason a favour after he kindly drove us to the Lake District a fortnight ago when our car broke down on our honeymoon. I am going to go and have a word with him and bat my eyelids."

Lotty literally took no notice of what was said, acknowledging only the fact that her competition was actually happily and recently married, and therefore no competition at all. Yay!

"Alithon here has already rung down. I can tell you that Bruthe has passed his breathalyther test and that he is just being spoken to about hith conduct."

Alison winced and wondered why Mason had never taken the hint to call her simply Ali.

"Look, Alison, I am really sorry. Bruce generally doesn't mean to be so rude. We were actually on a stake-out of a couple of suspects regarding the Evangeline DuVoir case—Greg and Melissa."

"From the *UK Chronicle*?"

"That's right. I own a detective agency, and we were being slightly delayed when we were stopped by your husband. We lost the car we were tailing. It was our fault anyway; Bruce had run over your husband's police bicycle. I am so sorry."

"Oh, don't worry yourself. I've heard all about you from Mason here, and you are very highly thought of by everyone upstairs. My hubby is probably a bit put out as that's the third bike he has had either run over, stolen, or thrown into the river."

Alison flashed Lotty a lovely smile and walked through the doors to the holding area of the station. Lotty looked at the floor, both embarrassed and ashamed at her jealousy. Alison was in fact a very nice woman.

"Tho, how isth the thleuthing going?" Mason laughed.

"Yes, take the mickey all you like. At least I was trying."

"Oh? I'm not then?"

"No, not at all. I didn't mean it like that." Lotty stared at the floor and shuffled her feet.

"Chill out. I'm joking with you. Look, you are going to have to get uthed to the fact that not every thtakeout goeth to plan. I have to be glad that you at leatht took my advice and didn't go alone." He winked at her, causing her to stare even harder at her shoes.

"I'm just really annoyed that Greg and Melissa got away, because I wanted to know where they were going and what they get up to in general."

"They drove home right after leaving the floatation plathe."

"How do you know that?" Lotty asked, shocked.

"We've also been following them. Alithon's huthband cycled to the building when one of the unmarked cars called through to the station to tell uth that they had followed them there. I then had a different unmarked car follow them home."

"Talk about duplication of work. Perhaps we should liaise more to find out what we're both doing?" Massive hint.

"Abtholutely. We can call each other every day, and then we'll know whath what. Anyway, I am going to drive you home. Bruthe is going to get a lift back to hith car from Alithon. I've already arranged it with her upthairth."

"OK, great. I would really appreciate that, as long as it's not too much trouble for you. I have some notes here that Bruce has obtained which you will find make up a pretty comprehensive biography of Greg. It should save you a lot of work." Lotty handed over the notepad and felt butterflies when DS Andrews touched her hand to receive the notes. Lotty had it bad.

"Is it not rude for me to just leave Bruce here on his own?"

"He won't mind. Time isth getting on, and you really need to get to bed. I'm guething that you need to be at work tomorrow?"

"Yes, unfortunately."

As DS Andrews drove Lotty back to her house, she gave him a brief synopsis of the background notes on Greg that Bruce had obtained. This was more to pass the time as she had started becoming increasingly more tongue-tied in his presence and couldn't think of anything else to talk about. As he pulled up outside her house, she remembered the rules of the game and tried not to sound too desperate by asking him in for coffee.

"Well, thank you for the lift. I'd best get to bed."

"Alwayth a pleathure, Lotty. You thertainly make my life interethting."

Voices screamed in Lotty's head: *Think of something cute to say!* As Lotty leaned into the car and bent down, the effect on her bodily functions, aggravated by the wine earlier, resulted in a quiet but extremely audible belch just as she opened her mouth to speak. The accompanying waft of winey bile was an added bonus. DS Andrews tried really hard not to blink despite the burning in his eyes.

"Well, night then, Lotty. Thleep tight."

As his car drove off into the distance, Lotty remained standing there, staring in disbelief at the cruel hand that fate had just dealt her.

Lotty retreated to her house sheepishly and watched *Dirty Dancing* in bed. She fast forwarded "She's Like the Wind" and then drifted slowly off to sleep.

CHAPTER 31

Lotty awoke from a very long and pleasant sleep. She rubbed her weary eyes, which were still covered in the now congealed make-up that she had forgotten to remove yesterday. She yawned dramatically and managed to enjoy the start of her day for all of fifteen seconds, until she remembered the events of the night before. She was utterly mortified. She put her head in her hands and physically cringed as she sat upright in bed.

It took an awful lot to embarrass Lotty. The last time that she even had come close to feeling like this was when she attended a postsurgery consultation with her very attractive hip surgeon and had to sit in his office staring up at the X-ray that had just been taken of her hip, which showed the tampon that she was currently wearing in all of its glory. Her consultant had sat merrily talking about the X-ray and pointing out how her hip cartilage had improved to an acceptable level, while Lotty sat red-faced and tried to look anywhere but at the tampon that was slap bang in the middle of the black-and-white representation of her crotch area. Coming a close second was the time she had attempted to adjust her heart rate monitor around her chest before a packed stationary bike class, having forgotten that she wasn't wearing a bra at the time. Having decided earlier that day when getting ready in the changing rooms that it would be fine to attend the exercise class without a sports bra, she soon realised she had forgotten it. Lotty had decided that when it came to her being topless, she was similar in anatomy to a twelve-year-old boy, so there was nothing to bounce around and get in the way. There was just enough, sadly, to flop out shamefully as she had raised her T-shirt to adjust the band linked to her sports watch. The ensuing look from a rather elderly gentleman who had the misfortune of having been looking in her direction at the time seemed to be more pity than shock. A really close third was the time Lotty had to have her bowels checked at a posh private hospital and found out that the toilet flush had stopped working after her stomach had produced the output from her enema. It's amazing how she had always been so terrible at DIY until faced with the worry of letting a plumber in to see *that*.

Lotty chose not to sit and wallow in her shame and to embrace the day ahead. She needed to focus. She got up, showered in a hurry, and drove to work at the laboratory. As she got out of her car, her stomach churned. She had such bad pains from when she hadn't been able to pass any solids since taking too much antidiarrhoeal medication a few days before, on the back of her food poisoning. She was starting to feel very bloated. Being quite used to it, she allowed herself to forget about it for a while.

CHAPTER 32

Lotty was greeted in reception by Arthur, who literally walked her straight back out of the building with his arm gently around her. Lotty warmed even more to Arthur when he was in daddy mode.

"Lotty, you are having some days off. I am starting to get into terrible trouble with the human resources department. You can send me the formal requests in the personnel system when you have the time. I am not having any arguments on this."

"But we are making strides on the Farmer Gardener case, and the case of Evangeline is really heating up."

"You mean the chemistry between you and DS Andrews is heating up."

She blushed and shuffled her feet. Arthur hoped she was in fact embarrassed and not about to break wind again; he was acutely aware that there were two reasons that Lotty started to shuffle her feet like that.

As they both stood outside in the crisp morning air, Arthur's mobile phone rang. He recognised the number displayed on the screen.

"Jonathan! How the devil are you?"

Arthur could feel Lotty staring intently at him. She either was about to break wind again or was being impatient. Arthur hoped it was the latter. He could cope with her moods, but her flatulence could take out an adult bear at forty paces.

Lotty stood waiting impatiently as Arthur nodded a lot into the phone. "Thanks, Jonathan. Take care. I'll speak to you soon." He disconnected the call.

"Well, that was Jonathan. The blood panels have come back showing extremely high levels of a substance called interferon-beta."

"Never heard of it." Lotty shrugged and looked puzzled.

"Well, nether had I, if I am perfectly honest with you. Jonathan explained that interferon-beta is a protein-based medication that is used to treat multiple sclerosis patients. It has been documented to successfully reduce somewhere between 18 per cent and 38 per cent of relapses associated with the condition."

He continued, saying, "The drug is used to slow down the rate of advance of the disease in patients. It is synthesised in two ways, with both methods using human gene sequencing to create the substance in either the ovaries of the Chinese hamster or bacterial cells called *Escherichia coli*. It's only found in injectable forms, so whoever killed Evangeline had been injecting it into her food or beverages initially."

"And then they, or someone else, injected her with it as well?"

"Well, I can only assume right now that the poisoner chose to build the drug levels up slowly to start attacking her kidneys, then used the party as an opportunity to inject a lethal dose."

"So this was premeditated?"

"Yes, I suppose so." He shrugged. "Jonathan also said that the panels indicate that Evangeline had been poisoned several times by the drug, given how much is still present in her system. It would have really taken its toll on her fragile kidneys. With Evangeline's weak kidneys already in distress and unable to filter out any toxins, poisoning of a protein form would mean that waste was building up in her kidneys to a dangerous level. She would have, over time, begun to become drowsy, confused, and sweaty, with a feeling of nausea."

Lotty felt like that at the start of every period she had. She scratched her head, moving her hand down to play with her hair thoughtfully. It was at this point that her chunky silver charm bracelet that so often adorned her wrist got stuck firmly in some strands of her hair. She looked panicked.

"Do you need a hand?" Arthur asked, moving in closer towards Lotty. Scrutinising her, he noticed that she was now wearing quite the look of worry as more strands of hair started being pulled out of her head as she frantically tried to free herself.

"No, do carry on." She yanked so hard that while her bracelet was freed, the violent motion of her arm resulted in Arthur's being punched quite violently in the face.

"Oh my god, sorry. Please don't fire me!" she begged, joking yet extremely apologetic. Only Lotty could manage to physically assault her boss with her jewellery.

He kindly shrugged off the incident, mainly out of male pride as he was now in a great deal of pain and was fairly sure that there was going to be a bruise. Patting Lotty's arm to reassure her, he went on. "Apparently, interferon-beta is rather a high-end drug and only found in specialised chemists. I'm not sure how easy it would have been to obtain or even to get a prescription for."

"It would surely also require a relatively detailed knowledge of the drug or the disease by the murderer?" postulated Lotty.

"Indeed. They also would have needed to know that Evangeline's kidneys were as fragile as a Premier League footballer's ego after his hairdresser finds a grey hair." Arthur gently rubbed his face. The place where Lotty had whacked him was started to sting now. "And you are correct by the way, Jonathan also found an injection mark on Evangeline's corpse after you left him the other day. The mark suggests that the medication was injected directly into her kidney."

"But that doesn't make sense. Are you now saying that Evangeline was poisoned by something in her wine glass *and* directly via lethal injection?"

"Yes. Someone really didn't like her at all, Lotty. Not at all."

Lotty exchanged pleasantries with her boss and went back to her car, where she started to formulate a plan. She didn't like the idea of having time away from work. She rang Bruce.

"Hello, my darling. Thanks for helping last night. I finally escaped the police station after apologising to everyone and eating humble pie. It was very late by the time I got in."

"It does serve you right for being catty. I have a day off from work. I want to look into our next suspect on the shitlist for the Evangeline DuVoir case."

CHAPTER 33

Several hours later, Lotty and Bruce were sitting in the reception area of Sir Ralph's headquarters.

"So how did you swing this?" she asked.

"I told him that you found him attractive."

"Please tell me you're joking."

"Look, Aunt Molly would have been the first person to tell you that you very often have to tell a little white lie when you are investigating people. This really isn't your job anyway. You are only doing all of this to impress DS Andrews, because you can't remember what a penis actually looks like."

Lotty pretended to look shocked. She tried very hard, but her Botox injections from the week before had just set that day and she was only managing to create an expression in the lower part of her face. The resultant look was clearly of concern to Bruce.

"You're not going to break wind again, are you?"

"Look, I am not *always* doing that. What is wrong with people? Everyone around me thinks I do it all the time. It's IBS."

"Darling, we are all forever on high alert around you. You once nearly took my eyebrows off. And I am worried about lighting matches whenever you've eaten purple sprouting."

"Right, can we stop and focus on the task at hand, please? Essentially I now have to swoon over someone who thinks I should be grateful I get to vote and who is going to be impressed that I can tie my shoelaces on my own?"

"That's the long and short of it, yes."

The lift door opened. Sir Ralph waved and walked towards them.

Lotty smiled back at Sir Ralph and tipped her head to one side in what she hoped was a shy and coquettish manner.

"Lotty! Bruce! How lovely to see you both. Do come on up."

They all crammed themselves into a very small lift. Lotty felt sure that Sir Ralph had picked this specific lift to transport them up just so he could grind up against her. Despite fighting the urge to recoil from Sir Ralph's touch, Lotty continued in her role-play and lolled her head to the other side flirtatiously.

"Lotty, when we get up to my office, I can have my assistant find my massage therapist's phone number if you would like?"

Sir Ralph immediately felt her eyes boring into him and wondered what he had done wrong.

"He's an absolute bloody deviant," Lotty whispered to Ralph.

As they walked out of the lift, Sir Ralph guided them through his luxurious open-plan office and into an area bedecked with velvet chairs. Lotty was clearly in the wrong business; all the chairs in her work canteen smelled like something had died on them. They would also give you a bad case of haemorrhoids if you sat on them too long.

"It's so nice of you to visit!" effused Sir Ralph.

Bruce beamed his award-winning smile back at Sir Ralph. "Well, we were just passing, and Lotty was very *keen* to pop in and see you again. Weren't you, Lotty darling?"

"If you say so."

Sir Ralph grabbed her arm with his. Lotty wondered how hard she could twist his arm behind his back before snapping it off.

"Lotty, why don't you and Bruce join me tomorrow evening at our work gala? It's black tie."

Before Lotty could respond, Bruce answered for her. There were several reasons why she was single, and her inability to interact with humans when she didn't feel like it was rather high up on that list.

"We accept! If you could just email me over the details, we'll be there with knobs on!"

Sir Ralph looked a mixture of pleased and worried. Given how often he had spent time in Bruce's company, he wasn't quite sure how literally Bruce would take that phrase. He wondered if it was too late to retract his invitation. Then again, that would mean he wouldn't be able to woo the beautiful Lotty.

Sir Ralph called his timid-looking assistant over and barked some directions at him to extend the invitations formally over email. Lotty could tell from looking at the assistant that he also hoped Sir Ralph would fall down the nearest staircase.

After a brief tour around Sir Ralph's headquarters, where he took every opportunity to showboat at them, Lotty and Bruce managed to escape and go home to their respective houses.

CHAPTER 34

It was two o'clock the following morning when Lotty sat bolt upright in bed, very sweaty and in a great deal of pain. As she tried to get out of bed to go and get some painkillers to help with the cramping, she was met with such acute stabbing in her abdomen that she simply allowed herself to drop on to the floor. Arabella started licking her face, managing at one point to glance her raspy tongue over Lotty's left eyeball.

Lotty rang Bruce.

"Darling, what's wrong?"

"I am in so much pain. I think there is something wrong. I need you to come and take me to the hospital. It could be my Appendix."

"No, I am calling an ambulance. I'll meet you at yours. If you have already left your house by the time I arrive, make sure you text me where they are taking you. But I am assuming it will be to the main town hospital."

He rang off. She reluctantly called for an ambulance while she clutched at her side and cried pathetically. She tried biting her lip to distract herself. As she remembered the paramedics wouldn't be able to get to her, she managed to drag herself forward on all fours and slowly make her way down the stairs. This was made an even more difficult task because Arabella had assumed it was a game and was now weaving between her arms and underneath her torso, while intermittently headbutting her. After several minutes, although to Lotty it seemed like hours, Lotty finally had dragged herself down the hall, down her stairs, and down her hallway and had managed to unlock the front door just as the paramedics were arriving. After a whirlwind of giving her name and answering many other questions, Lotty was put into an ambulance and covered with a thick blanket.

CHAPTER 35

It seemed like an eternity for the ambulance to weave its way through the roads, even though there were no other cars at this time of night, until eventually arriving at the hospital, where an extremely dishevelled Bruce was already waiting, concerned, outside the doors of the emergency department.

"Just hang on, darling. We will have you right as rain very soon." He squeezed her hand.

Lotty started to cry and wished she hadn't; it had prompted Bruce to enter full drama mode. As Lotty was taken down the corridors to her own private cubicle, Bruce started to dial various friends to alert everyone that she was very poorly.

"Hadn't we better wait until I have been checked over before we start calling people and worrying them?"

Bruce ignored her and took an incoming call from her mother.

"Yes, darling, she's in a terrible state. I bet it's another kidney stone, but she thinks it's her Appendix. More surgery. … Yes. Yes, I shall. … Yes. … OK, will do. … I'll call you with an update later, but perhaps you should start booking flights?"

He rang off.

It was at this point that a very attractive male nurse appeared around the cubicle curtain. He coughed gently to indicate his presence to Lotty and Bruce.

"Hello," they both chimed.

The nurse suddenly felt very self-conscious with both pairs of eyes now staring intently at him. Bruce's eyes had wandered down to the nurse's crotch.

"It's Lotty, isn't it?"

"Yes," she whispered. The dashing male nurse was now not even being enough of a distraction from the pain she was feeling in the lower half of her body.

"Lotty, I need you to put this gown on." The nurse handed her a backless hospital gown. "I'll be back shortly, and then we can perform some tests."

"I need you to contact a doctor immediately and order a blood panel for me. Go and get someone now. I think I've been poisoned."

Bruce looked confused and panicked as the nurse shot off down the corridor.

"What the heck are you talking about, Lotty?"

"Look, Arthur told me that Evangeline's murderer used a substance called interferon-beta to kill her. The penny has just dropped that this could be why I am unwell."

"It sounds like something out of a James Bond film. Do you think you're starting to hallucinate?"

She ignored him and continued. "They've already started to target me. Maybe they found a way to poison me. I may be starting to exhibit signs of organ failure!"

Bruce now shot off down the corridor after the nurse.

CHAPTER 36

Several minutes later, Bruce had returned with a doctor in tow—another attractive male specimen. Bruce was considering having someone back over him next week with his car so he could return to the emergency department himself.

Lotty had started to undress herself in order to change into the hospital gown. Because of the pain, she was having great difficulty. It was just as Bruce and the emergency doctor appeared that she was bent down, navigating the final stage of the process of removing her socks, now that she had battled to get the gown on.

"Oh my god, don't look, it's a black hole!" shouted Bruce at the doctor. Lotty shot back up, embarrassed.

Bruce had clearly already explained what was going on as the doctor wasted no time in rushing over to Lotty and gesturing for her to sit on the bed. He grabbed her trembling arm, applied a rubber tourniquet four inches above her elbow, and proceeded to concentrate. "Make a fist," he barked.

"Very firm, isn't he, Lotty?" She rolled her eyes.

The handsome doctor worked fast, given what Bruce had told him, and rubbed the pale inner crease of her arm with medical alcohol. He proceeded to hold her lower arm tightly as he drew the skin around the area taut. "Just a small prick coming."

Bruce went to say something but was stopped in his tracks by a reprimanding look from Lotty. *Don't, Bruce.*

After several phials of blood had been drawn, the doctor handed Lotty a small clear sample pot.

"I need you to pee into this while I finish up here. We need to hurry."

"Shall I rub my stomach and pat my head as well?"

He smiled.

Lotty attempted to pee while sitting down, holding the cup between her legs and beneath her hospital gown with the arm not being worked upon. There was a loud gushing noise, accompanied by the sound of liquid hitting the floor. As the doctor cleaned her arm and applied some cotton wool and a plaster, he looked at her, concerned, and took the now full sample from her.

"The porter is coming right now, and we are going to have an X-ray performed. While I survey those results, the team will prep you for a scan. If you have been poisoned, I want to know what with and how your body is responding. I'll send some cleaners in to mop the floor when they're free."

Lotty thanked him and continued to sweat profusely. She wasn't sure if the heat she felt on her face was because of the poison or because she just found the doctor so attractive and yet had just urinated all over the floor in front of him. She was also very certain some of it went on his expensive-looking shoes. He wasn't a patch on DS Andrews though. Nice to look at, but probably no substance.

Eventually, a tired-looking porter came to the cubicle and whisked Lotty off to have her X-rays. She was feeling so unwell now that she was starting to lose all her patience. She felt sure that there was no valid reason why she was being wheeled to the theatre lying on her front with the back of her gown completely open and showing everyone her backside. She was wheeled into a cold, dark room and left on her own. She felt vulnerable, tired, and sore, rather like Bruce felt when he returned from one of his sauna parties in Brighton. She once made the mistake of asking him if he'd had a nice time, but never again; she was still unsure quite why a butt plug needs a hole in it, and she would never again make the mistake of asking why said hole existed.

Lotty started to drift off to sleep when a kind-looking X-ray technician patted her arm gently. "Wake up, my darlin'." She had a thick Cornish accent and deep brown, joyful eyes. Her hair was drawn back loosely in a bun at the back of her head. She reminded Lotty of Aunt Molly.

Lotty smiled. "I'm so sore."

"I know, dear. We can't give you anything for the pain if you have been poisoned. We need to analyse what it is first before we can do anything. Don't be scared. I'm Jeanie. I am going to be doing your X-rays today."

Lotty relaxed somewhat and allowed Jeanie to help her lay face down upon the gurney.

"Now, I need you to lift your abdomen up slightly while I place this block under it. Try to breathe in slightly, dear." The pain hit Lotty like a truck, and she cried out. Jeanie patted her arm again.

After placing the block under Lotty, Jeanie disappeared behind a panel. Lotty heard a loud whirring as she started to drift off to sleep again. Jeanie reappeared next to Lotty and smiled kindly. "I need you to turn over," she said as she gently rolled Lotty over onto her back. Jeanie's Cornish lilt was beginning to make feel Lotty more relaxed and considerably sleepier. She felt sure that Jeanie should be doing the voice-overs for butter commercials. When Jeanie disappeared behind the screen again, Lotty heard more noise, akin to a small generator. Lotty closed her eyes, finally succumbing to the pain and fatigue. It was at that point that she fell very fast asleep.

CHAPTER 37

Lotty's eyes opened. She felt confused and weary. Bruce and the doctor were standing over her, staring. Bruce was holding an ice pack to his head. She wondered how long she had been asleep.

"Am I going to die?" she asked tentatively.

"I'm fine, thank you for asking." Bruce looked annoyed.

"What ... what happened?" She tried to sit up on her haunches, but the pain in her abdomen made it difficult, so she gave up and lay back down again.

"Well, Doctor Lassiter here was just coming down to see me to let me know that all that is wrong with you is that you're constipated from the antidiarrhoeal medication that you have been taking. Just as I was coming to check on you, I managed to slip in the puddle of your urine and banged my head on the floor when I landed, so thank you for *that*.

"Oh, and while we waited for you to wake up, he checked me over for concussion while I furiously texted everyone, including your mother, who was about to book a flight home from South Africa, that you're actually fine and just need to have a massive poo."

"Lotty, I just need you to drink this; it's a mild laxative. Bruce is going to take you home, and, well, *things* should start moving in the next few hours for you."

"Thank you, Doctor." Lotty looked suitably embarrassed and turned to Bruce. "Sorry, Bruce."

After being driven as the sun was rising, and having had to listen to several calls between Bruce and the various people in Lotty's life where Bruce felt the need to explain the reason for Lotty's trip to the hospital,

Lotty was finally home. She dragged herself to bed, got under the duvet, and closed her eyes.

Several hours, which seemed like only minutes, later, she woke up and felt frustration that while the pain had now gone, she still felt very bloated. Her stomach felt warm and uncomfortable. She pondered what she could manage to wear later for the party that wasn't too tight around her waist. She noticed the time and was about to go back to sleep when she checked her mobile phone and noticed a text had arrived from Bruce. She was worried about what it might say.

> I propose we both have a lie-in until later. The taxi will
> pick us up at seven. Try and poo.
>
> Love you,
> Bruce
> x

Lotty remembered about poor, hungry Arabella. She jumped gingerly out of bed and broke wind. She was unsurprised given how backed up she clearly was. Another thing to file under her list of reasons she was single. Lotty still felt somewhat nauseous, so pouring the gloopy brown meat and gravy from a cat food pouch into Arabella's bowl made her retch. "Bon appétit, Arabella!"

She stumbled back to bed and closed her eyes, oblivious to the fact that halfway through her second fitful sleep, Arabella had joined her. She also thankfully missed Arabella making far too good a job of cleaning her own backside and then immediately giving Lotty's face a gentle lick.

Lotty wasn't sure why, but she woke up briefly humming "The Lion Sleeps Tonight" to herself. Then she drifted slowly back to sleep.

CHAPTER 38

After stirring during the late afternoon, Lotty started to get ready for the party later. It took her an inordinately long time to pick an outfit that wasn't so tight around her middle that it would be uncomfortable given her "situation". Ordinarily, her outlook on life was that the less she was paying for the food, the looser her waistband should be. Due to the amount of exercise that she did, her friends often described the amount of food she could eat as "frightening". Thankfully this meant that Lotty owned several suitable dresses with accommodating waistbands (she was always ready for an ad hoc buffet). It was a long black diamante dress that she had picked from among these to wear tonight. Noticing it had some food left on it from the last time she had worn it (yellow in colour, crusty, and remaining unidentified), Lotty licked her finger and then dabbed at the stain with her finger to remedy the situation. Lotty, being a Gemini, often wavered freely between the border of lady and tramp.

Next, she carefully went through her significant shoe collection, choosing a suitably sparkly pair of heels and slipping them onto her tiny feet. Perusing herself critically in the mirror, she tried to frown, but the Botox proved this once again to be a challenge. She breathed in and looked at herself once more in her full-length mirror. Turning from side to side for one last check, she smiled.

The doorbell rang. Lotty proceeded gracefully down her stairs, tripping down the last couple of steps because she had miscalculated her gait in the heels she was wearing. A flustered Lotty finally opened the door to Bruce.

"Darling, you look gorgeous!" he cooed. "The taxi is parked on the other side of the road there. I thought I would come and walk you over and be gentlemanly." You could say many things about Bruce, but he did possess considerable charm.

"Are you wearing glitter, Bruce?"

"No. Why?"

"It's just that it's all over your face, mainly your lips." She pointed at said glitter.

"I think it's just transferred onto me from my hands perhaps. I met a friend for a quick one on the way and had the taxi meet me from there. He's in cabaret."

It was at this point in the conversation that Lotty knew she didn't need to know what type of cabaret or, indeed, how the glitter had transferred to his hands, or subsequently onto his lips.

"Shall we go?" She grabbed his arm. They walked towards the taxi.

"Have you been?"

"Been where?"

"No, Lotty. Have you *been*?"

"Can we not discuss this now? And no." She rolled her eyes as they got in and closed the doors. Lotty, in true Lotty style, had closed her side of the taxi door with several inches of her dress hanging outside of it.

CHAPTER 39

Arriving at the party in what Lotty would refer to as "being fashionably completely dead on time", they made their way to the reception area, where Bruce gave one of the young immaculate-looking party hosts their names. The host had been supplied with a very high-tech curly earpiece that made them look terribly important.

"What time is the Prime Minister arriving?" Bruce joked at the host. The host looked blankly at Bruce.

"Where can we put our coats?" Lotty asked, trying to both cover Bruce's poor humour and progress more rapidly to the free food part of the evening.

"Over there, madam."

After leaving their coats with the coatroom attendant, they both took a drink from one of the various silver platters being transported gracefully around the party by some of the fashionably well-dressed members of staff. Lotty sipped her champagne and finally took the time to look at Bruce's outfit. He was decked from head to toe in the most beautiful and expensive-looking dark blue crushed velvet dinner suit she had ever seen, complete with matching tie. Both of them felt pleased to be out and be *normal*; it was less than a year ago that a virus had caused a global pandemic and the world had ground to a halt. Bruce had passed his time watching what he referred to as "cultural films". Lotty hadn't dug too deeply into the content of the films at the time, but when she had dropped off some food shopping round to his house on one occasion, all the curtains were drawn, and Bruce had opened the door rather breathless. Having "key worker" status and not being able to work from home, Lotty had managed to maintain some semblance of structure in her life, but her social life had been obliterated with shops, cinemas, bars, and restaurants being closed for months at a time. Lotty was fairly sure during the pandemic that she had, in fact, read everything on the internet. She hadn't felt too concerned overall about her mental health until she caught herself greeting her toaster one morning. Even though considerable time had passed, the world still seemed grateful to be interacting with each other. Everyone seemed kinder.

Lotty turned to Bruce and sighed happily. "It's just so nice to be out and feeling glamorous again. Do you know, I think I must have watched hundreds of make-up tutorials during lockdown." Bruce, staring at the dark blue eyeshadow and bright red lipstick combination that adorned Lotty's face, felt certain that she could have possibly watched more of them.

Lotty sniffed loudly.

Bruce rolled his eyes. "Darling, quietly, please. We are in mixed company. What have we talked about? We don't sniff loudly in front of other humans."

Lotty didn't like Bruce when he was like this. "Champagne makes my nose run."

"Because you're quite revolting, darling."

"Er, no, because of the histamine in the wine *actually*; it causes fluids to leak out into the capillaries of my nose." She looked smugly at him.

"Oh, well, that is *much* less disgusting then, isn't it?"

Before she could snap back at Bruce, a very smartly dressed man tapped him on the shoulder.

"It's Bruce and Lotty, isn't it?" he asked. "I'm Fred Crane. Sir Ralph pointed you out to me in the office when you visited, just as you were getting into the lift to leave. He asked me to make sure that you were looked after, just in case he was too busy at the start of the party."

"How awfully kind! Yes, we just happened to be passing by and had stopped in to see him, and he shot us a last-minute invite. So kind. And what do you do for Sir Ralph, Fred?"

"I'm Sir Ralph's legal director for EMEA."

"I bet you've crammed a few skeletons into closets over the years!"

Fred didn't laugh at Bruce's joke but did manage to smile awkwardly and what he hoped was politely.

Lotty turned back to Fred after grabbing several canapés from a tray being swept past her at shoulder height. Her method of shoulder-barging several other nearby guests and blocking the path of the person holding the tray would have impressed a professional rugby player. "Have you worked for Sir Ralph long?" she asked, spraying Fred with a small piece of grilled goat cheese.

Fred wiped his lapel. "About three years now."

"It was awful what happened to his ex-wife. I was concerned that he would be upset, but I heard from Bruce that the split was rather bitter. Perhaps he's secretly rather pleased?" she postulated, adopting Bruce's "bull in a china shop" approach.

Fred now looked very awkward. He was expecting, at worst, to be making small talk with Bruce and Lotty, but he now felt rather like he was being interrogated.

"Well, not really. While Sir Ralph made no secret of how bitter things were between him and Evangeline, he needed her."

"What do you mean?" probed Bruce.

"Well, upon Evangeline's death, the shares in Sir Ralph's company that she received as a divorce settlement now transfer to Alexander, their son. Sir Ralph actually finds him much harder to influence than he did Evangeline. He's going to find business dealings considerably more difficult now."

Fred looked down at an imaginary watch and made his excuses to stop being probed. "Anyway, it was lovely to meet you both, but I am just going to have to leave you for a while. I am needed somewhere shortly for a presentation." He walked off rapidly in the direction of the bar.

Bruce and Lotty looked at each other.

"Well, that's one name off the suspect list, surely?" Lotty felt pleased that they had done what they had come for, and so quickly, and believed that now they could both enjoy their evening. "ABBA is on. Shall we dance?" She offered Bruce her hand. All bitchy comments were forgotten quickly, as was the norm between them. She now wanted to move on and enjoy herself.

Lotty and Bruce walked hand in hand towards the dance floor, stopping only once for Lotty to grab another canapé off a tray and cram it quickly into her mouth, chewing with her mouth open. That was another reason Lotty was single.

CHAPTER 40

Bruce and Lotty had been dancing together for hours. It didn't seem like hours to them; it was a whirlwind of fun that had flown by as if it were minutes. They'd had great fun overall, except for one moment during a can-can to "New York, New York" when Lotty had accidentally kicked Bruce quite violently on his shin.

As the music continued to play loudly around them, Lotty turned to Bruce on the dance floor, rubbed her stomach at him, then pointed at the toilets. It didn't take a genius to work out that the dancing had helped her stomach massage through the vast amounts of food that it had held captive for days. She felt a churning sensation that didn't bode well.

"Just go, darling. I'll be fine," he reassured her.

She walked towards the women's toilets, glancing back at him once to wave. "I'll be five minutes."

"I'm fairly sure you'll be longer than that," he said matter-of-factly.

As she continued to walk off, she saw Sir Ralph had finally found them and was currently walking towards Bruce.

Lotty hurriedly pushed open the door to the toilets and checked that she was alone. She felt this would require solitude and was thankful for the coverage from the loud music that was blaring in the next room. She looked at herself in the mirror and noticed that her make-up had started to run because of all her dancing. She opened her Alexander McQueen clutch bag and reapplied her blusher, lipstick, and eyeliner. She sprayed some of her perfume onto her neck and wrists, then looked at herself again. Now satisfied with her handiwork, she went into the bathroom, pulled down her underwear, and sat down. There was a considerable amount of pain. Nothing further needs to be narrated here to describe what Lotty experienced. Needless to say, *things* had righted themselves.

As Lotty flushed the toilet, she heard someone else come in, gasp loudly, and immediately leave again, slamming the door behind them. She was sure that she actually heard the person running off down the corridor at great speed. Lotty looked down at the toilet pan and became rather concerned with the amount of water moving upward, towards the seat. She opened the cubicle door and stood back. The water started to overflow onto the bathroom floor. Lotty felt panic. She wasn't quite sure what to do, so she chose to leave and make her way quickly to the reception area.

After gently elbowing her way through a considerable number of people, Lotty found herself at the cocktail bar. "A mojito, please."

As she waited for her drink to be prepared, she got her mobile phone out and checked her messages, wondering why she hadn't heard from her friend Mandy. She had picked up Mandy's concerned voicemail earlier and, not having the time to call her back, had sent her a quick text update to tell her that she had taken a laxative and everything seemed better. Lotty put her mobile phone back in her bag and took her drink, unaware that several miles away DS Andrews was still wondering why he'd received such a graphic random text message from Lotty that afternoon. He felt sure it must have been "text speak" and meant something much different from how it actually read.

Returning to the dance area, Lotty now saw Bruce standing next to Sir Ralph, who himself was chatting to a rather irate-looking man dressed in overalls and rubber gloves who was making the same dramatic hand gestures that a fisherman might use to describe his prize catch. The man pointed at Lotty, who turned sharply about-face and walked rapidly towards the coat area.

"Wait, darling." Bruce ran up to her and grabbed her waist. "So, do you think we need to figure out a way to let Sir Ralph down gently, or do you think you may have sorted that out yourself already?" He winked and laughed as they made their hurried exit.

CHAPTER 41

The following Monday morning, Lotty, Arthur, and Jonathan were gathered around a table in one of the meeting rooms at Lotty's place of work. Arthur had extended an invitation to Jonathan to drive over from his morgue to conduct a meeting to find out where they all were on the Farmer Gardener case. Arthur was feeling confident.

Jonathan grabbed a biscuit from the plate in front of him and dipped it into his steaming cup of tea. "Why have you got a bruise on your cheek, Arthur? It almost looks like a small key. What happened?"

Lotty shrank back in her chair, fiddling awkwardly with the key on her charm bracelet, and hoped Arthur wasn't bearing a grudge.

"Lotty happened." Arthur's hand moved to his cheek, which he rubbed gently. "So, here's where we are with the Farmer Gardener case."

Arthur got up and moved to the whiteboard that was set up on the wall by the large meeting table and picked up a pen. "In summary, we've found the murder weapon, the knife, on the farm, and it displays usable prints of Farmer Gardener. Additionally, we have a bag of bloodstained clothing found by the dustbin men, as well as bloodstained clothing found on the farm. The analysis of both sets of these clothes shows a DNA match to the wife's blood, using her twin as a reference sample. We have the receipt found on the farm where he purchased meat cleavers. We found the meat cleavers on the farm. We have evidence showing he purchased a considerable life insurance policy on his wife, and this insurance policy holds a missing persons clause that would enable him to claim after seven years, using the missing persons rule."

"What about the saw marks?" asked Lotty. "Where did we get with those?"

Arthur looked disgruntled as he continued. While he could apparently forgive Lotty for punching him in the face, he didn't like being derailed midflow when he was summarising. "Now, with regard to the saw found on-site, we needed to compare this with the cuts found on the undigested bone that was found in the pig's feeding area on the farm. The analysis proved to be successful as, thankfully, we weren't dealing with burnt remains."

Jonathan nodded wisely. Lotty nodded because Jonathan was nodding and she didn't want to feel left out. She did remember somewhere in the recesses of her brain that burnt remains were harder to work with when it came to performing cut mark analysis, however. She was good at the small area of forensics that she knew, hence her strong desire to start branching out into other areas.

"Jonathan's colleague, the anthropologist based out of a separate laboratory, has now sent me his findings." Arthur shuffled his papers to find the appropriate page. "This Hampshire-based laboratory used digital microscopy and micro-CT on the bone Lotty found on the farm. Both methods conclusively show that the marks found on the bone were made by the saw. It would have been highly fortuitous for us to have found an undigested bone from the stab site area to match to the knife we found, but at this point we are gathering a good pool of data to use as evidence against Farmer Gardener. Additionally, I have spoken to James today and learned we have now matched the DNA on the undigested bone to that of Grace Gardener. We can now proceed to hand over these findings to the lead investigator."

Jonathan and Arthur both looked at Lotty. She blushed. "I can ring him and arrange a meeting to update him, if you like?"

They both nodded and smiled. Lotty grabbed her mobile phone rather too desperately. Arthur waved his arm at her. "Wait. Before you do, we need to have a discussion about where we are with the Evangeline DuVoir case." She put her phone down.

Arthur threw the pen at Jonathan, who caught it and walked over to take Arthur's place in front of the whiteboard. "Now, after Lotty left the postmortem the other day, Laurence and I continued to conduct our full set of procedures on Evangeline's body. Given the amount of time the body

123

had sat in the fridge and on the table, an appropriate delay had occurred since time of death for a perimortem injury to be displayed."

"When you called, you mentioned it looked like an injection mark?"

"That's correct, located just in the region of the kidney." Jonathan drew a kidney on the whiteboard and marked an *X* in the area towards the middle of the drawing. "We used infrared photography to discern more intricate details of the mark. It is my conclusion that the small pinprick shows a cutaneous necrotic ulceration around the injection site."

Arthur and Lotty looked blankly at Jonathan. "Sorry," apologised Arthur, "that's a new one on me. Can you elaborate?"

"Essentially, the injection site shows evidence in the tissue around it of a severe local inflammatory skin reaction. It's observed from time to time in multiple sclerosis patients who are self-injecting with interferon-beta. So, this now suggests that Evangeline was being poisoned with interferon-beta both via ingestion and via injection. Given the progression of the reaction, I would say that the injection was carried out at the party."

CHAPTER 42

Lotty decided to go and see Teresa before she telephoned DS Andrews with an update. As she descended the two flights from the meeting rooms to go and see her friend, she felt rather self-conscious about the look on the face of one of the cleaners who was alighting the stairs towards her. Lotty wondered if the cleaner could see up her skirt; she'd been in a rush and had forgotten to put her pants in her gym kit this morning. Judging from the cleaner's face, he either had been having a really bad day or could currently see her winking at him from her lady garden. She tried taking narrower steps just in case.

Lotty eventually found herself at Teresa's desk, but Teresa was on the phone, sucking a lollipop. As Teresa let the confectionary play inside her cheeks, Arthur walked past and made the mistake of looking at Teresa. Promptly, he became so distracted that he walked directly into a nearby wall. He recovered himself and trotted off limping, taking a moment to glance back briefly, once again, at Teresa. He then stumbled awkwardly into a colleague's desk.

Teresa was nodding a lot and not saying much. She looked at Lotty and made a mock exhausted gesture. Teresa removed the lollipop from her mouth; it was accompanied by a long line of drool. Arthur had clearly chosen to take another glance back at the free display of soft porn being provided by Teresa as Lotty heard him crash into another desk, this one located slightly further across the office. Teresa placed the lollipop down, grabbed a pen, and wrote a note to Lotty on her pad: "This phone call will take ages. I'll call you later."

Lotty gave her friend a thumbs-up sign and walked back towards her own work area to sit down. She smoothed down her hair and coughed to clear her throat. She needed to prepare herself to call DS Andrews. Suddenly feeling very shy, Lottie smoothed down her skirt, got her mobile phone out, found DS Andrews' number in her list of contacts, then put the phone down again. She felt hot and nervous. An instant message displayed on her computer screen from Arthur: "Stop faffing and just call him. He can't see what you bloody well look like!"

She looked over at Arthur. He smiled reassuringly at her. Lotty wasn't used to talking to men whom she found attractive and funny. Her love life was nonexistent. She was very sure that more people had seen the Holy Grail than had seen her genitals, and she was more than ready for this situation to be rectified. One of Lotty's exercise instructors often talked about her participants needing to make time for "self-love". Lotty was bored of having to take that too literally. She smiled back at Arthur, picked up her mobile phone, and dialled. On the third ring, her call was answered.

""Mathon thpeaking."

"It's Lotty." Feeling her face turn crimson, she hid behind her computer. She was very sure Arthur was still watching, just to make sure that she had made the call.

"How have you been?"

"Fine, thanks. You?"

"Altho fine. Did you have an update for me?"

Lotty felt her heart flutter. She found DS Andrews utterly adorable. She wondered what he thought about her.

"So one of Arthur's administrative assistants is emailing the details over to you shortly as they are currently collating the two case file updates we have for you. With respect to the Farmer Gardener case, we have conclusive DNA and fingerprint analysis. We also have an excellent piece of work carried out on the cut marks, and additionally we have the evidence from the farmer's computer documenting a life insurance policy. It's time to proceed now."

"Thanksth. Great work! We will sthtart issuing a warrant."

She continued, saying, "Moving on now to the Evangeline DuVoir case, we are going to be sending over a file that documents that while Evangeline had been poisoned several times prior to her death by ingestion of a medication used to treat multiple sclerosis, she also had been injected with the same medication directly, most likely at the party."

"Probably when you thaid the lightsth went out?"

"Most likely. I wonder how they got the lights off like that."

"I've thurveyed the cabling mythelf. It would have taken thomeone highly profithent in electrics to rig what had been thet up. A timer had been plathed on one of the many boxeth leading from the temporary generatorth outthide the marquee."

"Even I could do that. I used timers on all the plugs when I had pet hermit crabs; I used the timers to turn the heat lamps on and off to simulate light and day in their tanks." DS Andrews chose at that point not to probe any further on why she used to have hermit crabs.

"Well, actually, it'sth more how they would have had to work out which of the many wireth and boxeth were feeding the interior main lightsth. That electrical thet-up was a meth and highly complexth."

Lotty's computer made a sound to signal that she'd received another instant message. She looked and saw that Arthur had sent her a lollipop emoji and an aubergine emoji. She ignored Arthur's "advice" and turned her back to the computer.

"Lotty, why don't we meet later thisth week? A bite to eat together maybe. We can have a proper catch-up and just, well, generally have a nithe meal together?" he offered hopefully.

Beaming, she agreed and rang off. Lotty chose to use the international signal of success at securing a date by thrusting her groin forward inappropriately at Arthur while simultaneously making a circle with the first two fingers of her left hand through which she poked the index finger of her right hand.

CHAPTER 43

Later that afternoon, as Lotty was exiting the building to find her car, she was accosted by Arthur. He made her jump, which caused her to break wind again.

"Nice. I've just been looking at your remaining days off in the system, and it still looks bad. I need you to take some more holiday. You aren't to come in to work for the rest of the week. If we need to speak to you, we will call your mobile. And if something urgent comes up, we may call you briefly into the office."

Lotty nodded reluctantly. "You know you are more than welcome to drive over for anything urgent?"

Arthur smiled politely, but he tried to avoid visiting Lotty's house in person. He had once been in her bathroom, when Arabella had decided to enter the house via the bathroom window. He was incredibly grateful that he was already seated on the toilet at the time.

"Still, kudos on getting your hot date. Maybe you can utilise your time off to preen yourself and do whatever it is that ladies do."

Lotty's general approach to getting ready for dates was to smell her armpits to check if she needed a shower first. She had also previously cancelled dates if there was a new episode of *Midsomer Murders* being aired. She felt differently about DS Andrews; she was excited to see him again. Her heart pounded harder in her chest at the thought of him.

Arthur moved towards Lotty and raised his arm to high-five her in celebration of her romantic success, but he didn't notice that she was using both her arms to carry her gym and work bags. Arthur subsequently slapped Lotty clean in the face, causing her to drop her bags. She was about to protest but realised that they were now quits.

She made her way through the car park to her car and got in. She felt a bit tired and confused and realised her blood sugar was low. After searching frantically through her car's glovebox and unfortunately finding that she had no sweets left in there, she set off quickly so that she could get home to eat. Having a very fast metabolism meant that Lotty's body went through any food that she put into it too quickly if she didn't eat correctly. Low GI wasn't just a fad for her; it was a necessity. As she continued her journey home while the dusk started to set in, she yawned and made a mental note to concentrate harder on the task at hand. She had once gotten all of the way home and passed out just as she parked in her drive, which had resulted in her ploughing her car straight into the side of her house before she could apply the brakes.

In order to remain on high alert for this trip, she wound down the window to let some fresh air in and turned the volume on her music up as high as she could stand. As she went to drive her car around a rather sharp bend, she saw in her peripheral vision a blur of brown fluff and, rather too late, noticed it was a young squirrel trying to cross the road. It was immediately afterwards that she heard and felt a rather squishy bump under her wheels. Lotty cringed and started to weep. She hated hurting any living creature, preferring most animals to humans, and started to feel decidedly guilty about what she had just done. She carried on until she got to a path that led off the country road that she had been driving down. She pulled over. Wasting no time at all, she executed a rather professional and rapid three-point turn and went back to save the baby squirrel. She was going to wrap it in a mohair jumper that she always kept in the car in case of being caught out in cold weather, and then she would drive the poor, defenceless, and now wounded little ball of fur to a local animal sanctuary. Lotty had taken several animals to that particular sanctuary over recent years, including a slow-worm that she'd been too embarrassed to tell the founder of the sanctuary had been brought into her house in two halves by Arabella.

Lotty slowed down and looked carefully for the squirrel. Her eyes scanned every inch of the gravel road carefully as she attempted to track down the poor little creature. Suddenly, she spied a furry tail. She applied her brakes, stopped the vehicle, grabbed her jumper off of the car seat, got out, and ran at great speed towards the squirrel. She stopped and looked down. While she wasn't a vet, she did feel that there was little help for the victim of her collision as she now noticed, upon further investigation, that its head was missing.

CHAPTER 44

Lotty drove home rather solemnly. She felt utterly wicked for having murdered a beautiful woodland soul. Once she got home, she parked her car and noticed that there was fur on the grille from earlier; she couldn't bring herself to look at it and shuddered again at the thought of what she had done. She put her work kit away in the garage cupboard and walked into her kitchen, failing to notice the fact that Arabella was now rather intently licking her car's paintwork. As Lotty walked through the house, she had an uneasy feeling that something was odd. She couldn't quite place why she was feeling this, but she was feeling it all the same. Having had no time to listen to her voicemail messages all afternoon, she was unaware the Bruce had left a message informing her that he had provided a spare key to her house to a security guard from his company. Said security guard was now assessing her interior for any points of entry that he felt were prone and would need attention to tighten security at her home.

Lotty stopped in her tracks as she heard a noise upstairs; there was someone in her house. She trained her ears on the noise, her head darting around as, once again, she had to try to remember more of her personal defence training. She was looking for a weapon. Her eyes landed on a lamp that was plugged into the wall next to her. She slowly and carefully unplugged the cord and made her way stealthily upstairs. She heard more movement. What the actual fuck? Who was in her house? Lotty was overcome with a sense of anger, and her hostility rose; she was sick of having her sacred home persecuted in this manner. Spying a movement out of the corner of her keen eye, she leapt aggressively forward and swung the lamp with all of her strength until it made contact with her prey. As she heard the glass of the lamp's fluorescent bulb shatter into thousands of tiny pieces upon impact (she had best clean that up before Arabella could tread in it), she also felt the metal in the body of the lamp bow slightly. Then the lampshade fell off, landing right upon the head of whomever she had just hit.

She heard a groan. Looking down at the stranger, she now spied that the person was wearing a work lanyard around his neck that displayed the name of Bruce's company. Oops.

It was at that very moment that the mobile phone in Lotty's pocket rang. She answered it.

"Hello?"

"Darling, did you find John yet?"

"Er, yes, I have indeed found John."

John made a moaning sound and tried to remove the rather elegant lampshade that was now rather firmly stuck on his head.

"Lotty, what's happened?"

"In my defence …"

"Oh God, here we go. What have you done to John?"

"I was not aware that John would be visiting. And why on earth was he inside my house?"

"Lotty, I left you a message positively hours ago now telling you that that John was going to be making a security assessment of your house. Did you not listen to it?"

"If I had listened to the message, do you think I would have attacked John with a lampshade?"

"You did what? Oh my God. Lotty, he was doing me a favour; he hadn't even asked to be paid."

John, albeit slightly more alert than a few moments before, projectile-vomited very loudly, and very far down Lotty's corridor.

"I'm not an expert, but John *may* be concussed." She felt guilty and was very aware that she was going to get told off by Bruce again.

"Right, I'm calling an ambulance for him. Go and make him a strong cup of tea and get him an ice pack. Then call me, please. If he's taken to hospital, the very least I can do is go with him, as can you."

Lotty heard Bruce hang up abruptly on her. She screwed up her face in disgust, not at his rudeness, but because she was disappointed in herself for expelling such a powerful warning fart during the attack on John that she would now have to go and check to ensure that nothing untoward had happened in her underwear as a result.

CHAPTER 45

Having made poor John a cup of tea, Lotty waited for the ambulance to arrive at her address. John, seated awkwardly in one of her armchairs, looked terrified; he was probably worried that she was going to hit him again. Lotty was of the opinion that John was being rather dramatic about it all. After the two of them had to make a considerable amount of small talk between themselves, the paramedics finally arrived and started to perform an inspection of John's head wound and general symptoms.

Pamela, the senior first responder who had attended, appeared to be a particular lovely woman. She had tried to be extremely diplomatic when pointing out to Lotty that she hadn't ever seen anyone assaulted with such a soft furnishing, and neither had she realised that someone could have their forehead cut open so deeply by an insulation sleeve.

Pamela was now assessing John's mental faculties by asking him to respond to a particularly diverse set of questions.

"John, can you just follow my finger? Good … OK, so can you tell me what day it is, please?"

Lotty, having spoken to John for several tortuous minutes prior to Pamela's arrival, was quite certain that even under normal circumstances, John would have struggled to answer that question. She chastised herself for being a bitch again, yet was reminded of the reason: she needed to eat. She left the small group of people who were crammed into her upstairs landing and jogged towards her kitchen. When she got this hungry, she would start dreaming about food. She was currently thinking about maraschino cherries, as she had stolen a couple earlier on that afternoon at work from a jar in the communal fridge. Upon her arrival into her kitchen, she grabbed a ripe banana from the fruit bowl and wondered why she could see Arabella looking at her car's tyres so intently as the vehicle sat in the garage.

Lotty chose to wait downstairs for the remainder of the medical assessment. As she peeled her fruit and swallowed it practically without chewing, she picked up her mobile phone and decided to pass some time and search the internet as to how maraschino cherries were made. Eventually, after studying the search results with gusto, she had ascertained three things: (1) eating maraschino cherries earlier was most definitely the reason for her blood sugar dropping so rapidly; (2) John may not have been hit quite so hard if she'd been more successful in maintaining her blood sugar that day and avoided the maraschino cherries; and (3) maraschino cherries probably counted as a negative towards one's five a day.

CHAPTER 46

After much investigation, the paramedics had finally decided that John was fine and required no onwards trip to hospital. Bruce had arrived at Lotty's house just as the paramedics were starting to load their medical equipment back into the ambulance. As Lotty waved the ambulance off, as well as Bruce and John (John understandably decided not to wave back), DS Andrews pulled into her driveway.

If Lotty could have seen his face better in the gentle light of the dusk, she would have noticed the absence of surprise on it; he was so used to seeing various emergency vehicles there that he felt that Lotty should start a loyalty card scheme. He was becoming comfortably at ease with her little foibles. While she couldn't see much, she could see that he was checking his appearance in his rear-view mirror, and she caught a glimpse of him straightening his hair and briefly smoothing some stray strands down neatly with his hands. As he alighted from the car, she tried to lean nonchalantly against her rose bush and fell into it.

"Thall we ask them to turn around and come back, or do you think one vithit is enough for today, Lotty?" he shouted across the garden.

She laughed and gestured for him to follow her into the house. Glancing back at DS Andrews, Lotty noticed him stop and bend down to pick something up by her dustbins that she'd left out that morning, albeit on the wrong day. It wasn't the first time she had made such a mistake, but she found it rather difficult to excel at practical matters when her brain matter was being consumed on a case.

"Your dustbinth haven't been emptied, did you know?"

"I left them out on the wrong day again, I think. I have done it before, and I am sure that I will do it again."

"Well, did you know that the bin bagth have been pulled open and ranthacked, prethumably by a fox?"

"Oh no, really? I'll go out in a bit with some rubber gloves on and clear it all up. Do come in."

As DS Andrews stepped through her front door, he handed her a vibrator. "Erm, I picked thisth pieth of rubbith up for you, ath it hath probably already attracted rather a lot of attenthon. I imagine that ith been on your drive for a while now, tho you may want to conthider moving to a new house to avoid the embarrathment."

Lotty had thrown the offending item in her rubbish bin last week, just after bin day, and replaced it with the one that she'd subsequently had confiscated as a lethal weapon by DS Andrews' colleagues several days ago.

"Wath that altho a gift for a friend?" he asked.

Lotty stared at it for a moment while she wondered what she could *possibly* say to rescue the situation. She eventually took hold of the bright pink plastic, replete with teeth marks from the local wildlife, and immediately threw it into the kitchen dustbin, choosing to ignore the question and forcing the conversation in a different direction to avoid having to look at, or talk about, her "personal aids" any further.

"How can I help you?"

"I wath hoping to chat further about dinner. We can have a nithe talk about the two caythess we have in common, and perhapth anything elth we have in common?"

She smiled. "What about Thursday evening? I have a few days off, and I can do some more sleuthing with Bruce. Then we will hopefully have some more suspects whom we can mark off the list. There's a really nice French bistro I went to with Bruce recently, if you would fancy that?"

He nodded in agreement.

"You and your colleagueth thood be rewarded for how hard you have all worked on bringing the cathe againtht that farmer to fruithon. You have all done a thuperlative job there."

"I think my dad would have worked night and day on that case. He positively despised domestic abusers; he worked tirelessly to have them convicted when those types of cases came up." Lotty's dad had indeed brought his A game very often to a case; conversely, he wasn't always perfect, and had once knocked a civilian off their pushbike as he and his assessor had left the test centre for his advanced police driving course.

"The evidenth isth piling up around him now. Did you hear he'th now in polith cuthtody?"

"No. That's fantastic news! I keep forgetting to tell you, but I think we can strike a line through Sir Ralph's name as a suspect in the Evangeline DuVoir case. The research that I conducted with Bruce the other day suggests that there is no way that Sir Ralph would want his ex-wife dead. It makes his operational activities much harder to conduct as she was much easier to control than her son, who now inherits."

DS Andrews looked suitably impressed at her handiwork. He sat down next to Lotty while the kettle boiled and acknowledged to himself that he now felt very comfortable in her company.

They spent many hours that evening chatting together over several herbal teas, until Lotty could no longer battle to stifle the yawns that signalled her fatigue had beaten her for the day. As DS Andrews walked out of her front door, he stopped, turned his head, and paused. Was he going to lean in and kiss her?

Lotty closed her eyes and waited for the soft touch of his lips upon hers, yet after several seconds nothing had happened. She opened her eyes again. He was standing in front of her, awkwardly holding his coat that he'd reached back around the door for, having taken it from the coat stand. He coughed, wished her a good evening, and walked off to his car, wondering if she should start wearing glasses to help her eye strain.

Lotty closed the door and gave up on another hapless evening as the lyrics for "Shut Up and Kiss Me" played through her inner monologue. She scaled her stairs, removed her make-up, and practically fell into bed.

CHAPTER 47

It was early the next morning, and after successfully having completed a ten-mile trail run at one of her faster paces, when Lotty arrived at Bruce's house. They had arranged to meet at his and then proceed onwards to Alexander Rowley's house together in order to investigate him as a person of interest in the murder case involving Rowley's late mother.

Lotty knocked on Bruce's door. When he opened it, she was greeted with the strong scent of vanilla.

"What are you cooking this early?"

"I'm not cooking anything, but I have just been presented with a glorious handful of cream buns."

She held up her hand in protest. "Just no."

Bruce leaned back into his house briefly and shouted, "Grant, you can let yourself out. Lotty and I are going to be out most of the day." He closed his front door and followed her to her car.

"Aren't you going to ask me who is in there?"

"I don't need to. It's *hopefully* the patisserie chef."

"Why hopefully?"

"Because that is the only reason I would want to imagine you eating a cream bun at this time of the day. I googled Alexander's company address, and it's already in the car satnav. Let's go. I want to get there in good time so we can be there to follow him if he leaves the premises at all."

They secured their seat belts and went merrily on their way. Lotty chose to ignore the icing sugar and the knob of butter that Bruce had on both knees of his trousers.

CHAPTER 48

They eventually came to a stop at a very posh-looking set of offices which, Lotty felt, truly encapsulated the lavish and self-indulgent aura that Alexander had projected when she spent time with him at the party. Outside of the building there were several majestic stone statues and an impressive pond that appeared to house a family of Egyptian geese, which had clearly decided that they were worthy of a life of luxury. As Lotty's eyes swept slowly across the rest of the offices' frontage, she spied a beautiful pair of peacocks strutting proudly across an area of perfectly cut grass. It had those funny dark and light lawn lines cut into it, she noticed.

They pulled up behind several other parked cars and waited. Bruce shut off the engine, turned to Lotty, and then pointed his finger at a perfectly clean Land Rover Discovery with private registration plates that was parked in a corner of the car park. The parking space had "CEO" written on an unnecessarily large, and even more unnecessarily gaudy, sign that was attached to the wall behind the Land Rover.

Bruce chose his words carefully, considering Alexander was the son of someone he knew. "He's rather *extravagant*, isn't he?"

"You think? The peacocks appear to have their own sleeping quarters over there, behind the bench, where those two security men appear to be eating sushi on their break."

"Do you think Alexander provides them with gold chopsticks?" Bruce joked.

"Probably. Right, I say we wait here. We have a great view for when he drives to his first appointment, if he has any. We can just follow him for a day or so and get an idea of what he is up to. I bet he's arranging a visit with his solicitor and bank manager to start counting his inheritance."

139

"I think you're going to be disappointed, Lotty. He really is *actually* quite a nice lad."

"If you say so, but anyone could give off a vibe that doesn't truly reflect their character if they try hard enough."

"Well, what I will say about you is that you are, at least, beginning to think like your aunt Molly. She always thought the worst of a suspect until she gathered the correct amount of evidence to prove herself wrong."

They sat and waited for hours, playing on their respective mobile phones until lunchtime, when they were rewarded with a glimpse of Alexander emerging from his office building carrying nothing but his wallet.

"Gucci probably." Bruce could spot a designer brand quicker than a bald eagle could spy a freshwater salmon.

Lotty started her engine and waited for Alexander to exit the car park. She tailed him, keeping just enough distance between their cars so as not to raise suspicion, but also to allow her to follow him without error.

After about five miles, Alexander pulled up and parked outside of what a large painted sign signalled was a palliative care centre.

"What do you think he's going in there for?" he quizzed.

"I don't know. You've spent more time with him and his family. Do they have any family members who are ill? Evangeline can't have been admitted there given her prognosis, right?"

"Right." Bruce scratched his head in thought. "Honestly, I'm clueless at this point. And I do feel that it would be in rather poor taste to go and ask any form of probing questions in such an establishment."

Having both agreed that this avenue of the investigation had been temporarily closed, they would go back and change, and follow him again later when they had eaten. Despite firmly holding to the belief that they were making headway along their journey towards a career in detection, they were still easily distracted, and Bruce had heard that there was a sale on at their favourite boutique.

Bruce started singing "Money, Money, Money" at Lotty, and they both dreamed about how much cash they were about to part with in the shop.

CHAPTER 49

Later that Tuesday evening, Lotty was putting her dustbins out again, this time on the correct day of the week. She had double wrapped her rubbish to combat the attraction of any more wild animals to the scent of her musk. Her neighbour had given her quite the funny look earlier when she arrived home, so she was fairly sure he was one of the presumably many people who had been rewarded with a glimpse of her *self-care item* as it had been left wantonly on her lawn for hours, also attracting bird strike. As she walked back towards her front door, she heard a loud and very distinct raspberry being blown at her. She assumed that it was one of the local teenagers who had seen her half-emptied bin bags the day before and was therefore now trying to mock her.

"Oh, piss off!" She spun around to give the "international sign of peace" to the prankster and was greeted with a clear view of where the noise had come from. Arabella was crouching perfectly still, trying to do her business. Judging from the look of concentration and anguish on her face, she wasn't proving to be successful and appeared to be suffering with a bout of constipation. After Lotty had trotted back into her house, she began to check her search engine for guidance on treating feline bowel issues, desperately hoping that DS Andrews would never see her internet search history.

Getting ready would take awhile. Lotty and Bruce had spent a considerable amount of time stalking Alexander earlier that day via his social media page and had deduced that he would be going to a strip club later called *All Bra One* with a group of friends in order to celebrate the upcoming nuptials of a member of the group. While neither Bruce nor Lotty could yet think of a plausible reason for them to be at the bar, they would certainly have concocted an idea by the time they arrived there. They were planning to accidentally meet up with Alexander to see if they could at least tag along for one drink to gather some more background for the investigation.

CHAPTER 50

It was coming up to eleven o'clock at night. Their plan had been more than successful. Both Lotty and Bruce were now seated in All Bra One's private members' lounge, surrounded by Alexander's group and being subjected to a resounding cheer, a response to the fact that the stag had just drunk a shot of tequila out of the shoe of one of the strippers. Lotty was 99 per cent sure that she was going to throw up at some point later this evening, but it would come as no surprise to her given that she vaguely remembered drinking a shot of whisky that also contained crushed peanuts and was blended with shaved ice, double cream, and blue curaçao liqueur. She felt herself belch, and the belch was accompanied by some warning bile. She swallowed, grimaced, and hoped not to relive the time she had once blocked a bathroom sink by throwing up into it after drinking too much vodka on an empty stomach. She made her way over to the bar area and sat down on a purple velvet stool that she then fell immediately off of. She got back on. There were a group of extravagantly dressed strippers sitting along the bar chatting amongst each other, having just finished their shift.

"We don't see you in here much. Can't say that about your mate though." The Amazonian blonde looked over towards Alexander. "That fella is in here more than I am, and I work here."

"Do you know him well?" asked Lotty, who was trying hard not to compare herself to the beautiful women who made up the group, as to do so would be depressing. Her front looked like their backs.

"Yep, he's actually quite sweet really. He drinks a fair amount but knows when he's had enough, and he tips well. He's got a kind heart. Talks about his mother a lot. He was in here the other day. I had to abandon a lap dance, he was bawling so much."

"About her death, you mean?" Lotty tried to awaken the sober person inside her so she could pay attention.

"God, yes. He was crying very hard. And I didn't have a handkerchief, so he had to use the hem of my nurse's outfit."

Lotty felt sure that while the stripper didn't hold any formal medical qualifications, she probably had her own take on what constituted a "kiss of life".

"He was going off about what he would do if he ever found out who did that to his mum. He's completely cut up about it, poor little sod. He's still going down to volunteer at a care home that his mum's friend recently died in. They'd met only recently because they had both undergone the same surgery and had got chatting in a hospital consulting room. He's genuinely a decent lad, you know?"

Lotty *didn't* know. Most of the men whom she had dated had turned out to be massive wankers.

It was clear to Lotty that she now possessed unequivocal proof that Alexander wasn't the one who murdered Evangeline. It was also very clear that the churning alcohol in her stomach needed to be absorbed by food.

Lotty, sipping gently on the champagne that she was holding, felt herself belch again. To the great displeasure of all of her friends, she possessed the innate ability to execute a champagne burp that would melt your eyebrows off. She had, long ago, taken to holding the glass in front of her face just as she was about to belch. This served to catch the smell and prevented it from escaping too far from her immediate person. This evening she had misjudged the placement of the glass thanks to her excessive inebriation.

"Has somebody farted? What the fuck is that smell?"

All eyes were on Lotty. She thanked the women in the group and stumbled slowly back to find Bruce.

Having decided that it was now time to leave and forage for food, Bruce tried to support Lotty as best he could out of the bar. He was now questioning his idea of one of them being sober, as he had become quite bored at one point and started watching a documentary on World War Two on his phone. Lotty belched again.

"Sweet Jesus, that one was straight from hell, wasn't it? How do you make those awful smells?"

He managed to get Lotty outside, where he gingerly leaned her up against an exterior wall.

"We need to get you some food. There's a kebab van over there."

He dragged the now very drunk Lotty across the road, ordered them both a large doner kebab, each with extra jalapeños, and waited for the food to be prepared. Getting Lotty over to the van had proved way more challenging than getting her out of the bar, and it seemed that the more time she spent smelling the food, the more drunk she became, because her stomach was being reminded of how empty it was. Getting her subsequently to his car had seemed almost impossible. The battle of opening his passenger-side door with Lotty in tow resulted in his dropping his car keys twice, the food once, and Lotty more times than he would ever admit to her, despite the number of times she would subsequently press him to explain the various bruises with which she would later wake up with. She would therefore also never find out why she found a slice of grilled halloumi in her shoe the next morning.

"Sit down and eat before we go anywhere. And don't even think about dropping any of that kebab in my car."

Lotty tried to focus on eating the kebab and not dropping it. She felt that the only way to achieve zero spillage was to eat it as fast as possible. She and Bruce sat in silence and ate their food, with Bruce watching her every move from the corner of his eye. Ten minutes later, both their kebabs had been demolished and Bruce was carefully peeling off a stray slice of tomato that Lotty had dropped onto his centre console.

Lotty's eyes closed.

She snored.

Lotty's eyes opened.

"I've put the roof and windows down so you can get some fresh air," Bruce shouted at her over the noise of the motorway. "You have been asleep for ages. Are you feeling OK? You look a bit green."

Lotty leaned her head out of the open window and vomited the contents of her stomach down the side of his car, as well as out onto the road beneath them. The wind had the unfortunate effect of picking up a large volume of her vomit and transporting it rapidly onto the lorry that was driving behind them.

Lotty's eyes closed again.

CHAPTER 51

Lotty woke up the next morning with a large chunk of chargrilled onion stuck to the side of her face. Her throat was decidedly dry, and her breath would disarm a Navy SEAL. While she bitterly regretted several of her life choices from the previous evening, she was very pleased that it had successfully closed the chapter on another one of the suspects. They had crossed Alexander off of the list.

Her mobile phone rang. It seemed a lot louder today.

"Hello?"

"Lotty, it'sth Mathon. I got a textht from you overnight to call you, and while I won't embarrath you by reading it out loud, I will confirm that we are both on the thame page, although I would like to sthtate that one of the thuggestions in your methage wouldn't be pothible unleth I were an Olympic gymnatht."

"Erm, OK?" Lotty didn't care. She was very hung-over and worried her eyeballs were about to fall out of their sockets.

"I've been conducting thome background checkth on thome of the attendeeth of Bruthe's party the other night. Melitha'th father isth an electrithan. He evidently tradesth as a Misthter M. Bantley, out of *her* home addreth. Thee doethn't live permanently with Greg yet, and the electoral roll hath hith electrical company regithtered where Melitha liveth, on the edge of town."

Lotty sat up against her pillows. A piece of pitta bread dropped from her nipple onto the duvet.

"Maybe Melissa's father was annoyed that his future son-in-law was being bled dry by Evangeline at work? He then bumped her off to stop the drain on his daughter's future wealth?"

"That could be a pothibility. I think it isth definitely worth adding him to the thuspect pool."

"I knocked someone else off the list last night. There is no way Alexander Rowley killed his mother. He is absolutely heartbroken. We went out with him and his friends last night and spoke to some independent witnesses at the bar that he frequents."

"Great work. Look, I've got to get back to work, but before I go, I jutht wanted to let you know I'm really looking forward to our date tomorrow night."

There was an awkward pause, as Lotty always became incredibly tongue-tied when presented with any form of compliment.

"Thank you?" she mustered before hanging up.

CHAPTER 52

If she breathed in too deeply, Lotty could still taste advocaat, despite having brushed her teeth twice. It had taken two strong coffees and two headache tablets before Lotty felt human again, and now she needed to hurry as Bruce was on his way over to collect her for another productive day of investigating. While she was waiting, she fielded a call from work, but it was only Arthur ringing her to ask if she would permit him to throw away something with her name label on it that was making the communal fridge smell quite bad.

"I think if it stays in here much longer, we are going to have to transfer it to the fumigator." As over the top as it sounded, Arthur had on many occasions ordered for various food items to be relegated there. He had also once suggested that Lotty be moved there, the day after their office Christmas party at an Indian restaurant.

Lotty's head was pounding because of her hangover, and her situation wasn't being helped by Arabella's insistence that it was the right time to start playing with her crinkly cat tunnel. The noise was really grating on Lotty's nerves each time the troublesome feline launched herself through it. Just as Lotty had decided that the toy should be confiscated, Arabella's spatial ability failed her, and she launched herself head first at the lounge wall.

Just as Lotty was frantically searching the internet to investigate if cats could suffer from concussion, she looked out of the lounge window to see Bruce walking up her drive. Walking regally next to him was a rotund basset hound. She put her shoes on and went out to meet him.

"Lotty, meet Tallulah!"

Lotty patted Tallulah's head and received an overly friendly lick on her hand. "Are you planning to elaborate on why Tallulah is here?"

The dog sat down on Lotty's lawn and started to pant in the morning sun. Then Lotty scrunched up her nose as a waft of rancid dog breath attacked her nostrils.

"Don't pull that face at her. She's an absolute sweetie. Aren't you, my darling?" Bruce leaned down to cuddle Tallulah, trying to hide the alarming noise that he made upon also smelling her breath. "She belongs to Grant, the patisserie chef. He is visiting his mother, who is in hospital today, and he asked me if I wouldn't mind. I do mind, but I'm taking one for the team today in order to ingratiate myself."

"She's quite large, isn't she? And what in God's name is he feeding her? Her breath is awful."

"Funnily enough, we haven't yet talked at great lengths about his dog's diet. Dog food? I saw him putting some in a bowl, and it was custom-made. I read it on the label."

"You may want to suggest to him that they add some parsley to it then."

"Why parsley?"

"Everyone knows that parsley combats bad breath in dogs," she said, exasperated.

"No, dear. Only people who spend their evenings watching game shows and animal documentaries because they've forgotten what it feels like to be touched by another human. Now, can we go?" Tallulah was beginning to look bored. Bruce shook her lead gently to indicate that they were about to start walking, or rolling in, Tallulah's case.

"Why are we walking, and where?" Lotty had just noticed that Bruce was dressed all in cream.

"The car is being valeted because you vomited a doner kebab all over it last night. And we are off to a charity cricket match on the rectory green in the next village."

"On a Wednesday?"

"Don't apologise, will you? It's really fine. Anyway, days of the week don't matter if you have enough money. I offered myself as an additional player when I heard from Ralph in a WhatsApp group I'm in that Lorna

Brannigan was looking for volunteers. Lorna helps run a charity supporting the homeless."

"Nicely done." They fist-bumped.

"So how are things going with Grant?"

"Really well, thank you. It has transpired that our meeting wasn't by chance."

"I thought you knew him from the restaurant you like. I assumed you had just met him there."

"Not at all. I hadn't even seen him before, as he rarely ventures front of house due to his workload. I had asked the restaurant to help with the catering. They weren't doing all of it, but I had asked them to provide some of the fancier dishes. He had apparently seen me coming and going from the kitchen window and had asked about me. So, when the owner told him about the job, he'd specifically asked to work the shift."

Lotty smiled at how pleased Bruce looked with himself. He didn't need anyone to inflate his ego; he made such a good job of that himself.

As they completed their journey to the next village, Lotty relished the morning sunshine and appreciated the gentle serenade from the birds up in the trees.

Bruce and Lotty eventually found themselves on the porch of a picturesque pavilion. Bruce left Lotty with Tallulah, while he went off to join the team. Lotty made her way to a group of women who were holding clipboards and starting to set up a picnic on a series of wooden tables.

"Can I help at all? I'm here with Bruce. Which one of you is Lorna?"

A perfectly manicured hand was thrust towards Lotty. "You must be Lotty! I'm Lorna. Can you start unwrapping the sandwiches for me? Thank you for offering to help. It's a case of having all hands on deck at these charity events. Do you often watch cricket?"

Lotty tied the dog's lead around a deckchair that was near to the tables. "I have watched the odd match with Bruce, and I used to go to Lord's Cricket Ground occasionally with my late father." Lotty replied, beginning to remove the plastic wrap from the various trays of tasty-looking sandwiches that were set out in front of her and making her salivate.

One of the other women in the group standing next to Lotty also started to help unwrap the plates. "These look fantastic. Do you think anyone would mind if we took a couple? I haven't had my breakfast yet."

Lorna smiled at her friend and nodded. "Help yourself, Marla."

Lotty watched Marla take a cheese and tomato sandwich in her hand and move it up to her mouth. As if in slow motion, Tallulah suddenly raced over, knocking a deckchair into Lorna as she did so and causing her to land upon the floor. The excited dog then leapt up to steal the sandwich from Marla and also knocked her completely off of her feet. It reminded Lotty of a great white shark breaching the surface of the sea as it hunted for seals.

Lotty proceeded to pick Marla up off the ground and then removed a small bowl of clotted cream that had landed on her head. Bruce walked over to them.

"Lorna, how the devil are you? I see here that chaos prevails, so I can only assume that you have spent more than a minute in Lotty's company. I always take her back to anywhere we have been for a second visit as she generally needs to return to issue an apology."

"I'm wonderful! Please don't worry about it. Lotty was helping lay the picnic out. Sorry about missing your party, by the way." Lorna flicked a stray strawberry from her heel.

"It was rather fortuitous that you didn't come, to be fair. It ended up being rather a late night after all the statements had been taken."

"It was rather shocking with all the business about Evangeline."

Another dog had just arrived. Lotty was now using all of her strength to keep control of Tallulah, who was trying to chase the other dog.

"Lotty here was pulled into the case from a work perspective. I'm assuming you've been contacted by the police?"

"Not yet, but they are going to be rather disappointed if they think that I was involved, as Evangeline's demise has created quite the financial predicament for me. I am actually going to be losing a lot of money now that she has died. And although we had our differences, I had known her a great number of years and I will actually miss her."

Lorna started to sob delicately into a handkerchief that she had pulled out of her pocket. Lotty moved closer and patted her on the shoulder.

"There, there. Let it all out. I'm sorry you've lost your friend." Lotty finally lost control of Tallulah and watched her run over to the other dog and sniff its bottom.

"I guess one would say that Evangeline was my frenemy. We spent an inordinate amount of time together. We were always arguing, but over the years, we grew older and forged a mutual respect for one another. We had actually started to work on a book together and were only a quarter of the way through. I can't finish it without her input, and the publisher wouldn't be interested now. They've already asked me to return the retainer now that they've seen her death reported in in the media. It was fifty thousand pounds each."

Bruce started to pat Lorna's other shoulder now, as he would have hated to have lost that amount of money.

"I'm so sorry, darling. Why don't you sit down here with Lotty and enjoy the match? We're about to start. Lotty will get you a nice cup of tea."

CHAPTER 53

Several innings and a substantial picnic later, Lotty and Bruce were sitting next to Tallulah on deckchairs as the trophies were being handed out. Tallulah had been left to sleep peacefully on the green after proving that she wasn't going to eat any more of the sandwiches or chase any more dogs. She was currently enjoying sunning herself in the bright afternoon light.

Lotty handed another cup of tea to Bruce. "That's one more person knocked off the list then. There would have to be an extremely compelling reason for Lorna to have done this to balance out the money that she is losing as a result of Evangeline's death."

Bruce stirred sugar into his tea and nodded in agreement. "She didn't to it, I don't think. Never say never, but it is pretty unlikely."

They both paused to allow for a break in their conversation for a round of applause that had just erupted. Someone had just been awarded "Man of the Match". Lotty recognised him as the rather handsome man at whom she had been making phallic gestures during the picnic by creatively working a celery stick into her cheek with her tongue. As she watched him walk back to the pavilion, she noticed him absent-mindedly tossing a cricket ball in the air and catching it. Tallulah, having also noticed this, shot up and sped towards him, knocking him forcibly to the ground in order to retrieve the ball.

Bruce stood up and shouted in frustration, "That blasted dog has only gone and knocked the bloody vicar over now! Lotty, why have you gone so pale? You're as white as a sheet, darling."

"Highway to Hell" started to play in her head.

CHAPTER 54

The following Thursday morning was sunny and peaceful. The only sound Lotty heard as she opened her sleepy eyes was that of her bedroom clock. The obsessive-compulsive side of Lotty found the rhythmic clicking of the hands very calming as they marched around the numbers on the dial. She lamented over the absence of the flock of parakeets that used to sing gleefully at her in the mornings from her neighbour's garden, until Arabella had forced her way into the aviary and killed them all. Lotty had tried smoothing things over at the time with small talk, but Mrs Grantham hadn't been at all interested that a group of parakeets was also known as a "chatter". Mrs Grantham had also taken great pains to point out to Lotty that it was now a moot point, considering she now only owned one half-dead parakeet that didn't appear to want to chatter much any more.

Lotty had awakened excited about her date with DS Andrews. The absence of sexual activity in her life meant that whenever she executed a karate kick in her weekly martial arts class, she was worried about the other class participants being hit in the face by a bushel of tumbleweed.

She picked up her mobile phone and dialled Bruce's number.

"Hello, dear."

"You know you're my favourite person in the entire world …"

"The answer is no."

"But I haven't asked for anything yet."

"It's definitely still no."

"Do you want me to find a boyfriend or not?"

"OK, you have my attention …"

"Please, can I borrow your car to take DS Andrews for our date? I just read a text from him that his pool car is being serviced."

"Are you sure it's not being 'therviced'?"

Lotty sighed. "Why are you being like that? Do you think I even care that he has a lisp? I have a rather off-putting stomach disorder, *and* I am clumsy and have less than average-sized breasts, but he's still lovely to me. Everyone is unique, is special, and should be loved. Nobody is 'different'; it is just that we are all equally not the same."

Bruce sighed down the phone. "Lotty, you're right. I'm sorry. Look, that was just a little joke, but he doesn't deserve to be joked about. He does seem an exceptionally wonderful man, and I genuinely do like him. I'm sorry if I offended you. And of course you can take my car. You will need to go and pick it up from the valeting company as they don't do drop-offs."

"Thank you. I love you, and I accept your apology."

"You still haven't apologised for vomiting in it, by the way."

"Goodbye."

CHAPTER 55

Lotty was sitting in a taxi, on her way to collect Bruce's car. He had texted earlier to update her that the valeting company was aware that she was picking it up on his behalf. Lotty hadn't driven his car before and was rather looking forward to a change in engine power. She was sitting with her head jammed subtly out the window and gasping for fresh air. As lovely as the taxi driver was, he was completely unaware of how strong the stench of his body odour was to his clientele. Lotty was struggling to justify how he deserved a tip because there was no air freshener hanging in the vehicle anywhere to mask the smell. She had therefore been eagerly watching the in-car satnav in order to count down the miles left until they reached their destination. Extremely grateful when the car pulled up at an industrial area on the outskirts of South Oxfordshire, she thanked her driver while holding her breath. She begrudgingly tipped him a modest 10 per cent and hoped that he would use it to purchase some deodorant. Lotty was a Gemini and therefore only nice to others half of the time but she was working on that.

Lotty saw Bruce's gleaming white F-Type R convertible parked in front of her, the newly polished paint shining bright and receiving a final polish from a man dressed in grubby overalls.

"Are you Lotty? I'll need to see some identification before I allow this little beauty to leave. I've really enjoyed cleaning this one."

Lotty allowed him to check her driving licence and was then handed the keys to the vehicle.

The man pointed into the car's interior. "I've tried my best, but I'm not a miracle worker. I've had to work extra hard on the seats because there was rather a dodgy-looking brown stain there. I was hoping it was brown sauce from the kebab that I heard you hurled everywhere."

Lotty looked back at him, exasperated, as she was handed the key fob. "I can assure you that it definitely *is* just sauce. I'm not sure what you're implying."

"Well, anyway, I've left the roof and the windows down to air it out. I've tried my best with the smell."

Having ensured that the man used her own card to pay for the cleaning, considering that it was her own mess, she got into the car, put her seat belt on, and adjusted the seat to her height. She ran her hands over the smooth red leather of the interior cushion in appreciation of its finesse. Lotty loved driving; she'd inherited that from her father. He used to love a good car chase, although he was well known at the police station he worked out of for once driving a patrol car at great speed into an old-fashioned cement lamp post. He'd been taken to hospital at the time as the heavy light from the top of the post had become dislodged and plunged onto the bonnet of the car, resulting in him receiving a minor head injury.

Lotty turned on the engine and felt the guttural vibrations beneath her; it was quite a good car for single people. She drove the car carefully along the roads to town, being cautious as she wasn't used to driving it. She was, at points, unable to help herself and would occasionally press down hard on the accelerator to enjoy the immediate pickup of the five-litre V-8 engine. Upon finding an open stretch of straight road, she pressed her foot down as hard as she could and felt her neck snap back from the force of the acceleration, but her thoughts, once again, danced back to the memory of the departed squirrel from a few days earlier, so she slowed back down.

Lotty made her way into town and idled the car in the high street, until she saw a parking space become available. She expertly reversed the car, parked it parallel to the kerb, and shut off the engine. She needed to visit the chemist, she decided, surveying the puffy bags under her eyes that were a result of her continuing hangover. The dehydration from the alcohol consumed earlier in the week had meant that the area under her eyes was not as pretty as she would like it to be for her date, or indeed to see any other human. She had tried to resolve the situation with a cooling cucumber eye mask earlier that morning, then she had tried placing a cold spoon under each of her eyes, but nothing was working. A fruitful search on the internet had made Lotty aware that make-up artists favoured the use of haemorrhoid cream to reduce the effects of puffy eyes. They often had to use the product when celebrities turned up after a heavy night out on the town. After overcoming the initial apprehension of having to go and buy bottom medication (it wasn't the first time), Lotty had resolved herself to this being her last resort. She would have worn her sunglasses to go incognito, but she had just realised that her glasses were in her *own* car; she would have to just brave the shame of people thinking she had piles. She decided that she might ask for the cream loudly to turn the tide on people feeling embarrassed when they asked for things at the chemist. She had recently been prescribed testosterone gel for a hormone deficiency, initially having felt embarrassed, but she had gotten over it after the chemist had been so kind about it. The chemist was inwardly impressed at how the gel was working on what he thought was Lotty's transition to becoming a man. It was shortly before her lip wax had been done the last time.

Lotty enjoyed a slow meander down the high street, looking into the windows of the various shops. She was beginning to enjoy her enforced time off. She ducked into a coffee house, ordered a hazelnut Americano, and spent the time to sit down and enjoy it in situ with a portion of cacao porridge. Lotty felt it was always best to be seated when she was drinking coffee, or else it generally got thrown down her sleeve as she walked, and she had once nearly blinded a small child who had walked underneath her hand at rather an inopportune moment. She needed to work herself up to be confident enough to go into the chemist and get the cream. She swirled her spoon around the porridge thoughtfully, making lines as the metal cut through the smooth oats, and hardly noticed a waitress come over to her. "Are you not enjoying your breakfast, madam?"

"It's lovely. Sorry, it's just that I'm working myself up to go and buy pile cream."

Having been left alone by the waitress to play with her porridge some more, until she couldn't possibly put her shopping expedition off any longer, Lotty made her way back out into the busy high street.

The waitress came over to clear away Lotty's crockery and thought that Lotty should really be avoiding oats for the time being. Eating the porridge couldn't have been helping her piles.

As Lotty walked up towards the chemist, she was unaware that she had been spotted by DS Andrews. He was in town picking up his trousers from the dry-cleaners. He wanted to look his best for Lotty when he saw her later. He was surprised as he saw her navigate her way up the high street, not because she was there, but because she didn't have her skirt tucked up into her knickers and hadn't tripped over her shoelaces. Having found her clumsiness rather endearing, he decided to follow her to say hello and to see what chaos she would cause today. He sped up after her.

Lotty made her way into the chemist and suddenly became rather hot and nervous. She moved along the various lipsticks sitting on the shelves on her right-hand side and pretended to be looking at them. After eventually noticing that the shop was now devoid of other customers, she made her way to the counter.

"Can I help you, madam?"

Lotty heard the tinkle of the shop's bell as she started to reply to the chemist. *Damn.*

"Erm, I'd like some haemorrhoid cream, please."

She felt someone tap her on the shoulder from behind.

"Hi, Lotty, it'sth lovely to thee you."

Lotty turned to see DS Andrews' perfect face staring back at her. Her own face turned a deep hue of maroon at being caught in the act of buying something embarrassing. She suddenly became very flustered and felt unable to think straight. Having not seen DS Andrews for a few days, she shot her hand out to greet him. Having misjudged the distance, she punched him firmly, and with great accuracy, in his penis.

CHAPTER 56

Lotty and DS Andrews had agreed that she would pick him up, in Bruce's car, from his house around seven in the evening. She considered herself very lucky to have met someone so kind; he'd been more forgiving than most about being struck in his manhood at the chemists and had even insisted on paying for her haemorrhoid cream as a chivalrous gesture. He had listened to her explanation as to why she was buying the cream, but he hadn't fully paid attention as he kept having to double over in intermittent bursts of pain. Lotty felt he had gone above and beyond being gallant when he took the time to hold the shop door open for her with the hand that he wasn't using to protectively guard his groin.

It was now Thursday evening. Lotty had just honked her horn to signal to DS Andrews that she was waiting outside his house. She had spent several hours of her afternoon getting ready for dinner. Apart from a shower, most of her time had been spent trying to perfect feline-flick eyeliner with her kohl pencil, but she had abandoned that after several failed attempts that had left her looking like Ming the Merciless. She had ended up favouring a natural make-up look because she wanted to show her true self. She had even had her outfit approved by Bruce over a video call; he'd described the final look as "mildly desperate, but not quite mad cat lady", which was indeed a compliment coming from him.

DS Andrews sat down in the car and handed Lotty a beautiful bunch of red roses held together by a white velvet bow. She blushed. He kissed her lightly on her cheek.

"Handsth on the wheel, please. At leatht then I know you are conthentrating on driving, but altho you can't punch me again." He smiled at her. "You look beautiful."

Bruce and Lotty had taken a moment during their FaceTime to role-play an appropriate response to being paid a compliment, were the situation to arise. "That's lovely of you to say. Thank you, DS Andrews."

"It thmells a bit like thick in here. Can you thmell that?"

Lotty panicked, as this type of snag hadn't been covered in the role-play from earlier. She chose to smile politely and shake her head innocently.

"I think, given how our relathionthip is progrething, it would be fine to refer to me ath Mathon." He winked at her, and she felt the hairs prickle on the back of her neck. She smiled and started the car. Feeling rather self-conscious about driving in front of a police officer, she chose to fix her eyes on the road ahead as the car started to pick up speed.

"I thought I would have the roof and windows down as the weather is so nice. It's not too loud for you, is it?"

"I might jutht put the window up tho that I can hear what you're thaying." Mason pressed his finger against the button and watched a perfectly round slice of jalapeño stuck to the glass, which the car cleaner must have missed, slide slowly upward past his eyes.

"It's fine. I'll put the roof up as well." Lotty touched a button on the inner console and then put her hands back on the wheel.

Mason heard very little sound from the prestigious mechanics of the car roof as he saw it glide effortlessly above him. As he observed a large chunk of what looked like a tomato flying at great speed past his face outside the window, he was unsurprised; after all, it was a car that *Lotty* was driving, so anything could happen. He chose to sit back and enjoy the decadent journey to the bistro. He took the time to check that the window was now fully up to ensure that he wouldn't be hit in the face by any chunks of salad.

CHAPTER 57

Lotty and Mason had spent several glorious hours in each other's company; they had joked together over an exquisite chateaubriand that they'd shared and were now enjoying their dessert of apple tarte tatin. Mason had been expecting for Lotty to be set alight as the waiter stood next to their table flambéing the dish, but it transpired, to his delight, that the preparation was uneventful. The dessert was placed in front of them with vanilla ice cream oozing into the puddle of sweet caramel that adorned their plates. Mason picked up his spoon and started to eat. Lotty chose to take her time with her dessert as she wanted to discuss the Evangeline DuVoir case further.

"Do you think it is worth investigating Susan Gibbons further, Mason?"

"The woman whom Evangeline'th firtht huthband wath having an affair with prior to hith death? I don't think tho, no."

"How old would she be now? Have you even bothered to track her down?"

"Thee would be about Evangeline'th age, tho late thixties. I haven't done any digging. Thee'th tho far removed from the cathe that I don't think it would add any value at thisth point. Try the dethert. It'sth quite wonderful."

He picked up his spoon and offered it to her. His romantic gesture of feeding her made Lotty feel fuzzy on the inside. She didn't want the evening to end. She also didn't want the dessert to end, as it was amazing. She savoured the mouthful, closing her eyes and relishing the mix of the sugar and salt in the caramel sauce as the sticky liquid danced across her tongue. After picking up her own spoon and finishing her dessert before

Mason finished his, she reached into the handbag and popped a fennel tablet into her mouth. It was this herb alone that helped her remain socially acceptable in public after a meal. Taking the tablet meant that she was less likely to belch or fart in the car on the way home.

"What about the Farmer Gardener case? Is he still in police custody?" she asked, putting her digestion medication away.

"He'th been charged. Everyone at the sthtation isth very happy. After we got him into a cuthtody thuite and put all the evidenth in front of him, he broke down. He had been planning her murder for a long time. He really hadn't conthidered how difficult it would be to dithpothe of her body. That final part derailed him, so he began to make mithtaketh. It was all becauth of your laboratory that we found thuch overwhelming evidenth of the murder. A family liaithon offither is currently working with Grace Gardener'th twin to help her with how to move on from here. It isth now in the handsth of a prothecutor. The family can now go ahead with planning the funeral."

"As sad as it is for everyone involved, I feel better knowing that Grace's family can now grieve and have closure. That's why I really value what we do, providing answers for families like that."

As they sat in this moment of quiet reflection, Mason's hand reached over to Lotty's and held it tightly. Lotty smiled at him, looked into his eyes, and wondered what he was thinking. She was unaware that he was thinking about when it would be appropriate to tell her that they needed to send her vibrator to her place of work to be processed for fingerprints, in case her attacker had left any on it during their struggle. Instead, he leaned over the table, kissed her passionately on the mouth, and pretended to ignore her knocking her coffee cup to the floor.

CHAPTER 58

It was Friday morning. Lotty was bounding round her gym with positive energy. She was feeling fantastic about her date with Mason and felt confident that her crotch might get a bit of an airing soon. She had met someone who didn't seem to mind how awkward she was at navigating life without falling over, or in, something on a daily basis. She felt unstoppable today, coming to the end of a frantic training session with her personal trainer, Jamie. Lotty's exercise compulsion disorder meant that her trainer had to approach his sessions with her differently than he would those with his other clients. Instead of motivating her to exercise more, he was there to ensure that he gave her the functional training her limbs needed to cope with the extreme amounts of cardio that she put herself through. He was a support beacon for all of his clients, and Lotty was honoured to call him a friend. Their session had been relatively accident-free, apart from an incident where she had thrown a weighted ball onto a bounce mat and it had returned at great speed into her stomach before she could catch it.

Lotty completed her third and final round of goblet squats and leaned against a wall to rest. Her stomach wasn't feeling all that great from eating pastry the night before. Gluten was not her friend.

"OK, Lotty. That's us done for the day." Jamie was gesturing for her to lie down on a stretching mat that he had laid upon the floor, away from any obstacles that she could concuss herself with. "Time to stretch!"

She put her kettlebell down on the weight rack and went over to the mat next to Jamie. She lay upon her back and got ready to breathe deeply. They had a strict regimen of stretching at the end of every class as Jamie was very aware that Lotty never stretched on her own, ever. He was surprised she hadn't yet ripped a ligament. He knelt in front her, in between her legs, took her left leg in his hands, placed it carefully upon his shoulder, and pushed his own knee forward into her inner thigh to lengthen her muscle. He recognised the look of worry on her face all too late and was unable to move diplomatically out of the way in time to prevent her from farting directly on him. He truly earned every pound per minute that he charged Lotty.

"Sorry."

"Don't worry, I'm used to it by now. How was your date? I was excited when I got your text. I am always happy to move sessions around your love life because it's such a rarity!"

"He kissed me. He's lovely. He messaged me earlier asking to meet up later, but I have a wine tasting with Bruce and I wanted to give him the low-down on how last night went, without Mason listening."

"Does Mason also like doing exercise?" He pushed gently into the stretch and tried to hold his breath just in case.

"He was playing football near where he used to live, but he hasn't joined a local team since moving here. And he runs like me, but it sounds like he is way faster."

"Ask him to go running tomorrow. Then you will be in your comfort zone and will feel less awkward."

"That is such a good idea! Thank you. I shall text him after I've showered. I'll invite him to run with me on Bruce's estate." Lotty thanked Jamie again, walked off towards the changing rooms, and bumped her head on a shoulder-press machine.

Lotty danced along to the music playing from the gym speakers—"Whoomp (There It Is)".

CHAPTER 59

Lotty needed to keep the momentum of her investigation going. There would be very little additional evidence presenting itself until they had an appropriate suspect to home in on.

She had asked Bruce to invite Greg and Melissa to this evening's wine tasting so that she and Bruce could dig deeper into their backgrounds. Lotty had a funny feeling about them, worse than the funny feeling that she got after eating a whole baguette. Something was off about Greg and Melissa, but she couldn't quite put her finger on why she felt this way …

Lotty was sitting with Bruce in the wine bar near his house. As they waited for Greg and Melissa to arrive, they were drinking champagne.

"So, when are you seeing Mason again?" Bruce helped himself to one of the Kalamata olives from the glass dish in front of him.

"I'm running with him tomorrow. Is it OK if we park at yours and run around the estate?"

"Of course. So, did he kiss you? I don't need all of the gory details while I'm eating. Just a brief overview will suffice."

"That's a bit rich coming from you. I always get the graphic details of your sexual exploits. He kissed me, and he held my hand."

"Lovely, dear. I'm pleased that you will probably get the cobwebs between your legs cleared soon." He looked at his watch impatiently, then at the door of the bar. "Greg and Melissa should be here any minute."

Two clean glasses sat next to the bottle of champagne that Bruce and Lotty had been sharing; their bottle of Bollinger La Grande Annee Brut was chilling in a metal bucket in front of them.

Bruce finished the rest of his glass and sighed contentedly. "Two thousand and twelve, a lovely year." He dragged his bar stool closer to

Lotty and ran his fingers through her hair. "Your hair is looking dry, dear. Why don't you think about having your friend Teresa dye it darker again? Considering that she isn't a hairdresser, she did a cracking good job last time."

"I'll think about it. I guess it does need something doing to it."

Lotty's eyes turned to the door as Greg and Melissa entered the bar holding hands. She waved them over.

The couple unlinked their hands and walked over to sit between Bruce and Lotty, which involved a lot of shuffling of bar stools. Bruce poured them a drink each. "Thank you for coming at such short notice. We fancied a bit of company this evening."

"Thank you for having us. I love wine tastings." Greg smiled as he took his glass from Bruce. "Cheers!"

The entire group raised their glasses and clinked them (everybody feels awkward doing this; you are not alone). Lotty noted that Greg wasn't completely against drinking alcohol after all..

"Greg and I have been unable to sleep since the Evangeline incident. It's all so terrifying. What if she wasn't the intended target and one of us was?" Melissa dramatically flicked her hair extensions in the direction of Lotty, who rescued her glass from their path. Several strands of Melissa's hair made their way into Lotty's mouth.

Lotty chose not to divulge any of the case information that she had, especially pertaining to the idea that Evangeline *must* have been the intended target, considering she was also being poisoned before the party even took place.

Greg helped himself to an olive. "The source we have at the police station would only tell us that Evangeline was poisoned by injection. It seems rather ghoulish. Lotty, would you care to give us any more information to make tomorrow's edition?"

She shook her head. "Absolutely not. I'm afraid that is more than my job is worth."

"Fair enough. No harm in asking. I won't be drinking too much this evening. Since my stint in rehab, I only feel comfortable having the odd sip these days."

"Perfectly understandable, old chap! Even more for us, eh?" joked Bruce.

Lotty stealthily executed her champagne burp technique, belching into her glass, then leaned over Melissa to grab an olive. Melissa followed suit and gasped. "Yuck! What's that funny smell? Those olives must have gone off."

Lotty refused to look directly at Bruce, feeling sure he'd caught her stifling her burps. She didn't want to have his eye-rolling drag down her mood. She was in love.

A rather formidable-looking woman with jet-black hair, and covered head to toe in Gucci, walked into the bar area, clapping her hands loudly. "Ladies and Gentlemen, can I have your attention, please? My name is Cordelie. I will be the sommelier to guide you all through this evening's tasting. The first wine being circulated around on trays will be your first sparkling wine of the evening. It is a Pierre Péters Cuvée de Réserve Blanc de Blancs grand cru champagne."

Several smartly dressed members of staff appeared carrying trays of glasses, each filled with a small amount of the sparkling wine. Lotty grabbed a glass and was about to drink out of it, when Bruce placed his hand over the top of her glass and shook his head. "You're meant to wait," he whispered. "Behave, darling," he implored.

Cordelie shot Lotty a look that could freeze lava, then continued with her narrative. "Blanc de Blancs is the go-to wine for the hardened champagne drinker."

Bruce winked at Lotty. "I know that when I get home, I'll probably be quite har—" Lotty glared at him. *Hypocrite.*

Cordelie carried on, saying, "This superlative interpretation of a sparkling wine is only made from white grapes, especially the Chardonnay grape. A Blanc de Blancs champagne, as opposed to a Blanc de Blancs sparkling wine, indicates that it is produced in the Champagne region of France."

Lotty wondered when they would be allowed to drink anything; she was already bored. *I wonder if Mason would like to come to the next wine tasting?*

"Please take a sip of water, if you have one near you, and especially if you have already drunk alcohol this evening. This will alleviate any dry noses from alcohol and will allow you to enjoy the smell of the wine. If you would now like to take a sip of the wine and feel how it tastes as it touches your tongue, be careful not to swill your glass beforehand as we don't want to disturb the bubbles."

Lotty already felt out of her depth; she had already been swilling her glass and hadn't bothered with the water. She also took more than a sip of the wine.

"Remember, you're driving tonight, Lotty, so no more alcohol for you."

She glared at Bruce and spat her drink into one of the metal spit buckets that had been supplied to each table. She turned to Bruce. "It's OK, I won't swallow." She pulled one of Melissa's hair strands from her mouth and also placed that into the bucket.

"Reminds me of a trip I had to Ibiza last year," joked Bruce. Greg laughed riotously until he was shot a look of reproach from Melissa.

Greg turned to Lotty. "You and me both, Lotty. I am the designated driver tonight as well. Melissa doesn't really like to drive. I haven't even been in her car once!"

"Greg, this wine is lovely. Could we ask at the venue about serving this at the wedding?" Melissa rubbed his hand, clearly now feeling guilty for reprimanding him in company.

"We could. It really is very good. It has a smooth aftertaste at the back of your throat, instead of the normal acidity that often comes with sparkling wine."

Lotty grabbed some more olives and moved closer to Melissa. "So, how are the wedding plans going?"

"Good, thanks. Greg is helping a lot, so it hasn't been too bad. We haven't even been together that long, so it's been quite the whirlwind for me." Lotty felt a sudden pang of jealousy at not being engaged herself, and fought the overwhelming urge she was having to punch Melissa right in her perfect mouth.

Lotty watched Melissa's hand on Greg's and could understand why Greg didn't mind their "no sex before marriage" rule as Melissa had hands like shovels. Lotty was worried Melissa would completely detach his thingy with brute force, given half the chance.

"I felt it was the least I could do to help Melissa. She's had a terrible time. A bride planning a wedding without her mother is very upsetting. She has struggled somewhat."

"Lotty has just lost her father. I'm so sorry to hear about your mother, darling."

Melissa waved her hand. "It's fine. You don't want to hear all about that. It's going to put such a dampener on this evening." It was then that Melissa started to cry. She walked off towards the bathroom. Lotty went to follow. Greg grabbed her arm.

"Lotty, she is so upset. She doesn't like to talk about it much, but that's both her parents she's lost now. Her mother passed away of a terminal illness shortly before I met her. She really clams up. Maybe she'll talk to you." Lotty had a sudden uneasy feeling that something wasn't right, but she shrugged it off.

Lotty ran towards Melissa to try to catch up. She was nearly at her side as Melissa went into the men's toilets by accident.

"Oh, hi, Lotty. I'm so upset. Wrong door." She smiled, but then started to cry again. "I guess I should have brought my reading glasses with me."

"Don't worry, I've done it before. I once caught Bruce peeing, and he was ever so embarrassed. Come on, let's go and get your face cleaned up and forget about our bereavements for a bit. You can enjoy some more fizz."

CHAPTER 60

Lotty and Mason were in Mason's car, on the way to Bruce's estate.

"Arthur texted me to say there were no prints on Evangeline's wine glass, by the way. It's just a shame Bruce wasn't using the metal goblets he has used to serve drinks in the past."

"How tho?" Mason placed his hand upon her knee in a tender manner. Lotty's heart performed a pirouette. She composed herself and responded to his question.

"We can sometimes use the chemical residue from a print to perform an advanced analysis because the residue acts as an electrical insulator. We can therefore pass currents through it to highlight a print. It's called an electrochromic image."

"Fathinating sthtuff! We never found a thyringe to protheth for printsth at the crime thene. The murderer muth have sthmuggled it out of the party in thome manner."

"Did you not search everyone when you took their statements?"

"We did, tho I have absolutely no clue how it wath removed from the marquee area without the officersth finding it. We have even uthed detection dogsth to go back over the area theveral times thinth, uthing the thent of interferon-beta on a pieth of material. None of the searchesth have turned anything up, unfortunately."

They turned onto Bruce's drive and parked up.

Mason was wearing compression leggings as it was a rather cold morning. As he started to stretch next to his car, Lotty was distracted from her own stretching as his leggings left little to the imagination. Trying to make her secret inspection less obvious, she bent over, touching her hands to the floor, and looked back between her legs to steal another glance at his "gentleman's parcel".

Once they were satisfied that they were suitably limbered up, they turned on their respective running watches and started out. It was quite early into their run, but Lotty was already beginning to struggle with the pace somewhat. She felt self-conscious that her breathing was making her sound as if she were in the middle of a dirty phone call.

"Do you think we can slow down a bit?" she panted at him.

"Of courth. It'sth too fatht for me at this pathe anyway. I wath jutht a bit worried that you may be a rather fatht runner. I can thlow down a bit now."

"I was hoping for more of a tempo run today."

Lotty wasn't the fastest of runners unless she was running a timed race; she preferred to slow down and enjoy nature when she was out exercising. She was, however, an experienced road runner and trail runner and had also participated in a phenomenal number of obstacle course races. Her dedication to a race was only challenged if, at any point, she saw a dog; she always had to stop and pat them. She had once bent over suddenly after seeing a cute miniature schnauzer puppy and caused the runner behind her to be launched spectacularly into the air. Latterly, Lotty had stepped back from obstacle racing as she had been put off when she contracted leptospirosis from a river. There was nothing less glamourous than having to throw up into a bowl while also sitting on a toilet. During that sickness, she had been caught short on a car journey and had been forced to throw up into a shopping bag that turned out to be made of hessian fabric. It had led to a rather distressing stain on her previous car's upholstery.

Lotty and Mason made their way through endless fields, navigating the undulating ground under their trail shoes, and eventually came across a stile between two fields.

Mason slowed down to a stop, paused his running watch, and jumped up onto the stile.

"Here, why don't you grab my hand?" He offered it to her chivalrously as she stopped to pause her own running watch.

"No, it's cool. You carry on. I need to tie my lace anyway."

Mason stepped over the stile and started to check their split statistics on his watch. Lotty made her own way over the stile behind him.

It was at that point that Lotty spied Bruce, also walking in the field. He was across the other side walking hand in hand with Grant, accompanied by Tallulah. Lotty, raising her hand to wave across the field, lost her footing and fell dramatically onto the stile, directly onto her pubic bone. She gasped quietly so Mason wouldn't turn back to see what she'd done, then remained gingerly straddling the plank of wood as she tried to recover herself.

"Come on, Lotty darling, it's only your *mini* carry-on!" she heard Bruce roar across the field at her.

Alerted by the noise, Mason looked back to see Lotty struggling across the wood. He ran over to help her. As he ran towards her, Lotty could hear the tune to "Knock on Wood" playing across her thoughts.

CHAPTER 61

Lotty and Mason were in Bruce's kitchen, having been invited there for a post-run snack. Lotty was already regretting her decision to go back there because Grant had already made a joke about Lotty banging her "knick-knack" against the wrong piece of wood that morning.

Grant and Bruce had left Mason and Lotty alone to help themselves to food and drinks, and were discreetly keeping an eye on them both through the glass doors of the conservatory in the next room. Lotty could feel their eyes on her; they were clearly making sure that she didn't make a complete arse-head of herself.

"What would you like to eat?" Lotty asked.

"Nothing too heavy jutht after a run, thanksth. Perhapth a glath of milk?"

"What about a protein shake? I keep some here at Bruce's as I run here a lot. There are tons of flavours. What about pistachio?"

He nodded at her eagerly.

"I did have some wheatgerm shots here somewhere …" Lotty had a made a note never to try the wheatgerm even after she'd gone to the effort of buying it. Bruce had provided her with a rather too detailed account of what he felt wheatgerm tasted like, and it had put her off somewhat.

Lotty leaned her head back out of the cupboard. "Scratch that. It seems that Bruce has already finished the wheatgerm. What about if I put some bee pollen and a pinch of beetroot powder in it?"

"Thoundsth great!"

Mason wandered down the hall that ran parallel to the large ornate conservatory in which Bruce and Grant were sitting. He shouted back down to the kitchen at Lotty, "Thesth paintingsth are amathing; they mutht be worth a thmall fortune! I hope Bruthe hath a good alarm thysthem."

She decided she had best shake the drink by hand so that the sound of the blender wouldn't drown out what Mason was saying. "Of course. It's one of the stipulations on his house insurance that he must maintain a high-end security set-up. He spends thousands of pounds a year on it."

Due to recent events, Lotty had been thinking more about updating her own home alarm; the one she had was rather antiquated, and Arabella probably did a better job at preventing house intruders than the alarm did. Lotty finished adding the various ingredients to the milk and screwed the lid on. She walked up towards Mason, vigorously shaking the lidded cup. Her head turned towards the glass, and she saw Bruce and Grant mimicking her hand movement back at her and guffawing at one another. Lotty clearly hadn't placed the lid on the cup firmly enough. It flew off, covering the startled Mason in the liquid brown mess. This served to send Bruce and Grant over the edge. Bruce slapped Grant on the back. They looked to be in pain with their laughter.

"Sorry!"

"Don't worry." Mason wiped his finger down his face and smelled it. "Mmm." He placed his finger in his mouth and tasted it. "I can definitely tathte thomething fiery. It'sth lovely. Isth it ginger?" He wiped his hands on his trousers.

"It's black ginger powder."

Bruce appeared next to Lotty in the hall. "Whatever is it for, dear?" he asked in an overly exaggerated and sarcastic manner.

She glared at him. "How awfully strange that you're the one who purchased it online and yet you don't know what it's for," she spat back at him.

Mason was now scanning the screen of his mobile phone. "It thays here on Google that it'sth a natural herbal remedy from Thailand and used to maintain an erection."

"Oh, is it?" replied Lotty innocently, in what she hoped was her most sincere tone.

Grant walked out of the conservatory, put his arm around Bruce, and pointed at Mason in a manner that Lotty felt was overly dramatic. "*The Great Masturbator!*"

Mason looked indignant. "I would really rather that you didn't thpeak like that in front of my girlfriend. Furthermore, I can't even remember the latht time..."

Bruce held up his hand, signalling for Mason to calm down. "Firstly, Lotty says worse things than that to her own mother, and secondly, he is referring to the piece of art behind you." He started to gently dab at the large splashes of smoothie that were now covering his favourite piece. "It's called *The Great Masturbator*, and it's a copy of a painting that Dalí did in 1929. He gifted the original after his death, and it's now hanging in a museum in Madrid. Thankfully, it's often hard to tell if you've spilled anything on a Dalí."

"Lotty! Do you have any idea how much that is worth?"

"That one's a piece of crap, anyway."

"Well, thank you *very* much for your valued critique. It's just that despite the fact it's only a lithograph print, it actually cost me several thousand pounds. It's a highly valuable piece of crap."

Lotty wasn't really paying any attention; she was far too excited about the fact that Mason had just referred to her as his girlfriend. She didn't even notice Bruce rubbing the lithograph so hard that it eventually plummeted to the floor, or Tallulah then running over and licking the protein shake off it.

CHAPTER 62

The next morning was drizzly and wet. Lotty was comfortably snuggled under her warm duvet, watching the drops of rain patter against the glass of her bedroom windows. She desperately wanted to go outside for another trail run; this was shorts-wearing weather for any regular runner. She had made other plans, having booked another stationary bike class at her gym. Until recently, she had considered describing her relationship status as "in a long-term relationship with my bike" when asked for it on forms that she was filling in. She had been spending so many hours of the week on a bike that padded shorts were no longer helping, and she had been forced to start rubbing Vaseline into her "foo-foo" before every class in order to stop the burning sensation.

Over the years, Lotty had engaged in other forms of activity that were slightly less energetic. In her late thirties she had enjoyed taking part in adult ballet classes. Even Lotty's mother had been excited about the classes because, for once, Lotty had chosen an activity that was much more civilised. There had even be a dance recital that all her peers took part in to mark the end of their season, but Lotty's mother had embarrassed her somewhat by shouting "I'll never get *that* time back!" when she had exited the auditorium. The hapless Lotty had also tried pole dancing, and had worked her way up to Level 3 status, but she'd been asked not to return after she suffered a leg spasm halfway up a pole and had accidentally kicked her instructor's front teeth out.

Reluctantly, she got up and packed her gym kit into her rucksack, then made her bed. She sauntered off towards the bathroom to get ready and was completely oblivious to the car parked across the street from her house.

Inside the car, someone dastardly sat watching her every move through binoculars while carefully planning her untimely demise.

Lotty turned the shower on to heat up, wound down her bathroom blinds, and experienced an inexplicable feeling of unease. She shuddered.

The car drove slowly down the road. Inside the car, the murderer was listening to "Psycho Killer".

CHAPTER 63

Lotty was changing at her gym. She was also hiding. The UK police commissioner was also a member there, and Lotty had embarrassed herself when their paths last crossed. It was on a day when Lotty was experiencing delayed-onset muscle soreness (DOMS) in her legs, thanks to Jamie having made her repeatedly drag a barrow that he was standing on across either side of the gym floor. As a result of her DOMS, Lotty had had difficulty bending or sitting down that day. She had accidentally dropped her towel on the floor of the changing room and was innocently picking it up, while naked, by leaning back against a locker and slowly sliding her back down it while pulling her legs gently apart. That was when the police commissioner had chosen to walk into the changing rooms and gasp in horror. She'd actively avoided the commissioner ever since.

After ensuring that the coast was now clear, Lotty bounded up the steps, taking them two at a time, towards the treadmill for a gentle walk to warm herself up. A muscle pinged in her groin as she was halfway up the staircase, so she slowed herself down again to a walk. Lotty would often pull a muscle when she wasn't careful. If she pulled a muscle too badly, she would have to go back to see her sports therapist. Last time, one of his other patients had tried walking into the treatment suite during her session and had been shocked to find her having a fist lodged firmly at the tops of her thighs, which then prompted some very inappropriate rumours to circulate around the gym afterwards. As much as Lotty enjoyed treadmill workouts at the gym, she had to exercise extreme caution when engaged in this particular activity; she had once lost her footing during an interval session because she'd been too engrossed in singing loudly to the Macarena and had been catapulted off the end of the machine and into the police commissioner. The commissioner's security detail had been much more forgiving of Lotty than the treadmill itself. Lotty had spent the following three days walking round with carpet burns on her anus.

As Lotty alighted the treadmill, she turned on the integrated television screen. It defaulted again to the adult channel. It wasn't the first time that this had happened, and it left Lotty wondering who these people were who felt it was appropriate to watch such a thing while running and in public. It also gave a whole new meaning to the term *bashing a run-out*. Lotty unlocked her mobile phone, scrolled to her favourite walking playlist, and immediately launched into a resounding rendition of "Smack My Bitch Up" by the Prodigy, until she noticed a more mature gentleman on the next machine looking very concerned. She changed the television channel to something less pornographic and then used the buttons on the console in front of her to increase the gradient to make it moderately challenging. She proceeded to set about her walk for a few minutes, ensuring that her arms were swinging strongly by her sides to get her heart pounding.

She felt a strange sensation, and the hairs on the back of her neck stood up. She shrugged the feeling off and put it down to the sudden rush of adrenalin coursing through her veins.

She didn't notice the murderer brazenly watching her from the cafeteria area and plotting how to attack her next.

CHAPTER 64

Having taken the time to limber up enough, Lotty grabbed her water bottle from next to her treadmill and made her way to the bike studio. She walked over to the bike area and slipped into her cleat shoes. She placed her signature against her name on the participation sheet that was placed on the wall, worried that the man standing next to her looked quite disgusted as he came closer to her armpit to sign his own name. She made a note to remember her deodorant next time. Having abandoned the chest-mounted heart rate monitor after her boob-flashing incident, she now owned a watch that measured her beats per minute using a built-in green light. She had been forced to disable the built-in function that informed her favourite contacts with an alert text if she had fallen over, because she fell over a lot. Lotty had once made a hospital packed with waiting people laugh their heads off when she was forced to admit to the check-in staff that she had broken her ankle playing badminton because she had fallen off a stool that she had been standing on after being hit in the face by a stray shuttlecock. She had returned to the same hospital less than a month later with suspected deep-vein thrombosis after her left leg had swelled up on an aeroplane journey from a holiday in the Philippines. Having been caught short without toilet paper at the airport, Lotty had used one of her compression socks to wipe her "lady garden" and had forgotten to remove the other sock. Bruce had once proclaimed that Lotty should either be escorted daily by a health and safety officer or simply dress herself from head to toe in bubble wrap.

The energetic class instructor had just turned up and was high-fiving everyone as he walked across the studio and towards his own bike at the back of the class. Lotty was prepared this time and avoided a smack in the face as she returned the gesture to him without incident. After passing Lotty, the instructor turned back around and shouted at the class, "Have you brought your A game, people? Are you ready to go?"

Everybody made a whooping noise and started to clap. Lotty appreciated that some people may enjoy this jolly American style of class, but she preferred a British one, where everyone would turn up and queue quietly and then tut a lot for no reason. It should be ended with a gentle clap at the end, which incidentally was how Bruce described his last trip to Greece. While some folks occasionally consummated a holiday romance on the beach, Bruce had once been informed by the surgeon performing his colonoscopy that an alarming amount of sand had been found quite far up Bruce's back passage.

The instructor started to navigate the room again for another round of motivating high fives and backslaps with the other participants, as Lotty wrestled with her warm-up jacket, trying to remove it over her head.

"Have you brought your A game, Lotty?" He patted her on the back. The impact helped her to release the final section of the jacket that had been stuck halfway over her head. It also served to dislodge a pair of her oldest and most threadbare pair of knickers that had clearly gotten stuck to the jacket while in the tumble dryer.

"Yes, and I've brought my pants as well, apparently." Correctly assuming that the rest of the class wouldn't want to look at them for the duration, Lotty picked her pants up and tried to cram them into the small coin purse that she carried around the gym with her. They didn't seem to fit at first, but it's amazing what one can do when backed into a corner. She got onto the bike and clipped her cleat shoes into her pedals, forgetting all about her pants. She would be reminded about them later when she managed to launch them into a three-egg omelette that she was paying for after class in the cafeteria.

CHAPTER 65

Lotty was perched on a chair in the kitchen at Teresa's house. Teresa lived on her own about fifteen minutes from Lotty's house. Teresa had tried having lodgers in over the years to help pay her bills, but her general demeanour scared them off within weeks. Her last, and final, lodger had handed in his notice because there was a strong draft in the attic which buffeted the sex swing that lived up there back and forth. The noise kept waking them up, and their error in judgement from going up to the attic to see what had been causing the noise meant that they would now never be able to go to a playground ever again without breaking out into a cold sweat.

Teresa and Lotty were chatting and eating chocolate-covered digestive biscuits. Lotty was thoroughly enjoying them and ignoring the fact that the wheat they contained would be coming back later to haunt her. If Lotty had been eating those biscuits when she was attacked in her home the other day, she would have needed only to lift the duvet, and the assailant would have been knocked completely unconscious by the acrid odour. She was praying that Mason didn't have a particularly keen sense of smell.

Teresa had just dyed Lotty's hair bright red, and Lotty vowed to ensure that they got any chemicals out of her hair before her farts set in, for fear of setting Teresa's house alight.

"Should we not have done the colour after the perm, Teresa?"

Teresa dipped her biscuit in her cup and tried giving Lotty her most reassuring look, but Teresa had only just realised the mistake, now that Lotty had pointed it out.

"It's fine. It doesn't matter what order we do it in; it's going to look amazing."

"Why are we perming it, again?"

"It said in one of the magazines I was reading at the nail parlour that curly hair is back in."

Teresa was now only allowed manicures when she went to have her nails done as the proprietor had been forced to ban her from having pedicures after she'd gone there without wearing any underwear on purpose. The attractive man from whom she liked to have foot massages had been forced to complain to his manager and had used the phrase "it was like looking into an abyss". He was eternally grateful that he was slightly short-sighted.

"How much longer until we need to wash it off?"

Teresa looked at her watch. "Just a few more minutes. By the way, I was chatting to some folks down at the lab, and they have performed their second confirmatory tests on the interferon-beta that they found in the glass at the crime scene."

"Using liquid chromatography–tandem mass spectrometry?"

"Yes. It just means the lab is now ahead of the game for when the case goes to court for the various legal teams to review the evidence that we submit."

"We just need to pinpoint the murderer now. Bruce and I have been working down the list of suspects, and we've knocked quote a few names off."

"Who do you want to finger for it?" Teresa winked. Lotty could see why Arthur was always loath to allow Teresa into a courtroom environment as an expert witness. It would be hard for the lab to maintain their professional reputation if Teresa were unleashed on a judge or a panel of jurors. She had been allowed in once but had embarrassed Arthur after giving far too detailed an account of what a suspect had been looking at on the internet. The judge presiding over the case had been forced to stop Teresa midflow as she was explaining the particular content that could be found on a website called FetishFisting.com. One of the jurors in the case had sworn never to do her washing up wearing rubber gloves ever again.

Teresa also had a pet cat, a Bengal called Monty, who was so large that he had his own gravitational pull. Teresa and Lotty had spent numerous hours in the past conducting video calls on their mobile phones with their respective cats on the screen "chatting" to each other. It was for that very reason that Teresa had suggested they try speed dating. She was worried that they were both one bottle of lavender perfume away from achieving "mad cat lady" status. Monty had just sauntered into the kitchen and finished what was in his food bowl, and was now sitting in front of Lotty, staring intently at her. She started to feel rather awkward.

"What does he want?"

"He just wants a bit of fuss, I expect. He likes to play hard to get though."

"Well, I don't know about hard to get, but he certainly looks hard to pick up. I thought he was going to be put on a diet by the vet?"

"He's just very fluffy, that's all."

"Even shaved, he would have probably fed you during the entire pandemic, and that ended up lasting more than a year."

Monty continued to stare at Lotty. Teresa handed Lotty a small tub of cat treats.

"Here, shake his treats at him and he will jump up on you."

"Is that wise? I don't want both my legs broken."

Lotty shook the biscuits. Monty didn't budge. Teresa stood up, took the tub from Lotty's hands, and placed it onto Lotty's lap.

"Go on, Monty. Jump."

Monty leaped into their air. Lotty grunted when his eleven-and-a-half-kilogram body crashed onto her lap, knocking the cat treats all over the floor.

"Maybe instead of registering him at the feline weight clinic, you could just have him reclassified as a seal?"

"Don't listen to her, Monty." Monty, having removed himself from Lotty's lap, had followed the treats on the floor and was now hoovering them up.

"Right, let's go. Time to wash you off!"

Lotty followed Teresa over to the sink and let her shampoo the colourant out. Teresa gave Lotty's hair two thorough washes, conditioned it, and patted it with a towel. She sat Lotty down and started to pull a brush through the strands. "It's a beautiful colour. It's a crying shame that red doesn't last too long as it's a man-made colour. We will just need you to top it up regularly at home." She handed Lotty a mirror.

"Do you not think I look a bit like a traffic cone?"

"Absolutely not. I think you look divine."

"What if Mason prefers blondes?"

Teresa tutted at Lotty and rolled her eyes. "Mason can sod off. We dye our hair for how *we* want to look, not for how others want us to look, dear."

Lotty surveyed herself in the mirror again. She felt worried she looked a bit like a James Bond villain.

Teresa had already started to prepare the perming treatment. She was pulling open various bottles and mixing powders into them. She went quiet while she read the instructions, furrowing her brow.

"Is there something wrong?" Lotty felt concerned now.

"Not really, but it does say we should maybe have waited to colour your hair after we curled it. You were right."

"Should we leave it then?"

"No, chill out. It's just one of those overly cautious warnings that companies have to put onto products to cover their backs."

Teresa was already working on Lotty's hair again, so Lotty now had little choice in the matter. Lotty closed her eyes, crossed her fingers, and hoped for the best, while Teresa proceeded to drag a brush through the mop of bright red hair on Lotty's head.

CHAPTER 66

Lotty had endured over an hour of Teresa pulling violently at chunks of her hair, which were then curled tightly around plastic curlers and coated in a disgusting-smelling perming lotion. The smell was so bad that it had caused Lotty's mascara and eyeliner to run; she now looked like Alice Cooper. The two women had been playing Monopoly for the last hour while waiting for Lotty's curls to set.

"Right, come on, you're back up." Teresa gestured towards the sink.

Lotty carefully stood up so as not to knock over the board game pieces and went over to the sink. Lotty hadn't been too invested in winning the game after noticing that Teresa had been cheating. Having noticed Teresa steal money from the bank repeatedly throughout the game, Lotty was avoiding touching any of the notes that Teresa had been handing over, as Lotty had seen where Teresa had hidden them. She felt the best approach would be to burn the game when she got it home. She had been forced to bring her version of the game over after Teresa had warned her that *her* Monopoly board had been subjected to a certain incident during a game of Strip Monopoly. Lotty made Teresa promise never to bring it out to play with at family gatherings, as it was very hard to disguise the smell of what had been "spilled" onto it.

There was a lot of splashing and tutting as Teresa proceeded to rinse the perm off. She had become alarmingly quiet. Lotty started to worry.

"Have you ever considered dying your hair pink, Lotty?"

"No. Why ever do you ask?"

Teresa sighed and handed Lotty a mirror. "Because I have accidentally dyed your hair pink."

Lotty stared into the mirror with her mouth open in disbelief. She had ridiculously tight curls that made her look a bit like Kevin Keegan. Additionally, her hair was so bright pink in colour that she looked like a stick of cotton candy.

"The perming lotion must have stripped the chemicals in the red hair dye out of your hair. Sorry."

"Can you fix it?"

"I think so. I once fixed my own hair nicely enough after dying it green accidentally."

"I've got to be honest, I feel like you could have told me that story before you let me do something so dramatic to my own hair." She sighed despondently, looked into the mirror again, and picked at her curls gingerly. "It feels so weak and brittle."

"It's just the mix of chemicals. We can put an intensive conditioner on to fix that. That's the easy bit. Just wait there while I go upstairs and find a spare bottle of brown hair dye that I know I have in my bathroom."

Lotty decided that she would take Teresa's advice and wait there. She certainly wouldn't be leaving Teresa's house as she currently looked like a reject from a computer game commercial.

It was a further hour of sitting with various lotions and potions on her hair until Lotty was allowed to see Teresa's handiwork. One hair mask, one brown hair dye, and some cutting later, Lotty looked presentable again. Teresa had been forced to cut quite a substantial amount of Lotty's hair off to repair the damage, but it now looked quite good. Teresa was forgiven.

They had just finished clearing up all of the debris from Teresa's impromptu hair parlour when Arthur called Teresa on FaceTime. Teresa picked up her mobile phone and accepted his call.

"Hello, both! I thought I would call you as I knew you were going to be together and I wanted to give you a quick update on the DuVoir case. Lotty, are you still enjoying your time off?"

"Yes, thanks. Do you like my new colour?"

"Did you lose a bet?"

"Oh, ha ha."

"I thought Teresa told me earlier that you were dying it red."

"There was a slight mishap with the colour. How are you anyway?"

"I'm fabulous, love! I've just finished chatting to some people in the laboratory, actually. It appears that the police officers who went to

Evangeline DuVoir's workspace at the *UK Chronicle* have come across a water bottle in her desk that contains chemicals."

"Interferon-beta?" asked Teresa, as she continued to style Lotty's hair. Lotty was yet to complain that her fringe looked as if it had been cut using a bowl for the outline.

"Analysis down at the lab indicates that interferon-beta was indeed present in the water that was in the bottle. Sadly, there weren't any fingerprints on the bottle other than those of Evangeline."

Lotty brushed Teresa's hand off. She was sick of having her hair pulled about and wanted a break from it. "So, we know at least how the initial poisoning was done then."

"Yes indeed. There was also evidence of a high concentration of antiandrogens present in the water bottle."

Lotty looked confused. "But isn't that used to treat things like prostate cancer and acne?"

Arthur nodded his head. "It's used to treat much more than that, dear; it's used in transgender therapy and can also be used to treat hair loss. There are several medical uses for it. I just can't think why it was also in her water bottle. It's a complete head-scratcher."

Lotty felt Arthur would be scratching his head even more if he'd just had it permed and coloured by Teresa. "Well, it seems to me that whoever was trying to poison Evangeline was trying to overload her weak kidneys as much as possible, but it does seem an eclectic mix of medications to have in one's house. Maybe the murderer just randomly ordered a load of strong chemicals on the Dark Web, knowing that whatever it was, it would eventually kill her."

Arthur looked puzzled. "Wouldn't they have ordered something more mainstream though? These medications are quite obscure. Unless they had some form of medical training, or had recently been around a lot of medication for some other reason."

Lotty clapped her hands together. "Alexander Rowley had been helping his mum a lot, and he is visiting her friend who is currently in a palliative care home. I'm just perplexed because he seems so upset about his mum's death."

Teresa grabbed her own breasts in a comedic manner. "That could just be a front. … Honk!"

Lotty nodded in agreement. A significant clump of her hair fell onto her lap. She picked it up. "Is my hair shedding from all the chemicals, Teresa?"

"No. Please stop panicking. That is just the hair I was cutting to fix the mess. I was trying to brush the loose hair out, but you kept tapping my hand away. Don't you think it looks nice?"

"It is nice. It's just, there is now a lot less of it."

Arthur paused for a moment to give them enough time to finish bickering. "The fingerprints on the desk aren't remarkable either. We found prints from Evangeline herself, as well as from Greg."

"Why would his prints be on there?" Lotty asked as she picked hairs off her jumper. She wasn't sure if they were hers or Monty's.

"Because Greg was there talking to her a lot as her boss. It makes sense for anyone's prints from the *Chronicle* to be there really. We found Greg's, and we also found Sir Ralph's and Alexander's. Both Sir Ralph and Alexander would visit Evangeline at work. Sir Ralph liked to pop in to see her to discuss business operations, considering she had that stake in his business. Alexander was renowned for surprising her at work with flowers or chocolates. The desks are cleaned every couple of weeks with a complete wipe-down, apparently. The final list of prints found were Greg's, Sir Ralph's, and Alexander's."

"Only every two weeks? That's a bit gross," exclaimed Lotty. She was grateful that the cleaners at her work had a much more regular cleaning schedule for desks. The last glycolic acid peel that she had done on her face had caused her to shed large chunks of skin onto her desk every time she scratched her face. She was unaware that the cleaners ran a monthly game of short straws to decide who would have the unlucky task of cleaning her desk.

Arthur wished them both a good evening and rang off.

Lotty took her mobile phone, held her arm up, pouted, then took a photo of herself to send to Mason for his verdict. She hit send, packed up her things, kissed her friend on the forehead, and thanked her for her help that evening. As Lotty sat down onto her car seat, her phone pinged, and she checked the message. It was Mason telling her that her eyebrow wax looked lovely. Mason had suffered the same panic experienced by most men when questioned if their partner looks nice; he had reacted as most men would by simply randomly picking something he knew *could be* embellished at a salon, without having any clue what had actually been improved. Lotty screwed up her face at his response and worried that she should go home and pluck her eyebrows; they were getting rather unruly, and perhaps he was hinting …

CHAPTER 67

The following day passed rather uneventfully. Lotty had taken herself to the cinema to watch two films back to back. Her father had often recommended that she try going on her own, having done it on numerous occasions himself, but she had never fancied it. Her overriding concern was that everyone would be looking at her, judging her for not having a date to bring. Most people did in fact look at her, but that was because she often had a piece of toilet paper stuck to the bottom of her shoe as she walked through the refreshments section. After her father's death, she had plucked up the courage to finally go to the cinema alone, and never looked back. Her favourite part was not having to share her cinema snacks with anyone. Her adoration of food and her inability to share it with anyone was legendary. She had once missed a stripper performing at her friend's hen party because as all eyes turned on him as he descended a staircase into the venue, Lotty had her back to the entire proceedings because the buffet had just been brought out. She had regretted nothing, despite hearing a story about how his manhood would have made quite the slapping sound if it had inadvertently hit someone in the face during the performance.

Lotty had recently started to enjoy travelling to one cinema that had a screen room where the seats moved, and sprayed water and smells, to provide a wholly interactive cinematic experience. Today she had made the unwise decision to pick snacks that were inappropriate for the experience. She had subsequently left the auditorium covered in nacho cheese and milkshake, which had left her with the strong smell of cheese on her clothing as she exited the cinema and rushed across the car park to avoid being chased by any stray dogs who might be attracted to the smell. Lotty was well versed in having to disguise her clothing after spilling food down it at the cinema since she had discovered the new cinematic seats, and her stubbornness about such incidents was the reason she had once remained sitting firmly in her seat during the last *Star Wars* film, despite having spilled a litre of sparkling water into her lap right as the film was starting.

Lotty had treated herself to a meal for one at her favourite Japanese restaurant and then returned home. She now found herself deeply engrossed in an eyebrow tidy-up. She was concentrating intently as she stared into her well-lit vanity mirror, carefully plucking away at the tiny hairs. Earlier that day, she had nearly bought herself a special tool to remove hairs, having seen that it was a mini blade that could be used to exfoliate, as well as remove hairs easily. Lotty knew her limitations; she was wholeheartedly convinced that she shouldn't be left alone to drag a mini blade across her own face. She was very careful with home beauty treatments after an unfortunate incident where she inflicted a rather serious vaginal burn upon herself during a random bikini wax. She was mortified explaining the injury to her doctor. The embarrassment had dragged on for several days afterwards because she had been prescribed several litres of saline water to spray on to her "minky" to alleviate the burning sensation caused by the urine as it passed across the burn area when she peed.

Lotty stood back and assessed her handiwork, concerned about a rather large gap in the hairs that she had left herself with because she had coughed and lost control of her hand. She looked closely into the mirror and tried to brush the remaining eyebrow hairs over to hide the gap, but nothing was working. She gave up, put her tweezers away, and decided to go for a night run.

Lotty went upstairs and got changed. After falling over when putting her sports socks on, resulting in her banging her head on a chest of drawers, she felt ready to go. For her solo night runs, Lotty exercised appropriate road safety and would only wear her headphones over one ear, pulling the other side to the back of her head. She also wore a high-visibility tabard even though she had once been mistaken for a police support volunteer by an old woman who was keen for Lotty to get her cat down from a nearby tree. By tomorrow morning, she would be lamenting not having extended her personal safety routine to making her running app posts private.

Lotty bent down, farted gently, and tied her shoelaces. She had recently taken to wearing running trainers that were half a size bigger than her feet actually were; this had been advised by Jamie, who had explained that when her feet swelled slightly from the heat of the running, her toes would have ample room so as not to suffer any further nasty injuries. Lotty had fainted at work a few months prior due to blood poisoning from a septic toenail. She had been rushed into hospital, where a doctor was forced to lance the giant blister that had formed under the damaged toenail. Lotty was sent home with a significant gap under the toenail, which meant that each time she placed her foot onto the floor to walk, she made a whistling noise. She had become used to having disgusting feet and had once heard herself referred to as "the Hobbit" when she was visiting her regular nail parlour. Having noticed it was now raining outside, she bounded up her staircase and grabbed her faithful Batman beanie hat.

CHAPTER 68

Lotty was eight miles into her run and had settled into a comfortable pace. Today she was concentrating on training to pee while running. Jamie had added this rather peculiar training requirement to her schedule because she was about to take part in a marathon. Lotty's damaged hips usually began to grumble after seventeen miles into any training run, and as a result, she would be unable to stop and urinate. Despite the darkness, she had spent quite a lot of time building up the courage to do her first pee. She had ducked into a bush that was alongside a main road, to take some of the awkwardness out of it, and had emerged feeling much braver, albeit with steam now coming off her legs. As she ventured off the main drag and down a road that led back to her village through the woods, she heard footsteps behind her. Whoever it was, they were running at quite a pace. She crossed over the road to see what would happen, and she heard the footsteps immediately follow her.

Lotty felt alarmed. She decided to fully deduce if she was being followed by crossing back over the road. Her heart sank as the footsteps, once again, followed her trajectory. Lotty afforded herself very little self-praise, but the one thing she was really good at was self-defence. As her adrenaline raced, she focused her thoughts and got ready to fuck shit up. Lotty had made many male and female sparring partners, including many much bigger than she, cry. When she had trained for one of her competitive bouts at a training camp in Thailand, someone had tried mugging her while she was a passenger on the back of a moped. She had broken the mugger's nose with a backfist and then clung to her handbag so tightly that she'd suffered a separated shoulder. When later she explained the incident to her mother, Lotty had confidently reassured her that Lotty's sole priority was guarding her passport within the handbag. The actual reason Lotty had stubbornly refused to let go of the bag was that it was her first ever Paul Frank purchase.

Lotty inhaled deeply to prepare herself, then swung herself around to throw her headphones with all her might at the person behind her. They missed their target but did act as a diversionary tactic. They had been launched at quite an alarming speed and contained so much perspiration that the smell was rather overwhelming for her assailant as the headphones whizzed past the individual's face. Lotty sprinted as fast as she could. Every training session that she had ever done with Jamie had prepared her for this very moment; she was now running for her life.

Lotty drove her arms forward and concentrated on her gait; she had no time to fall over today. She mentally counted each time her knees drove upward. She maintained her breathing as Jamie had shown her for interval training. She held her watch up to her mouth and shouted at it to enable the voice function.

"Dial 999!" she shouted into the watch.

Lotty heard ringing at the other end of the line. "Nine-nine-nine. What service do you require?"

"Help! Police!" she gasped, struggling to talk and sprint at the same time.

The silence as she was transferred seemed to last forever, despite its only being a matter of seconds.

"Police. What is your emergency?"

"I am halfway down Elvendon Road, running from Woodcote to Goring. Someone is following me. I need help. Please send a patrol car and stay on the line with me."

"I've dispatched a local car. Someone is on their way to you. I can hear that you're running. I am going to stay on here with you. Run like you've never run before. Just keep going. You can do this. What's your name?"

"It's Lotty. I'm a bit too out of breath to talk back to you."

Lotty took another deep inhalation to stabilise her output, focusing all her brain cells on making every footfall more precise than she had ever done in a race. This evening wasn't about a personal best; it was about crossing her imaginary finishing line alive. Lotty just tried to remember everything that Jamie had drilled into her about running efficiently. She continued to surge forward, every arm movement in perfect alignment, no energy being wasted. Actively casting her mind back to everything that he had taught her about the importance of breathing, she started to draw strong and measured breaths. She would remember to thank him when she got out of this alive.

"It's OK, Lotty. Stay silent and I can talk to you. Just keep running. A squad car is quite close to you. They have abandoned a burglary they were attending. They will be with you soon."

Lotty, able to hear the person behind gaining on her, felt the sudden urge to cry, but she stopped herself. She had been taught to use every single item on her person as a weapon, and she wasn't about to give up. If she went down, she would do so fighting with every last ounce of energy that she had left within her. She wore a running pouch around her waist for easy access to the sweets and energy gels she carried to maintain her blood sugar. She suddenly remembered that her house keys were also in the pouch. Lotty was rather lackadaisical when it came to throwing redundant keys away, and the set of keys on her person was weighty from all the luggage keys that she'd never disposed of. Her hand shot down to the set of keys. She whirled around and hurled them as aggressively as she could, having taken the time to aim as accurately as she could at her pursuer. They hit the person full force in the face. Lotty couldn't actually see the person's face because he or she was wearing a balaclava. Lotty's Batman hat flew off. She was forced to leave it on the ground. Because of this, she was *gutted*.

Lotty, feeling herself gain a second wind, sped up. She grabbed at her personal alarm that was in her pouch and enabled it, holding it aloft to try to get the disarming sound away from her ears. Almost able to hear the blood thumping in her veins, she was beginning to get a headache. Her heavy breaths were now being masked by the high-pitched squeal of the alarm as she continued her descent into her village. Between the intense waves of noise coming from the alarm, she suddenly noticed the lack of footfalls behind her and realised that whoever had been chasing her had now stopped. She slowed down to a trot and started to scan the houses that she could see lining both sides of the street now that she had emerged from the woods. Seeing a house with several lights on, she ran to the front door and pounded on it. "Help me, please. I'm being chased."

"Lotty, I can hear you are at a residence now. When they open the door and I know you are safe, I'll terminate the call," the dispatcher said over the phone.

"Thank you."

Lotty heard sirens in the distance. As the front door of the house opened, Lotty was overcome by a sudden rush of nausea. She promptly vomited on the lovely woman who had just opened the door to her, and all over her doormat. Lotty fainted into the pile of sick as the lyrics to "Running with the Night" flowed along her synapses.

CHAPTER 69

Lotty's rescuer had apparently heard the sirens in the distance and put two and two together. Waiting outside for the car to pass by, they had frantically waved their arms to flag down the police officers inside it.

Lotty was only aware of this as she was being told what had happened by one of the attending officers.

The door to the room that she was sitting in at the police station opened. Mason ran in, throwing his arms protectively around her. She hugged him back, relishing the smell of his aftershave, to which she was becoming very accustomed. If you were to ask Lotty, she'd tell you that it was one of the nicest smells on earth.

"Well, at leatht the guyth recovered your Batman hat from the road that you were running down."

She smiled and took the hat from him. "Sorry about smelling of sick."

"I hadn't even notithted." (He definitely had.)

She looked down at the hat; having it returned to her had cheered her up somewhat. Lotty had kept the hat as a memento from one of the Comic-Cons she had attended. She had queued to meet Val Kilmer and have a photo taken with him. She had spent many hours at Comic-Cons over the past decade and enjoyed having photos taken with her arm draped around a harem of her favourite actors, mainly male ones. Lotty wasn't being sexist, but it served as a cheap alternative to hiring male escorts. And there were also stalls selling cakes there; the only thing that could have made a Comic-Con better was if you could pay to have some of the guests lick the cake off you. Lotty had tried suggesting it, but the idea was yet to take off.

"What happened to your eyebrowth? There isth a big gap in one of them."

"It must have happened during the attack," said Lotty as she put her hat back on to cover her misshapen brow.

"My friend who returned that hat thaid it would need a cleaning ath it had landed in a pile of horth manure."

"Well, that explains the smell then, doesn't it! Thanks for telling me after I put it on my head anyway."

"I want you to thtay at mine tonight. I am fearful of you going back to your houthe at the moment."

"I can't do that. I've got Arabella to think of. Who would feed her if I wasn't there?"

"Can't Bruthe do that?"

"No, it's not fair on her to leave her being cared for by a stranger. She's very highly strung."

Mason was very aware of how highly strung Arabella was. The last time he had tried to pet her while she was sitting on his lap, she had dug her claws into his testicles without any warning.

"Will you at leatht let me thtay at yourth then? I'll be a gentleman and thleep on the thofa."

"Deal!"

Lotty took Mason's hand, and they walked to his patrol car. For someone who had just been attacked, Lotty felt weirdly content.

CHAPTER 70

Lotty had awakened early the next morning. She was preparing to attend a zombie run with Teresa. Mason had awakened with Arabella sitting on his head, with her least favourable end covering his mouth. He was firmly regretting not having his spare toothbrush with him. Noticing how firmly engrossed Lotty was in packing her sports kit, Mason decided it was an appropriate time to leave for work. He planted a gentle kiss on her face to avoid transfer of too much of anything that Arabella had left on his lips, and wished her a good day.

As Mason was pulling out of her drive, Lotty paused to wave him off. She noticed Teresa pull in. Noticing that she hadn't quite gotten her shit together, she then proceeded to speed around her house like a lunatic, grabbing various items for the run as she did so. As Lotty was finishing up, Teresa let herself in.

"Morning! I got your text. Do you really think this is a good idea after what happened to you last night?"

"I want to take my mind off it."

"By being chased by people dressed as zombies?"

"It will be fun. Come on!" Lotty grabbed her sports bag and followed Teresa out, taking the time to check twice that her front door was firmly secured.

Teresa turned to Lotty on the way to the car. "I've never done a zombie run. What actually happens?"

"All the participants are given a neon waistband to wear, and attached to that are three pieces of ribbon."

"Sounds a bit like morris dancing so far."

Lotty was now fairly sure that Teresa had never actually seen anyone morris dancing, as that wasn't what it was like at all. She continued: "There are volunteers at the race who have all been made to look like zombies. They have different themes to each area, so one particular patch of zombies may all be dressed as a wedding party, or perhaps an army patrol."

"This sounds bloody amazing so far. Pass us your bag. I'll throw it into the car boot."

Lotty passed her bag over to Teresa and carried on, saying, "Zombies have to grab at your ribbons as you run past them. If you lose all your ribbons, while you are allowed to carry on and complete the race, the medal that you achieve at the end will denote that you have not survived the zombie apocalypse. If you pass the finishing line with at least one of your ribbons remaining attached to your belt, then your medal will denote that you are a survivor."

"Seems easy enough to understand." Teresa started the car.

"It may be easy to understand, but it's pretty hard to finish the race with all your bands."

"Challenge accepted!"

CHAPTER 71

Teresa and Lotty were panting heavily and being chased by a zombie dressed as a restaurant maître d'. Lotty was suitably impressed by the speed he was managing to maintain, despite the drag from his jacket tails in the wind.

Teresa pointed at a gap in the bushes. "Quick, sharp left!"

Both women sped as fast as their legs would carry them towards the gap, and then they ducked down, attempting to remain still and motionless.

"I bloody well hope that you've not eaten bread for breakfast," Teresa whispered.

They watched the zombie search unsuccessfully for them, then lose interest and run off after another pack of runners. Seeing their chance to escape, they got back on the move, starting to run at a comfortable jog.

"So, Mason stayed last night, did he?"

"Yes, but nothing happened. He's very chivalrous."

"He does sound lovely. I'm really pleased for you. When are you seeing him again?"

"I don't know. I expect he'll call me later to check how I am anyway, so we can discuss it then."

Lotty was desperately hoping that they wouldn't come across any more zombies; they were nearly at the end of the race, and her throat was sore. Teresa had been successfully taking advantage of Lotty's fear from the events of last night and using her as a human hand grenade. She had spent the entire race shoving Lotty into the path of various zombies. They had been terrified because Lotty's fear had manifested itself in the form of screaming like a banshee each time any zombies tried to approach her.

Teresa's methodology had been working quite well so far, but she had been forced to apologise to a zombie bride after Lotty had gotten far too excited and punched her spectacularly in her tit. It was a bit surreal to see a zombie crying and clutching her at her boob. There was no end to the embarrassment that Teresa felt as a result of Lotty's clumsy nature; she once had had to explain to an attending paramedic how Lotty had drunk so much champagne on her thirtieth birthday that she had suffered an unfortunate leap-frog incident and had concussed herself by ending up jammed between a skirting board and a professional ice hockey player. Teresa wouldn't change anything about her friend though; she embraced her flaws because they accompanied great kindness and loyalty.

While they both eventually managed to cross the finishing line with one ribbon each intact, Teresa had suffered a punch in the ear during the final sprint through a dark warehouse and was confident it was Lotty who had punched her. She didn't care. She turned to her friend and held her tight, reminding herself that one can't put a price on friendship.

CHAPTER 72

Lotty had awakened invigorated from her fun day with the zombies yesterday. She had called Mason the minute she had gotten home.

"Tho how many people did you manage to injure, my thweet?"

"Just enough, and not too many." She laughed down the phone.

"Will I thee you thoon? I mith you."

"That's nice. I miss you too. Why don't you come over tonight?"

"OK, I have to go ath people here at the offith are waiting to talk to me. Are you really thure you were OK latht night?"

"Teresa stayed the night. I was fine, but I am touched by your concern."

"You can be touched by thomething elth later if you fanthy?"

"I feel sad that Teresa isn't here to give that one of her famous comedy honks."

Lotty laughed and heard Mason walking down a corridor as he ended the call. She was firmly in her happy place; several near-death experiences weren't about to shake her mood.

She started to make herself some breakfast, having recently discovered that the world would become a better place if you simply stirred peanut butter into everything. She also firmly held the belief that a meal was perfect as long as there was a significant enough volume of it. She regularly purchased meals for two, feeling confident that it wouldn't even touch the sides when she ate the whole thing herself. She had once made herself very unpopular at a Michelin-star restaurant by ordering herself two of each course on the tasting menu. She probably wouldn't have annoyed the staff so much, but she had also managed to accidentally set her menu on fire with the candle on the table, which had then set their fire alarm off.

As she was finishing her peanut-butter-laden porridge, she heard Bruce let himself in the house.

"Are you decent, dear?" he shouted from the hallway. He entered the kitchen as Lotty was loading her bowl into the dishwasher.

"What do you think I could possibly be doing that would involve me not being decent at this time of the morning?"

"There! That's your problem, darling. You shouldn't be constrained by what time of the day it is acceptable to be doing things."

Bruce's notion of a new relationship involved "doing things" that would often find one having to book an appointment at a chiropractor afterwards.

"I have just been having some food, nothing exciting. Let's sit down and have a catch-up on the DuVoir case."

"How are you feeling after the other night? Still a bit nervous?"

"Honestly, I am fine. I wish people would stop asking. You're almost making me feel worse. I do appreciate your concern though. Anyway, this morning I was scanning through the crime scene notes from the party and I noticed something rather peculiar."

"Go on," Bruce said as he helped himself to a glass of milk. Arabella looked at him with daggers; that was *her* milk. She left the kitchen in search of his shoes; she would go and vomit in one of them to teach him a lesson.

Lotty picked up a pile of papers from the worktop she was standing at. "It says here that they never recovered Evangeline's mobile phone."

Bruce took a sip of his milk and paused thoughtfully. "Maybe she hadn't taken it with her to the party. It's not that remarkable. I sometimes leave mine at home if I want some proper downtime."

"But I saw her holding it that evening. She was dictating into it. Either that or she was on loudspeaker, and the latter is highly doubtful considering the music was so loud. She definitely didn't have headphones in. She can't have been on a call."

"Either way, you're saying that someone also took her mobile phone?"

"Correct. And we need to think about how they did it and, more importantly, why."

"They just would have smuggled it out in a bag or a pocket, no?"

"No. Mason confirmed that the people were searched; it is also documented here in the notes. The police searched every bag, pocket, and coat as people gave their statements. That's why it took so long for people to be able to leave."

"I don't see how the mobile phone could have been removed then."

"They removed it in some manner, and they also took the syringe that was used to poison her apparently. They've still not recovered that. So, did you get my text about Emmanuel?"

"That explains why the police have been walking up and down my land for days with search dogs then. And yes, I got your text. I have been doing some digging via my security team again." Bruce started to consult his own notes that he'd brought with him.

"Is that what the notes are for? I was concerned they were diagrams of the things that I should be doing on a weekday morning with Mason!"

Bruce chuckled and winked at her.

"I printed off the email from my team before I left my house today. There isn't really anything of note regarding the agent. Apparently, while it is claimed that Evangeline did fire Emmanuel, our sources indicate that it was more a mutual parting of ways."

"What sources?"

"Some of the other reporters at the *UK Chronicle* have rather loose lips, apparently. For enough money, they are more than happy to dish the dirt on their colleagues, especially when it's someone whom they all found deeply unpleasant. I can't see how investigating Emmanuel would add any value to our investigation, but I am more than happy to have her followed."

"What was the reason they gave for this parting of ways?"

Bruce pulled up a chair and sat down at the kitchen table. "Emmanuel has been telling her other clients that she had started to find Evangeline's techniques rather unethical."

"Gosh, what on earth was she doing that was so bad it was considered unethical, considering she was a gossip columnist?!"

"Precisely. Nothing was elaborated upon, however. And that is all I have to offer, I am afraid."

"I think we can park Emmanuel for the time being. What about Bernard Chilton, the late first husband?"

"I haven't started looking into him. I thought we could take Tallulah with us to the registry office and do a bit of digging. I have left her asleep on your lawn. I didn't want to bring her in and upset Arabella."

Arabella was in a permanent state of upset; bringing a dog into the house would have pushed her even closer to the edge. Lotty had once had to dog-sit for a friend, and Arabella had reacted by randomly peeing everywhere. It wasn't a huge issue until Bruce came round to visit one day and stepped in one of the puddles with his new suede brogues.

As Bruce, Lotty, and Tallulah got into Bruce's car, Arabella was watching them from the bedroom window. She knocked an ornament onto the floor, watching it smash into hundreds of pieces. She did this because she was a cat and for absolutely no other reason.

CHAPTER 73

Lotty continued to hold Bruce's shoe out of the window so that it could air. She smelled at it.

"It's OK. It doesn't smell. It was just a bit damp and stained. I have got most of the cat sick cleaned off with the tissues, but it will need a better wipe when you get it home." She waved the shoe at Bruce. He tapped her hand away.

"I'm trying to drive, sweetheart."

"Do you think we should have allowed Tallulah to eat some of our drive-through?"

Lotty was staring at Tallulah, who was looking a bit peaky after being allowed to polish off a burger of her own.

"She'll be fine. It's not like we gave her a milkshake or fries."

"She looks a bit green around the gills, and I think that smell is coming from her bottom."

"Oh, do stop panicking, dear."

Lotty watched Tallulah vomit the burger all over Bruce's back seats. Some of it even fell spectacularly into the back seat cupholder.

"What was that splashing noise? And what is that smell? Dear God, open more windows—and quickly."

"It's your turn to pay for your car to be cleaned, apparently."

Bruce adjusted his rear-view mirror and gasped. "She's bloody eating her own sick now!"

"You can't fault her logic; she's trying to be helpful."

"That is utterly revolting. My car is going to look like a rubbish dump by the time I try to sell it on."

Tallulah was sick again.

"Right! This isn't funny now."

Lotty tried to hide her laughter behind her hand. "She's eating it again."

"Is this entirely normal behaviour?" asked Bruce.

"I'm a cat owner; honestly, I don't know. Do you want me to check the internet?"

"This is getting …"

Lotty interrupted him. "She's being sick again. … Oh, no, I think she's done."

They pulled into the registry office car park. Bruce jumped out of his seat, put his damp shoe on, and set about wiping the car seats down with the remainder of the paper tissues he kept in there.

"Darling, can you go and tie Tallulah up outside the front of the building while I dispose of these in the bin? They're now covered in dog and cat vomit." He held the papers at arm's length as if they were going to explode.

As Lotty crossed the car park with Tallulah in tow, a car shot across the tarmac behind her, driving far too fast. It nearly hit her. She only avoided being run down by managing to jump out of the way just in time, dragging the dog with her. She panicked until she noticed the driver of the vehicle was a mature gentleman wearing thick glasses on his nose, his head being far too close to the steering wheel. He clearly couldn't see and had not done it on purpose.

Bruce burst out laughing as he crossed the car park and started to walk alongside Lotty. "Are you OK, dear? Well, if we need to report your death from a car collision, we are certainly in the right place."

As he continued to laugh heartily, tickled by his own joke, he walked head first into a rather demure woman who was leaving the building, sobbing into a handkerchief as she did so. She stopped crying just long enough to stare at Bruce with utter contempt, then strike him full in the face with her handbag.

"I do apologise, madam. I am so sorry for your loss," exclaimed Bruce, as he unsuccessfully ducked from the surprise attack.

The woman composed herself and awkwardly retained eye contact with Bruce as she walked to her car, turning her head back to do so. The situation became even more awkward as she was then gently knocked on her hip by the car being driven by the elderly gentleman who had just nearly run Lotty over. He was currently engaged in a seventeen-point turn to park his vehicle, and he hadn't seen the woman apparently.

Bruce and Lotty tied Tallulah to the pole, remaining solemnly quiet for the duration, and walked into the registry office.

CHAPTER 74

It was less than twenty minutes later when Bruce and Lotty were leaving the registry office again.

Bruce turned to Lotty as she undid the knot in the lead that had kept Tallulah in place during their absence. Tallulah licked Bruce's hand to signal her happiness at being rescued. He was getting rather concerned at how attached he was becoming to Tallulah. If he were being honest with himself, he'd have to admit to having become more attached to her than to Grant.

"Well, that got us absolutely nowhere, Lotty. What a wasted trip!"

"It isn't just my fault; we *both* forgot to bring the information about Bernard."

"I find it ridiculous that in this day and age, these places don't have computers so you can search for someone by surname. I couldn't remember his date of birth. At my age, I am lucky enough to remember what I ate for breakfast this morning."

"Maybe that member of staff would have helped us if you hadn't called her a fascist?"

"Well, I think it's utterly ridiculous you have to stand behind a line to queue. There wasn't anyone else there. And it's not a bloody airport."

"But did you need to tell her that you would shove a pen up her arse? And I'm just not sure the accompanying hand gesture was entirely necessary; I am fairly sure she knew what you meant."

"Lucky you rang Mason instead. Has he sent you the email with the details yet?"

They sat down in the car. Lotty leaned into the back seat to clip Tallulah into her doggie safety harness. Lotty had noticed that the harness was now a firm fixture in Bruce's car, even when Tallulah wasn't in it. She felt a significant romance was brewing between Bruce and Grant, and that pleased her. Not only did Bruce deserve someone nice, but also this meant that Lotty would get free cakes.

Lotty checked her mobile phone. "OK, here we go. He's just sent it."

"We are all ears, aren't we, Tallulah? Especially you, with your big floppy gorgeous ones!"

It was now Bruce's turn to lean into the back of the car. He gently played with Tallulah's big ears and gave her a loving scratch.

Lotty rolled her eyes and read out the information from her tiny screen.

"Not much of interest—a bit like Emmanuel. As we know, Bernard's body was never recovered, and Evangeline had him declared legally dead before she married Sir Ralph. There was an investigation into the wreckage that was found from the boat, and it was deemed that nothing malicious had occurred. It was noted in the information Mason found that the assumption was that Bernard's boat hit some rocks. There was significant damage to the boat. The engine was recovered, and that all looked fine. The coastguard had received an SOS from Bernard when he had run into trouble and told them he was caught in a bad storm."

"A giant dead end—coincidentally the same nickname I'd given your genitals over the years. Did you ever hear from Sir Ralph, you know, after the party and such …"

"No, and I don't care. It's not like I wanted to hear from him anyway."

"I just can't think why you never heard back from him after flooding the toilets at his party with a massive poo. Funny, that."

CHAPTER 75

Later that afternoon, Bruce had parked the car outside Melissa and Greg's house. To optimise Lotty's continued holiday from work, they had decided to circle back on their main suspects. So far, they had hadn't seen Greg or Melissa, but they had spent a good thirty minutes finding fault in their curtains.

"These binoculars are fantastic, aren't they? Have a look. The quality is top-notch."

Bruce handed Lotty the binoculars.

"Is it time for another pee?" Lotty asked, nodding her head at Tallulah.

"She is fine. Stop fussing. Is this because you need to pee again? I think we have run out of cups. And that one you filled over there is leaking a bit. What did you drink today? You have the bladder of a male rhino. I never want to hear you doing that again; that splashing noise is going to haunt me to my dying day. Hang on, I see Greg's car is on the move."

Greg drove his car out of his drive and indicated to turn in the other direction. He drove off up the road. Lotty and Bruce popped back up into the upright position, having ducked down when Greg left to prevent being seen.

"Shall we follow him, Lotty?"

Just as Bruce finished talking, Melissa emerged from the house, looking furtively about her in every direction, clearly checking that Greg had already driven off. She looked down the road and then ran quickly back into the house, her extensions flying around as she turned her head to check to her left and right.

"She's looking very suspicious. It's like she's checking repeatedly that no one is watching her."

They watched Melissa, now wearing a dark coat, leave Greg's house again. She ran at great speed to her own car and got in.

"Get your head down again!" Bruce shouted.

They both ducked down until they heard that Melissa had driven past. Bruce sat up, quickly started the engine, and followed her car. Lotty was still in the crouched position when the car throttled forward, catapulting her back into a seated position. She looked down.

"My urine has spilled everywhere. Sorry."

"Why don't you just take a massive shit in here? It's about the only thing that hasn't happened to my lovely car this past week."

"I said sorry. You drove off too fast."

Their surveillance of Melissa started to lead them through town. Lotty turned to Bruce. "She can't be going to work then, as that was the turning to the *UK Chronicle* back there. Where do you think she's going?"

"I hope it's an illicit rendezvous because, so far, nothing in the pool of suspects has been even vaguely interesting."

They watched Melissa turn her Mercedes left into a council rubbish dump. She drove in.

"I think we should park outside here. Driving this car into there is surely going to attract a lot of attention."

"Bruce, you're such a snob. Rich people have rubbish to dispose of as well, you know."

"Yes, but more often than not, they have someone whom they employ to do it for them."

Bruce parked his Jaguar just outside the exit to the rubbish dump and passed Lotty the binoculars. "Here, take a look at what she's doing, quickly."

"Clearly, she is going to be throwing rubbish away."

"It might be a dead body for all you know," he exclaimed excitedly.

"In the middle of the afternoon, at a rubbish dump?" Lotty held the binoculars to her face. "She's taking a black bin liner out of her boot."

"And?"

"Stop being impatient. OK, so it looks to be a bag full of men's clothing that she's throwing away. It's probably just Greg's clothes."

"Absolute nonsense. She's up to something. She was acting very strangely back there. She kept checking no one was watching, including Greg. She was looking up the road to check he had driven off."

Bruce slapped his thigh. The vibration knocked another cup of Lotty's urine over.

"Firstly, get those cups out of the car and over into that bin. Secondly, I bet she's having an affair. Evangeline found out, and Melissa killed her to stop Greg finding out."

Lotty jumped out of the car and walked the two cups over to the dustbin to dispose of them. Her synapses were still firing when she got back into the car and fastened her seat belt.

"She might be having an affair with someone from the party. Alexander, perhaps? She is a lot younger than Greg."

"Why does it have to be someone from the party? This isn't an episode of *Murder, She Wrote*. Not everything has to be tied up neatly in a bow."

Lotty glared at Greg. She would put up with most of Bruce's nasty commentary, but she wouldn't be able to forgive someone being derogatory about her favourite television programme.

"You've crossed a line." She wagged her finger reproachfully at Bruce. "Don't disrespect my queen."

Bruce chuckled. "Melissa's getting back into her car. Let's follow her."

They waited until Melissa drove past, then proceeded to follow her again.

Nothing of further interest was discovered by Bruce and Lotty during the final course of the afternoon. The same couldn't be said for the local park-keeper who was engaged in his daily rubbish collection in the area near to where Bruce had parked his car. The keeper discovered, to his horror, that people threw anything away. He also discovered that you can't get a urine stain out of nubuck leather.

CHAPTER 76

Lotty picked up her coconut-infused soap from the shower pan, where she had just dropped it. Her hands were shaking; she was feeling extra clumsy this evening because she had the distinct impression that she was going to be having sex shortly. It had been so long that she couldn't even remember what a penis looked like, let alone what she was meant to do with one. Bruce had looked quite terrified several months previously when she had voiced her concerns about this to him. She had felt the need to explain that it was more of an observation than a cry for help. She was in an absolute dither and simply couldn't concentrate. She had been trying to piece together the final parts of the puzzle pertaining to Evangeline's death. Something was really bothering her. A few little things that she had seen over the past few days were trying to knot themselves together in her cerebral cortex to form a solution. The thought of her impending romantic encounter with Mason was making it very difficult to see what the knot was showing her. She continued to lather herself luxuriously, to try to relax. *If I can relax my body, I can relax my thoughts.*

Lotty got out of the shower and dried herself off, screwing her face up in thought. She was starting to get frustrated at how her brain was failing her. She absent-mindedly grabbed her can of mousse and sprayed a ball of it into her hands before scrunching it through her hair. Suddenly detecting a strong familiar smell working its way up into her nostrils, she looked down at her orange-stained hands. She jumped quickly back into the shower to wash the fake tan off her hair, then dried herself for a second time.

Having remembered that her clothes for this evening were still in the tumble dryer, Lotty walked back downstairs. She continued to try to focus her thoughts as she navigated carefully over the sleeping Arabella halfway down the stairs. She walked purposefully into her freezing cold garage and started to retrieve her favourite clothes from inside. Turning and seeing her shovel leaning against the garage wall, she stared at it, her brain cells yearning for her to make some sort of connection. *You're trying to remember. Relax.*

The shovel.

Lotty grabbed a bottle of champagne from her wine fridge in the garage. She had decided that in order to ease her nerves, she would just have a few glasses this evening—nothing mad, just enough to take the edge off.

Lotty walked the bottle and her clothes into the kitchen and got dressed there. Arabella came out to meet her. She started to meow. Lotty bent down to stroke her fur. She loved how Arabella had cute little tufts of untidy patches near her ears; it made it look as if Arabella were wearing a wig.

The hair.

Lotty stood up sharply, nearly making a connection, which she then lost because she heard Mason at her door. She opened the door to find him holding a giant box of chocolates and some champagne.

"You look utterly beautiful, Lotty."

Lotty blushed and looked at her feet. "You look jolly nice yourself. Have you come straight from work?"

"I went home to change, then I thwung into town to get thesth for you. I wath going to pick up thome oysthterth, but the fithmonger was clothed."

"Oysters give me a bad stomach."

"Of course they do. Is there anything that doesn't?" He walked into the hall and kissed her firmly on the mouth.

"It gets even worse if I eat shrimp."

"Oh, thtop with your thexy talk!"

"Something is really off with Melissa. She was acting really weird today. She was acting really suspiciously when we followed her to the rubbish dump, and she was throwing a load of men's clothing away."

"It'sth funny you thay that, becauth I think thee uthed to be known under a different name. I had finally gotten around to performing thome thearchesth on her today. Nothing. I wath going to hand it off to some junior officersth tomorrow becauth it doethn't look like thee will be eathy to thrathe."

"My thoughts are muddled tonight. I feel really discombobulated. Something is really nagging me about Melissa now."

Lotty took Mason's hand and led him to her sofa. They sat down. Mason wrapped his arms around her. "If you try too hard, you thimply won't remember. Try to conthentrate on thomething elth."

Mason unsubtly looked at his groin and smiled sweetly.

"Shall I go and get our food first?"

"Oh, go on then. You've pulled my arm."

"I can pull something else later, if you like."

Lotty winked at him and walked sexily to the kitchen, which she ruined by tripping over the remote control that was lying on the floor.

CHAPTER 77

Lotty and Mason were sitting at her dining room table, sharing a giant bowl of Carbonara, eating with only one hand each because they were holding hands with each other. Mason was currently engaged in trying to use his left hand to twirl pasta around his fork and had managed to drop most of his meal on the floor. He felt something rubbing against his legs and thought his luck was in, until he looked down and noticed that it was Arabella trying to clean herself because she had tagliatelle stuck on her head.

"Thisth wath lovely, my thweet, but I am quite full up now." Mason put down his fork and poured himself another glass of orange juice.

"Are you sure you won't have even one glass of champagne with me?" Lotty asked, finishing her third glass of the evening.

"I can't when I'm on call."

He felt sure that at least one of them should remain sober this evening to ensure things went well. Sexual things. And that person wouldn't be Lotty, who was now so drunk that she had cross eyes. She had also lost most of her inhibitions and had fallen into her bookcase earlier that evening when she was trying to dance seductively with Mason. As much as he was enjoying the dancing, he felt it may have been considerably more romantic if she hadn't farted repeatedly during their salsa.

"I think you need to drink some water and eat some more pasta. You are a tad drunk." He kissed her gently and went out into the kitchen to get their garlic bread out of Lotty's oven. He had taken over the latter part of the culinary duties because Lotty would often set fire to things while stone-cold sober; he shuddered to think what she may do while rat-arsed.

When he returned, Lotty was downing a jug of water that she'd found on the table. He smiled. At least he knew she listened to his advice.

"I'll be back in a bit, Lotty. I need to go to the toilet."

Lotty spent the next twenty minutes trying not to notice that Mason was clearly having a poo. Instead, she chose to continue to drink her water and finish her pasta. She was starting to feel a bit less drunk.

Mason returned to sit down next to her.

"You're bleeding on your hand."

"It will thtop in a minute. It'sth jutht a thmall thcratch. I caught my hand on your toilet door."

Toilet door? Come on, think, Lotty. Fire your brain, accept the memory, tie that knot ...

"Whath wrong? It lookth like you've theen a ghostht."

She clasped her hands to her face in frustration and bellowed, "I need to sober up. My brain is trying to tell me something important. Just then, when you were mentioning the toilet door, it made me remember something weird. I just can't quite remember what it was."

"Maybe I can take your mind off things?"

Mason put his arm around her and kissed her neck. Lotty, feeling her nipples immediately stand on ceremony, was worried that they would catapult her bra across to the other side of the lounge. She kissed Mason hard on the lips. Their tongues locked together as she held his face between her hands. As she started to gently nibble on his lower lip, he started to undress her. First her skirt was on the floor, then her shirt, followed by her bra. She moved her hands down to his shirt and started to return the favour. She slowly undid each button while still engaged in thrusting her tongue firmly down his throat. She was concerned that he would choke on her tongue, but he didn't seem to be complaining. His shirt fell to the floor, landing on Arabella, who had been staring at them both, wondering why they weren't paying attention to her. She also wondered why they were making the same noises she did when she was trying to clear her constipation. Arabella moved farther away and settled onto the rug to fall asleep.

Lotty removed Mason's belt and pulled his trousers down, followed by his boxer shorts. Mason felt his boxer shorts get stuck under his left foot, so he tried to kick them off with his right. He shuffled his left foot into a better position and felt the boxers get launched rapidly to the other side of the lounge. He peered over and noticed that Arabella was now looking disgruntled because of now having a pair of pants on top of her head. He tried to ignore this and went back to concentrating on the fun he was having with Lotty. He was moaning with pleasure now as she played her tongue down every inch of his chest hair and back up again. Mason pulled Lotty closer and gripped her firmly between his hands, pausing only briefly when a significant chunk of her hair came away in his hand.

"Sorry, that's just breakage from all the colourant and perming lotion still," she whispered into his ear.

Asserting inwardly to himself that he refused to be put off, he laid his lips once more upon hers, grabbed at her hand, and moved it towards him.

"I want your fingerth wrapped tho tight around my dick that you leave fingerprints."

Lotty unfurled her fingers from around Mason's now very erect penis and stood up quickly.

"I've got it!"

"I haven't gotten it yet." He sighed mournfully.

Lotty ran over to her laptop bag, which was in the corner of the lounge, and ripped it open. She set her laptop onto the table and opened it up. The lights came on. She entered her password, then turned to look at Mason. He appeared to be embarrassed. There were many reasons why he thought their first sexual experience together would prove awkward, but standing next to Lotty with an erect penis while he waited for her laptop to attach to her laboratory's virtual private network wasn't one of the scenarios he'd imagined.

Arabella jumped up onto the table to see what was going on. She felt confident that if only she hung around long enough, someone would pat her on the head. She sauntered over closer to the laptop and stared at Mason's proud manhood. He noticed, and moved his hands down to afford himself some dignity. The stubborn feline steadfastly refused to avert her gaze.

"Will thisth take long?"

"I wouldn't do that if I were you. She likes licking people's hands, and yours are rather close to your more fragile parts at the moment."

Mason stood a bit farther back from the table, still gazing at Lotty's screen, yet managing to maintain his peripheral gaze on the cat, for safety.

Lotty jumped out of her seat, startling Arabella and causing her to jump off the table and plant her claws firmly into Mason's waist, clinging to it as if she were abseiling.

"Ouch!"

Lotty ran over and gently peeled Arabella from Mason, and placed her gently upon the floor.

"Melissa's fingerprints weren't on Evangeline's desk."

"And?"

"Greg and Melissa are glued at the hip, yet she has gone to great pains to avoid her fingerprints being on that desk. It doesn't add up. Something about her is really bothering me now …"

"What do you want to do?"

"When we followed her from the rubbish dump earlier, she was driving back to Greg's. Let's go and break into her car. I bet we can find something. If we don't find anything, we can have Bruce bribe someone at the *UK Chronicle* to let us in to search her desk. His security team have got some good contacts down there. For the right price, we could definitely gain entry."

"Can't we jutht gather thome more tangible evidenth and obtain a thearch warrant, like normal people? I could get into trouble."

"I'll go on my own. I don't expect you to get into trouble. If I manage to crack this case, I could really make a name for myself as the new head of my detective agency. This is really important to me, Mason."

"We can't tell anyone we did this, but I'll come with you—if you think you will find something."

"We should probably get dressed first?"

They didn't end up getting dressed first. In fact, they left the house a good hour later, with Lotty grinning like a Cheshire cat, having left a buttock-shaped impression, as well as several pubic hairs, in the garlic bread.

CHAPTER 78

Mason and Lotty were crouched down at the front gates to Greg's driveway.

"Greg's car isn't here. What if he returns while we are doing this?"

"We will hear him. It'sth perfectly thafe. If he comth, we can duck into the buthteth and leave. At wortht, he will think thomeone pried hith gate open."

"Melissa must be waiting for him to come back as she doesn't live here yet. He has probably therefore only popped out for a short visit. And it's nearly midnight. We really need to hurry up. I feel like a ninja."

"You don't remind me much of a ninja. Your thirt is on inthide out. Won't we thet their exthterior lightsth off?"

"I texted my on-call technical team while you were driving us here. They hacked Greg's home security system and turned the security lights off. It's quite a long drive, so I also changed my social media profile to show that I'm in a relationship."

"Oh my god, Lotty. Pleath never tell anyone that. Well, the latter part isth fine. I'll change mine later."

He gave her bottom a loving squeeze, then realised how hazardous that could have been, considering she had been eating the garlic bread while waiting for him to get dressed.

Lotty pulled something out of her mouth. "Why have I got pubic hairs in my mouth?"

"Can we conthentrate?"

Mason gestured to Lotty to follow him. They crouched down onto their haunches and moved swiftly towards the large gate that stood proudly at the end of the driveway ahead of them.

"My lovely boffins have unlocked the gate too. We just need to pull it gently apart, like this, and squeeze through."

"Thlowly doeth it. We don't want it to creak."

"I imagine that's what Bruce says to Grant in bed."

They giggled, and crept forward through the gate and down the long drive. Lotty ensured that she followed Mason's lead, staying close to the ground. She noticed that he was avoiding the patches of lawn where the moonlight played upon the ground, in order to remain as hidden as possible.

They approached Melissa's car.

"This is hers, the Mercedes."

Lotty removed a metal tool from the small backpack that she was carrying, proudly showing it off to Mason. "This was in my father's surveillance kit. It will unlock the car."

Lotty inserted the long metal shaft of the device into the car's lock and watched it snap in half and hit Mason in the eye.

"Thall I try it? I can probably thtill manage it becauth you only parthially blinded me."

Lotty allowed Mason to take the tool from her and gently work it into the lock, moving his fingers adeptly clockwise until they both heard a clicking sound.

"Don't take thisth the wrong way, darling, but can I do thisth bit alone, for fear of you acthidentally honking the horn."

She sighed in agreement and watched Mason climb carefully into the car.

"Are there any bags to look through in there?" she whispered.

"Nothing. Hang on, I'll try the gloveboxth." Mason opened the glovebox and looked inside. "There are thome paperth in here." He handed them to Lotty.

"I just need to use my head torch to see what it says."

"That will be too bright. Here, uthe the glare from my mobile phone thcreen."

She took his mobile phone from him and started to read the papers.

"These are banks statements from her father's electrical company. They are addressed to Mel. That must have been her dad. She is probably just terrible at throwing stuff away."

Lotty placed the bank statements on the floor. "What else is in there?"

Mason passed her a bottle. "There isth thisth bottle and a mobile phone."

Lotty took the bottle from him and gasped. It was as if all of the gears churning away in her head all clicked into place at once.

"The shovel in my garage earlier, it made me try to recall something strange. Melissa has hands that are like shovels! The bathroom door—you know, when you scratched your hand. The other night, Melissa tried to walk into the men's toilets instead of the ladies' ones."

Mason started at her blankly.

"This bottle is cyproterone. It's used to reduce masculine traits in transgender women. If Evangeline was ingesting this, it would have elevated her levels of enzymes. These are the antiandrogens we found in her water bottle. No wonder Melissa never drives Greg anywhere. She has quite the stash in her glovebox. I worry that I keep a spare pair of knickers in my car."

Mason felt it was best not to ask why Lotty felt the need to drive everywhere with a spare pair of pants.

"Thisth mobile phone turnsth on, but it hathn't got a thim card in it."

"Use your own SIM card." She handed him his mobile phone back.

Mason used the metal shaft he had used on the car lock and pried open the SIM slot on the mobile phone in his hand.

"OK, it'sth working."

"That must be Evangeline's mobile phone. Find the dictation app."

Mason scrolled through the apps and pressed the screen. They heard music blaring through the speakers.

"Turn it down. That's too loud."

"I can't hear anything but background noithe and muthic."

"That's the end, at the party. Rewind a few seconds."

"Melissa was born a male."

"Evangeline knew! I thought she was talking about an email when I heard her dictating. She actually said *male*. It must be a secret that Melissa would kill to keep."

"There isth another bottle here." He handed it to Lotty.

"It's hard to read with only the interior car light, but this looks like the interferon-beta. The name on this label is probably her mother's. I can only assume that the terminal illness that we know she died of was multiple sclerosis. So, she had all this medication already."

"We need to pack everything back away in here. We need to get out of here before Greg returnth home."

The loving couple were so engrossed in each other, and in the task of getting everything back away in the glovebox, that they didn't see Melissa watching them with daggers from one of the bedroom windows. She let the curtain fall back into place in front of her and started to hatch a plan.

CHAPTER 79

"Why are we driving to your work?"

"We know who the killer isth! We need to tell thomeone."

"You're going to get into a lot of trouble though."

"Lotty, it wath bad enough to have done what we did tonight. I can't now allow a murderer to remain on the looth."

"Maybe we could say that I broke into the car on my own, then told you about it? And that's why we are now driving here together."

"We can do that, yeth. Well, you did tholve the cathe after all. I'm tho proud of you. I'm a lucky man."

He squeezed her hand reassuringly.

"I feel bad. Whatever we tell people might paint you in a bad light. And I would never want anything I have done to be detrimental to your career. Let's ring Bruce. He'll know what to do."

Lotty dialled Bruce's number. Bruce didn't pick up.

"That's weird. After what has been happening, Bruce turned his ringer up to full blast and said that he would pick up for me no matter what he was doing or what time of day it was."

"He and Grant are probably jutht having it off. Relax."

"No, you don't understand. When my father died, Bruce promised to always look out for me. This isn't like him at all. Even if he and Grant were doing that, he would have picked up. We exchanged some texts a while back, just after you and I left Greg and Melissa's. I gave him an update, and he said that Greg had just left Bruce's house. He had popped round to drop off a thank-you gift for being invited to the wine tasting the other night."

"Call Greg. I'm thure you're panicking about nothing."

"But I don't know his number. Do you have it?"

"Down there on the floor isth my notebook. You'll find it in there."

"We both have a lovely clean car. This notebook is literally the only thing in here other than us."

"I don't have any underwear in mine though."

Lotty ignored him and dialled Greg.

"Lotty, how the devil are you? I'm just driving back from seeing Bruce."

"I'm great, Greg, thank you. Sorry to forgo the pleasantries, but it was Bruce I was trying to get hold of actually. I'm worried about him. He isn't picking up his phone."

"I'm sure he is fine, darling. He and Grant were just making a nice hot chocolate as I was leaving."

"OK, thank you. I'll try ringing him again. Have a pleasant evening."

"Well, I was going to watch a late night film with Melissa, but she passed me a while ago, travelling in the opposite direction. I expect she's been called out on a work assignment. It must be close to Bruce's as she passed me heading into his village."

"OK, I've got to go. Sorry, Greg."

Lotty hung up and turned to Mason. "You need to drive me to Bruce's house—now."

CHAPTER 80

Lotty was on the verge of tears. She felt the need to pull herself together in order to reflect the professional image that she had been trying to forge for herself recently.

"Melissa is going to Bruce's to hurt him, I just know it."

"Why Bruthe?"

"I think because she hasn't succeeded in hurting me so far."

"What would hurting Bruthe achieve?"

"I guess she wants to upset me enough that it derails the investigation for a while, giving her a chance to regroup. Or enough time to marry Greg before he finds out her secret."

"I don't thee why being tranthgender isth an ithue. The world hath moved on. Love isth love."

"Maybe he is antiquated."

They parked outside Bruce's house, next to Melissa's Mercedes. Lotty turned to Mason with fire burning in her eyes.

"All I know is that she's a massively vindictive bitch, and if she has harmed even one hair on Bruce's head, I'm going to kick her in the ..."

"Can't we call for backup, or do you want uth to go in right now, on our own? Thee might be armed."

"We can't wait for anyone. I'm going in."

Lotty leapt out of the car and ran towards the house, with Mason following closely behind. The front door had been left suspiciously open, and they could hear shouting from inside.

Lotty tore towards Bruce's conservatory, where all the noise was coming from.

"Bruce, Greg, are you OK?" Lotty was shouting as she sprinted into the room.

Mason ran up behind Lotty and stopped. Ahead of him was absolute chaos. Grant was tied up on the sofa, and Melissa was lying prone upon the floor because Tallulah had Melissa's leg in her mouth.

Lotty's mouth fell open, partly in shock and partly with pride, as Tallulah growled like a rabid werewolf until Melissa stopped struggling.

Bruce appeared surprisingly calm; he had his mobile phone in one hand and a champagne glass in the other.

"I've just called the police, darling. Do you want a drink?" He pointed at a bottle of Bollinger that was chilling on the table near Grant. "There are more glasses in the cabinet over there. I would suggest one of my coupe glasses, to truly honour that it's a vintage Bollinger."

Melissa looked up. "Can you get this fucking dog off me?"

Mason crossed the room, stepping over Tallulah as he did so, and placed a pair of handcuffs around Melissa's wrists. He patted Tallulah, signalling her to stand down. Melissa's leg was now bleeding from the large dog bite around her ankle.

Bruce pointed at the rug she was bleeding on. "If you could be careful, that was rather expensive, and it's an absolute bugger to get dry-cleaned."

Mason bent down towards Melissa. "I am arrethting you in connecthion with the murder of Evangeline DuVoir, and for common athault. You do not have to thay anything. But it may harm your defenth if you do not menthion when questhtioned thomething whith you later rely on in court. Anything you do thay may be given in evidenth."

Melissa spat up at him. "Fuck off."

Lotty walked over to Grant and pointed. "Melissa tied poor Grant up."

Bruce handed Lotty a full glass of champagne. "Well, this is a bit awkward, but it wasn't Melissa. I did that."

Lotty removed the unpeeled banana from Grant's mouth, and turned to Melissa. "Why kill Evangeline? There is no shame in being transgender."

"I know that. I'm proud of who I am. But she was going to tell Greg before the wedding. She had been blackmailing me to keep it quiet; she knew how fanatical Greg was about having children."

"You can adopt," interjected Bruce.

"He wouldn't want that; he is keen to enjoy watching a natural

231

childbirth. I have seen how narrow-minded he is when we meet someone who needs a surrogate. I just wanted to marry him and get some cash under my belt. I wasn't marrying him for love, so I didn't really care that he wanted children."

"But why inject Evangeline with the drugs?" Lotty asked, perplexed.

"She started to bleed me dry with the blackmail. She found out about me because she likes to dig deep into the background of anyone joining the *UK Chronicle*. She likes to gather secrets so she can use them to her advantage. I saw her watching me at the party when I was trying to slip some more of my medication into her drink. I thought no one was watching at the time. I knew it would come to this, so I started to carry the syringe round as my backup plan."

"And becauth you are a qualified electrithan, you knew how to fixth the lightsth to go off."

"Precisely. I used to do electrical contracting, I owned my own firm. And during the blackout, I smashed the memory card she always carried with her. She made a big song and dance about the fact that she used it to store all her blackmail material on."

"How did you sthmuggle her mobile phone and the thyringe out?"

"I wound the syringe up into the knots under my hair extensions."

"What about the mobile phone?" Mason asked.

"I put it into my underwear when no one was looking."

Lotty looked appalled. "I've been touching that this evening!"

CHAPTER 81

It was several hours later, and the sun had started to rise above the wall of trees that lined Bruce's garden. The rays of morning sun danced upon Bruce's forehead.

Bruce put his arm around Grant as they both looked out from the conservatory, watching Mason and Lotty hugging endlessly on the lawn. It was being made somewhat less romantic because Tallulah had wandered out to join them and kept sniffing at Lotty's crotch.

"I did wonder why Melissa had such big hands," Bruce said thoughtfully. He turned to Grant and kissed him firmly on the mouth. "I just don't see how Melissa felt the need to do all of this. I know Grant, and he is supportive of me and the whole LGBTQ+ community. He truly loved Melissa."

"It was having the children, I guess. Even the most open-minded people have certain things they find hard to change their feelings about. We should all be respectful of one another's views, even if we don't agree with them ourselves. Adoption is fantastic. Maybe something for us to ponder in the future?"

Bruce smiled at Grant and felt utterly content. "Shall we drive round to Lotty's while they're busy being loved up? I heard there were leftovers, and I absolutely adore cold garlic bread for breakfast."

Printed in Great Britain
by Amazon